THE GIRL WHO

NEVER WAS

skylar dorset

sourcebooks
fire

Published by Sourcebooks Fire, an imprint of Sourcebooks, Inc.
P.O. Box 4410, Naperville, Illinois 60567-4410
(630) 961-3900
Fax: (630) 961-2168
www.sourcebooks.com

Library of Congress Cataloging-in-Publication data is on file with the publisher

Printed and bound in the United States of America.
VP 10 9 8 7 6 5 4 3 2 1

For my parents, who are perfectly
ordinary, in the most extraordinary way. Which
makes me very lucky.

CHAPTER 1

One day, my father walked into his Back Bay apartment to find a blond woman asleep on his couch. Nine months later, I appeared on his doorstep. One year later, my aunts succeeded in getting him committed to a psychiatric hospital.

This is how the story of my birth goes.

My father says my mother was the most beautiful woman he had ever seen. I always ask how she ended up on his couch. *Where did she come from?* I ask. *Why was she there? Did you know her?* My father always looks at me vaguely. *The most beautiful woman I had ever seen,* he tells me, and then he tells me the story of my name. *Selkie,* he says. *She told me to name you Selkie.* And I ask, *How did she tell you?* And he replies, *She etched it into a snowflake, sighed it into a gust of wind, rustled it through the trees of autumn, rippled it over a summer pond.*

And my aunts sigh and say, *That's enough.*

And when I ask my aunts about my mother, all they will ever say is that she was "flighty."

When I was little, I used to think maybe my mother would come to take me away. Aunt True and Aunt Virtue aren't exactly my aunts. They are my dad's aunts, making them my great-aunts, and therefore old—older than I could pinpoint when I was young. Now that I'm older, I know that they're older than my dad, but I can't quite figure out exactly how much older. Dad was their little brother's only child, I know, but the dates of births in my family are fuzzy. *Who wants to remember how old they are?* Aunt True asks me. I have never had a birthday party. Or an acknowledgment of my birthday. But I do have a birthday.

It is today.

I am sitting on Boston Common, watching the tourists get lost and the leaves fall, and I am thinking. The Common is the huge park in the middle of Boston. The story I have always been told is that it was originally a cow pasture and that the paved paths meandering through it follow the original cow paths, and I believe that; there is an aimlessness to them. I like that about Boston Common. I like that the place feels like it has no discernible purpose, in this age without cows. It is unnecessary, a frivolity in the middle of the city, prime real estate that isn't even *landscaped*, really, is just basic grass and some scattered trees. It is a place that just *is*, and I have always found, sprawled on the ground and looking at the buildings that crowd around it, that it is the perfect place to think.

I am, according to my birth certificate, seventeen today. I don't know whether or not to believe my birth certificate, though, honestly. Some days I feel that I must be much older than seventeen and that somebody got it all wrong: my addle-minded father or my aunts who don't keep track of dates. And some days I feel much younger than seventeen, like a small child, and I just want my mother.

I feel that way now.

I am thinking of my mother, of how I am told I resemble her. I have never seen her photograph, so all I can do is study myself in the mirror and draw conclusions from there. Tall, I suppose, the way I am tall. Slender the way I am slender. It must be from her that I get my pale skin that resists all of my efforts to get it to tan, since my aunts and father have naturally olive complexions. It must be from her that I get my blue eyes, my blond hair so light that it can be white in certain lights. I wear my hair long, and I wonder if my mother did—if she does still, wherever she is.

"Hey," says Ben, interrupting my thoughts. Ben works at one of the stands scattered through the Common. On hot summer days, Ben makes fresh-squeezed lemonade that he gives me for free. He brings it to me while I lie on the grass in the heat and read books and tell him what they're about. Now, at the time of year when it can be summer or winter both in the same day, Ben makes lemonade or sells sweatshirts, as the mood strikes him. It must be sweatshirts today, because he's brought me one, and he drops it playfully on top of my head, draped so that it momentarily obscures my vision.

I feel like I have known Ben all my life, but that's not true. I just can't remember the first time I met him is the problem. I have always come to the Common to be alone, alone among the strangers, and Ben has always been in the background of life on the Common. I don't know when we started speaking to each other, when he started bringing me lemonade, when we learned each other's names. It all just happened, the way good things just happen without having to be forced. Ben is—I think—older than me in a way that always makes me feel very young, but I don't think he does it on purpose, the way the college guys do when we cross paths on the T, Boston's sprawling and ever-crowded subway system. Ben is *effortlessly* older than me. He is tall—taller than me—and thin—maybe thinner than me too, honestly—and has a lot of thick, dark, curly hair and very pale eyes whose color I can never quite pinpoint, and for a little while now, I have been ignoring the attention of Mike Summerton at school because there is Ben. But I don't think Ben is thinking that way, and what's really kind of annoying is that, in a relationship where I don't ever remember even having to tell Ben my name, why should I have to tell him that we're kind of dating, even if he doesn't know it and has never kissed me? He should just *know*, the way he knew I'd like lemonade and that I was cold and needed a sweatshirt.

"What are you up to?" he asks me, dropping to the leaf-strewn grass next to me. Ben moves with an absentminded elegance. When he drops to the ground, it almost feels like he floats his way down. It sounds weird, but it's the only way I can think to describe it: a soft, fluttering quality to the way Ben moves. It is, trust me, very appealing. Ben never clumsily plops to the ground beside me. Ben always sort of *sinks* there. And you get the feeling, watching Ben move, that everything he does is very deliberate, no motion wasted. It makes it terribly flattering when he uses those deliberate, studied motions to come talk to *you*—terribly flattering and the slightest bit annoying. I am not known for my grace. Not that I'm the clumsiest person ever, but let's just say I know I'm never going to be a ballerina. My aunts say that I move with "Stewart stubbornness," trying to refuse to yield to hard objects or even gravity at times—that that is one thing, at least, that I did not inherit from my mother. I guess I have to take their word for it. In my head, whenever I imagine her, my "flighty" mother moves so fluidly she could be floating.

"It's wet," Ben says of the grass, and he crinkles his nose in displeasure, shaking his hands like a fastidious cat and all of his motions are so beautifully choreographed that he is painful to look at.

"Yeah," I reply, as if Ben is not painful for me to look at and is just a regular friend, hanging out on the Common with me.

Ben shrugs and takes the sweatshirt out of my hands.

"Hey," I protest as he puts it on the ground and sits on it. "I was going to wear that."

"You know I hate to be wet," he says. And he does. I do know this. He wraps the cups of lemonade he sells in thickets of napkins to keep condensation away from his hands. He complains vociferously whenever it rains. He has sixteen different ways of fending off dampness. I always ask him why he lives in Boston and sells things outside if he hates the rain so much; it rains here a lot. And Ben always shrugs. Ben shrugs in response to lots of things. Like whenever I ask him why he doesn't go to school. He is—I think—too old for high school, although he never confirms this. But why not college then? One of the two hundred colleges in the Boston area?

And Ben shrugs.

"Today is my birthday," I blurt out. I don't know why I say it just then. I never tell anyone my birthday. I expect Aunt True and Aunt Virtue to come running out of the townhouse to scold me about how polite people never reveal such personal information.

But nobody comes dashing across Beacon Street. The piano player outside the entrance to the T plays something tinkling and tuneless. Ben says, "Happy birthday." He does not ask me how old I am. I am glad for that. It seems weird to say that I'm seventeen when I feel so much younger than that. Then he says, "It's the autumnal equinox. You were born on the autumnal equinox."

"Not really. Well, I don't know. The autumnal equinox is different every year."

Ben shrugs.

I want to tell him that I would like to find my mother.

I don't.

Kelsey is my best friend. She has never been inside my house though. I don't allow anybody inside my house. The air in that house shouldn't be disturbed by outside people. Aunt True and Aunt Virtue wouldn't even know how to address a new person. They have been talking to the same people for *centuries* it feels like. "A proper Bostonian never talks to *strangers*," they tell me, and their definition of *stranger* means "every person on the planet except the four people we know." Life on Beacon Hill, for a certain type of Bostonian, has not changed in hundreds of years. Sometimes I think it will never change.

But today...today I think maybe change is right around the corner. I feel like even the air I'm breathing feels lighter.

Kelsey is waiting for me on the sidewalk, and I jump over the last two front steps to meet her. This is not really like me, and she lifts her eyebrows.

"I have a good feeling," I tell her.

She smiles. "Good. Me too." Kelsey always has a good feeling when we are about to go on what she considers to be an adventure. Kelsey likes adventures. She would have started looking for her mother ages ago had she been in my position. She adjusts the bag slung over her shoulder and tips her chin in the direction of the Common. "Let's go," she says.

My house sits right on Beacon Street, on the very outer edge of the higgledy-piggledy, charm-personified area of

Boston known as Beacon Hill, a place whose very streets were literally designed to try to keep the less desirable element out, set out in a rabbit warren that only those with the right breeding were supposed to know how to navigate. It seems strange to me, quaint, an entire neighborhood built so defensively, as if preparing for an invasion from the rest of the city. Beacon Hill is full of ancient brick townhouses that all hug each other, tipping drunkenly against each other on the unsteady land of a hill that was halved in height at one point so that its dirt could form the rest of the city. My house is no different, with unnecessarily large doors and dramatic, curved walls. Like the very poshest of the Beacon Hill houses, some of the windowpanes are the distinctive lavender that dates back centuries, to a defective shipment of glass once unknowingly used in Boston Brahmin Beacon Hill homes. The panes, months after installation, revealed a tendency to turn lavender in the sun and became the best sort of accidental status symbol. For a little while, there were imitation lavender panes all over Boston, none ever quite managing to duplicate the particular Beacon Hill shade. The fad for imitation eventually fell out of fashion. Now only a few of the originals remain, and tourists walk up and down the busy and chaotic thoroughfare of Beacon Street, almost getting hit by cars as they dart into traffic to get a better angle on our front windows. I feel sometimes like I live in a museum from the number of people constantly loitering around my front stoop.

We glance left and right before crossing Beacon Street, but without much interest: Boston pedestrians walk protected by the confidence that motorists would rather stop than face the lawsuit if they killed you. Once across the two lanes of traffic, we are directly on the Common. It is no surprise I considered it my front yard when I was growing up and no surprise that we have no outdoor area to our home. Why would you need one with so many empty acres right in front of you, kindly maintained by the city? My aunts have beautiful window boxes—another Beacon Hill necessity—but that is their only concession to nature. And they don't even take care of them, hiring out their care to gardeners. "Our kind does not *garden*," my aunts always say, ever the proper Bostonians.

Kelsey and I walk through the Common to the T station. It's windy, as usual, and Kelsey's hair is whipping in front of her face.

She sighs, pushing hair out of her mouth. "I should have thought to bring an elastic."

"Oh," I say and pull a rubber band out of my pocket and hand it to her.

"How clean is it?" she asks dubiously.

"I found it in with my aunts' yarn the other day," I assure her.

"I don't know what I would do without you," remarks Kelsey. "It's like having my own personal genie. If I didn't have you, I'd have to, like, *remember* things on my own."

I don't bother to say anything. I can't help the habit I have

9

of pocketing random things, and lots of times it comes in handy, like now.

Kelsey takes the rubber band and pulls her blond hair briskly back into a ponytail.

I look around for Ben, but I don't see him. I almost never see Ben when I'm not alone. Sometimes I wonder if he hides from me. Sometimes I wonder if he's a figment of my imagination. I've never told anyone about Ben, not even Kelsey. It's weird. For all I consider Kelsey my best friend, there's so much about my life I feel I can't tell her—can't tell *anyone*. My antiquated aunts in their time-frozen home seem too rarefied to be discussed with Kelsey, who exists for me in such a normal world. These are the worlds I straddle—home and high school—and it's hard for me to get the two to intersect. Football games and study hall and prom—I can't fit them into the other pieces of my life. And Ben exists in still another world, a world all his own for me, neither school nor home but a special slice of life. I could tell Kelsey about him, but somehow I feel like he would be less *mine* then. Which is both silly and selfish, but I can't help it. I have never told Kelsey about Ben, and I don't mention him now.

We get to the Park Street subway station. The T worker keeping guard at the turnstile frowns at us, so I make sure to make a big show of swiping my card. The T is always freaking out about non-paying riders. Sometimes they're so strident, you'd think they were fighting a war or something.

"And they'll just let you look up information about your

mother?" Kelsey asks me as we head toward the Red Line platform. The Red Line will take us into Dorchester, where the Registry of Vital Records is, the object of our mission today. I am determined to learn everything I can about my mother. I've asked Kelsey along because I don't want to be alone, and Kelsey is always game for an outing.

Someone steps in front of me, and I have to concentrate on darting around them. This is always happening at Park Street. There are always too many tourists around, all of them lost, all of them wandering around so confusingly aimlessly that they seem to pop up out of nowhere. Walking through Park Street station requires as much concentration as driving a car.

"Well," I reply, having completed my darting maneuver. "They're public records. Why shouldn't I be allowed to see them?"

"I don't know," she says. "If it was this easy, why didn't you ever do it before?"

Frankly, sometimes even I can barely understand my motives for the things I do. This used to frighten my aunts. I learned to cover whenever I found myself doing something inexplicable, like dancing to nonexistent music in my room or trying to read the language of dust motes. This is probably why I haven't mentioned to them my latest determination to find my mother. Well, that and the fact that my aunts obviously didn't like my mother.

To Kelsey I say, "I don't know. I'm seventeen now. I guess it's time."

"Seventeen?" exclaims Kelsey in delight. "Did you have a birthday? You should have told me! We could have celebrated!"

I take the Ben route and shrug.

Kelsey is silent a moment before saying, "But…why seventeen? What's the big deal about seventeen? Sixteen I could see, or eighteen. But seventeen's just…seventeen. Nothing big, nothing exciting. Just an in-between age."

I don't know what to say to that. Seventeen seems like a huge deal to me.

The Red Line gets stalled underground for a bit, which is not at all an unusual occurrence, but we eventually reach Dorchester. Dorchester is a decidedly different part of Boston than where I live. Everything about Boston can seem vaguely faded—it is a very old city by American standards—but Beacon Hill is so faded that it has come full circle to being fashionable again. There was a time period when modernizing Bostonians wanted to tear down Beacon Hill, all the lovely old homes with their lavender windowpanes, in favor of a new residential area with all the conveniences, like places for automobiles and electrical systems that weren't fire hazards. The less-modernizing Bostonians, Bostonians like my aunts, resisted the entire idea, and Beacon Hill survived its shabbiest era more or less intact, the same as it had been for ages, only the barest concessions to the passage of time, to emerge today as the type of place that gets thrown onto postcards.

Dorchester is at the point in time when modernizing

Bostonians wish to tear it down and start from scratch, and Dorchester doesn't have proper Bostonian inhabitants to insist upon its unchanging preservation, so some of that has happened. In among the older, rundown buildings are gleaming new ones, like the Registry of Vital Records. I don't like new buildings in Boston; they make you wince, like hearing a sour note in a song. The streets are also wide enough that cars easily fit down them, and you could be anywhere in America with streets like that. I don't feel at *home* here. I may be only seventeen—already seventeen?—but I'm most at home in the places where seventeen-year-olds were at home, like, two centuries ago.

The accents are at least comfortingly Boston, as proven by the woman at the front desk.

"I'm looking for information about my mother," I tell her, pushing across my identification.

The woman smiles at me kindly. "Okay. And what was her name?"

"Faye Blaxton," I say and spell the name for her. I know that much from my birth certificate.

The woman types into her computer. Then she looks back at me. "Was she born in Massachusetts?" she asks me.

"I don't know," I admit. "Maybe not."

The woman does some more typing—and then frowns a bit. "I can't find anyone by that name. At least, not in the right time period to be your mother. You're sure it's the correct name? And the correct spelling?"

I'm sure. But, just in case, I have her look up my birth certificate, and there is my mother's name on it, plain as day. *Faye Blaxton.*

"It could be a glitch in the system," says the nice woman at the desk. "A typo maybe. Or something."

"Yeah," I agree glumly. I don't want to sound glum. I want to sound like it's no big deal that I can't find my mother. I've done okay without her so far, haven't I? But I'd thought, well, that it'd be simple. *Oh, Faye Blaxton, she lives out in Malden.* And then, maybe, I would know that she'd never bothered to check in on her daughter, but I would also know that she *existed.*

"It's a dead end, maybe," says Kelsey when we leave, "but there are other avenues to explore!" Kelsey is all big-picture enthusiasm, which I know is for my benefit. "What do you know about your mother?"

One day my father walked into his Back Bay apartment to find a blond woman asleep on his couch. I can't say that. "Not much," I say. And then, truthfully, after a pause, "My aunts say she was flighty." I know my aunts mean it as a negative, but when I was little, I always had the impression that it meant my mother could fly, that she had deposited me on that Back Bay doorstep and then soared into the neverending sky.

"Your aunts knew her, then," says Kelsey.

"No," I reply. "Not really. Well, I don't know, actually. I think to them she's just a woman who left her baby on a doorstep."

"Wait, she really *did* that?" Kelsey asks.

I look at her in confusion because I've told her at least this much about myself, my family, my past. "Yeah."

"I thought you meant that *figuratively*. Like, that you just meant your mom gave you up or something. She *literally* left you on a doorstep?"

I nod. *With a note. A note etched into a snowflake, sighed into a gust of wind, rustled through the trees of autumn, rippled over a summer pond.*

"Well," says Kelsey. And then she doesn't say anything else.

We get on the T. This time there are no delays, but I feel like people watch me the whole way, like it must be common knowledge, written all over me: *I am the girl who has no mother.*

CHAPTER 2

You're supposed to go to Salem in October. At least, that's what Kelsey tells me. I go though, because *not* going doesn't seem like an option—one of those things I do without really knowing why. I don't particularly want to go to Salem, but I feel like I need to go.

Salem is crowded despite the fact that it's a cold and misty day. The sidewalks are so jam-packed you can't walk without stepping on someone's broomstick. I walk along, picking up dropped coins because you never know when they might come in handy. Mike and Jake are throwing pieces of cotton candy at each other. It's stupid, because you can't really effectively throw cotton candy and because it's causing chaos—people are glaring at us—and I wonder if Mike thinks this is cool and I'm going to be thoroughly smitten with him now. I try to imagine Ben ever throwing cotton candy around. I can't. It makes me wish Ben were there, but it's the sort of day Ben avoids like the plague, when he's dressed in at least one layer more than any normal person would wear and huddles under the meager shelter of the Park Street subway station entrance. I admit I kind of like weather like this. I've only started to dislike it because it makes Ben so miserable.

I look at Kelsey. "I've had enough," I tell her.

She looks at her watch. "The next ferry isn't until—"

"I'm going to go in here," I say. It's one of the plethora of witch museums littered all over the town, an old house, well tended, with a silhouette of a stylized witch in the fanlight over the door. There is a pot of bright bronze chrysanthemums in front of the door, but someone's knocked it over.

"'The Salem Which Museum,'" reads Kelsey from the dripping black letters on the sign swinging off the house. "They didn't even spell *witch* correctly."

I'd noticed, but the Salem Which Museum has the great advantage of, well, being only two steps away from me and so conveniently easy to disappear into. "It's fine. It'll be something for me to do until they get tired of…" I look at Mike and Jake. "Throwing things," I finish, because they've now moved on to throwing popcorn at each other. At least that works a little better than the cotton candy had. I decide not to think about where they'd gotten the popcorn.

"Are you sure?" Kelsey asks.

I nod. Now that I've seized on the idea, I kind of really want to explore this misnamed museum.

"I think I'll stick with them," says Kelsey, blushing. The reason for this blush is clear: Kelsey likes Jake. She thinks I haven't noticed this. It's silly because Kelsey has liked Jake for a while now. Maybe that's why Mike thinks I should like him. Maybe he thinks we should all just couple up.

"Okay," I agree amiably. "I'll hang out here and meet you

guys at the ferry." I reach for the door then pause, my hand on the doorknob, and look back at her. "Don't let Mike come in after me."

"You got it," says Kelsey, and then she hurries to catch up with Mike and Jake, who have tired of the popcorn throwing and are looking around for the next thing they can throw. Before they find it—or can spot me—I duck into the museum.

I'm in a tiny room with tiny windows and a short ceiling, typical for a house this age. The house is at least three centuries old, and I feel at home in it immediately. The light is murky, but that's because there really *is* no light today, more of a non-light. There's an open shoebox on an old wooden table right next to me, and there's an index card taped to it with "Donations Appreciated" written on it in the kind of proper Bostonian cursive that my aunts use. Except that the final flourish is a smiley face, and I think my aunts would die before using a smiley face. There is a single dollar bill in the shoebox and several dusty coins. The coins don't even look American. Next to the table is a softly ticking grandfather clock. As I walk in, it's just finishing up chiming nine o'clock. Not the right time. Grandfather clocks never tell the right time in my experience. My aunts' is the same way.

"Oh!" exclaims a voice to my right. The floor creaks in that way old wooden floors do, and I look up, startled. A man is bustling into the room from a doorway on the other side. He's dressed in gray corduroys and a bright red cable-knit sweater, and he's possibly in his early fifties, between my father and aunts in age, I'd estimate. He has glasses and graying brown hair that's sticking up a little, and he makes me think of professors and naps and my father, all at once. I have that feeling I get sometimes, of odd familiarity, instinctive comfort, being in this museum with this man. It's almost like déjà vu, although surely I've never been here before, never met this man before. "I'm Will," he says. "Welcome to the Salem Which Museum?"

He says it like it's a question, like he's not sure whether or not I am, in fact, welcome there. "Thanks," I say awkwardly, and then, because he looks so thrilled to have a visitor and because I feel bad, I dig my collected coins from the day out of the pocket of my jeans and drop them in the shoebox.

Will absolutely beams. Then he says, "What would you like to hear about?"

"Sorry?" I say because I have no idea what I want to hear about. I thought I'd just be able to wander around the museum, looking at displays.

"Well, here at the Salem Which Museum? The guest decides. Which type of museum are you looking for? That is the type of museum we are."

"Oh." I realize slowly. "The Salem *Which* Museum."

"That's us," he affirms, still beaming and now rocking back and forth, heel to toe.

The kind of museum I was looking for was a museum in which I could disappear. I wonder what Will would say to that. I look around the little room, trying to find the most obvious thing to ask about. I could ask about the Salem Witch Trials, of course, but I've heard that story a million times.

"Might I suggest," says Will, "family history?"

I blink, sure I must have misunderstood. I look down. I am wearing the Boston sweatshirt Ben gave me on my birthday. There is no sign around my neck proclaiming my motherlessness. What would make this man say that?

"The history of Boston," Will continues, "for all Bostonians are family. And you are a Bostonian, are you not?"

Yes, I am wearing the Boston sweatshirt, although how many Bostonians wear Boston sweatshirts? But I just nod.

"Oh, the words I could tell you about the history of Boston," says Will. "But better you read them for yourself. Written words—that's where the real power is. And, of course, the history of Boston depends on who has done the writing of it. Come along."

He scurries out of the room, through the doorway he came in.

I hesitate, then follow.

The room connects to a kitchen that looks as if it was last redone in the 1950s, and there is a huge iguana on the counter. I stare at it. It stares at me, reptilian eyes blinking without interest. Will's head pops through another door at the other end of the room and he notices my showdown with the creature.

"Oh," he says. "That's just Iggy."

"Iggy," I repeat dubiously.

"Yes. He's an *iguana*," Will points out, like I'm an idiot. "Come here," he says and disappears into the other room.

The other room turns out to be much bigger than the rooms I've been in so far, with a much higher ceiling. Maybe it was the carriage house or something. Whatever it used to be, it is now a storage space for books. They are piled sky high, toward the rafters above. I'm not sure how they're not toppling over. There are narrow windows way up there, and that's where all the light is, barely making it to the floor where I'm standing. Something about the room makes me shiver, makes me stand on its threshold, unwilling to step forward, unsure what might happen if I do. The air seems dusty and *different* somehow—difficult to breathe.

Will, in the meantime, is busy impossibly climbing an impossible pile of books. He plucks one off the top of an adjacent pile, shimmies back down, and tosses me the book. "About Boston," he says helpfully and then runs off to scale another pile of books.

"That doesn't look safe," I say.

"What?" he shouts down to me and then throws me another book, which I catch instinctively. "Also about Boston."

"Oh," I say, not sure what to make of this, but Will is already down that pile and up the next, and I'm holding two books so dusty that I can't even see their titles. I try to blow the dust off their covers, but the dust is so thick my breath doesn't even dislodge it.

"You should go read them," instructs Will, handing me

another book. He has apparently reached the ground safely once again.

I figure I've got time to kill. I look at the dusty floor. "Is there somewhere I can sit?"

"Oh!" exclaims Will, as if that never occurred to him. "You want to sit! Oh! Yes! Of course! In the front room!"

I edge back past Iggy and into the front room. There's a couch in there that doesn't look like anyone's sat on it since 1672, but it doesn't collapse when I sit on it, so that's something, I suppose. The fragile fabric probably crushes into dust underneath me, but it's better than the floor in the other room. I keep one ear open for the sound of books tumbling onto Will (*What will I do?* I wonder. *Call 911 and say a mountain of books toppled onto him?*) and flip open my books. The first one is some kind of epic poem about the first winter of the Plymouth Plantation, the second is a more traditional history, and the third, practically crumbling in my grasp, seems like some odd combination of the two, serious stories and anecdotes about kraken all mixed up into one. This is the one I decide to look through, and there, in the middle of it, is a list of Boston's first settlers. I look for Blaxtons, but there are none there. And then I decide to look for Stewarts. After all, I think, smiling to myself, my aunts have lived in the townhouse on Beacon Street since the beginning of time.

And then their names are there.

True Stewart

Virtue Stewart

Etherington Stewart

My aunts. And my father. Their names. Right there.

I stare at them for a long time. *Coincidence*, I think. The Stewarts *are* an old family, one of Boston's oldest. And the names True, Virtue, Etherington—not exactly modern ones. Maybe old family ones. Maybe recurring, from generation to generation.

I pick up the history and let it fall open where it wants, to a well-worn page in the middle, and it is a portrait of old, dour-looking people. The date of the portrait is 1753. I study it, wondering how many of these people were still alive when the Revolution broke out twenty years later.

I turn the page, and there are my aunts' faces, staring out at me. I blink, startled, but there is no mistaking it. It is them—as much them as a portrait can be. Their wide, deep, dark eyes, sorrowful and ageless under perfectly sculpted dark eyebrows. Their dark hair pulled back from their high foreheads. Their pursed, unsmiling lips. Their sharp cheekbones under unlined, olive skin.

I look at the caption. *True and Virtue Stewart*, it reads. *1760.* I look back at them, at their faces. *Family resemblance*, I try to think. *The Stewarts are an old family*, I remind myself. *Their names and features might be recurring.*

I flip through the rest of the portraits in the book. No Etherington Stewart turns up. Just True and Virtue, posed in stiff black dresses, looking exactly like the True and Virtue

Stewart in my house, the True and Virtue Stewart who have raised me.

I reach for the epic poem, let it fall open as well, and the first lines on the page are not even a surprise to me at this point. *The house of the Misses Stewart / Theyre brother late returneth / Frome an excursion to a newe settlement / Fulle of truth and virtue / Befitting of theyre names.*

I look from the poem to the portraits. I can hear Will humming to himself in his weird library place, and following one of my usual spur-of-the-moment impulses, I reach out and rip the portrait out of its book. I do the same for the lines of the epic poem. I pick up the history and thumb through it until I find the list of settlers again, and I rip that out as well. Then I fold the pages up and stick them in the kangaroo pocket of my Boston sweatshirt.

What have I done? I have *ripped pages* out of old, priceless books belonging to a *museum*. A really strange museum but *still*. And what am I going to *do* with these pages? What am I *doing*?

I'm finished here. I have to be before Will comes back and asks why I'm vandalizing his books of power, his museum's only exhibits. I get up and walk to Iggy's kitchen, and I call to Will, "Thanks for letting me look at the books on Boston! I'm leaving now!"

I step out into the mist without waiting for him to reply. Here on the streets of Salem, Halloween is still in full swing, witches roaming around, modern day and centuries old, like the pages of my family's ancient history tucked in my pocket. I hurry away from the Salem Which Museum, oblivious to the press of the costumed, festive crowds, preoccupied with the words of the pages in my pocket. *Stewarts, Stewarts everywhere. And not a single Blaxton.*

My aunts move through our house like ghosts. They always have, for as long as I can remember. They glide silently from room to room, dressed always in long-sleeved black blouses tucked carefully into knee-length black skirts with black boots gleaming underneath them. I find myself wondering now for how many centuries they have done this.

"How was Salem, dear?" Aunt Virtue asks me vaguely, because they are focused on other things. Mainly, the arrangement of the furniture. They are always convinced that the furniture is being moved on them—tiny, infinitesimal adjustments in its angles. They blame gnomes. This is the kind of life I lead: my aunts are genuinely convinced gnomes are real, as real a plague on Beacon Hill as the mice and rats are.

"Fine," I answer.

I'm not even sure they hear me.

"Insufferable gnomes!" curses Aunt True as Aunt Virtue tips a picture frame an unseeable amount of space to the left. She is standing tiptoe on top of a pink-and-gilt Queen Anne chair to do this. The house is an odd combination of styles, and I always assumed it was inherited from generations of Stewarts past. Now I wonder if Aunt True and Aunt Virtue have been collecting through the centuries.

This is madness, I think. *I'm losing my mind.*

"It looks better," Aunt True tells Aunt Virtue, and Aunt Virtue leaps down from the Queen Anne chair with a nimbleness that belies her age.

"*Damnable* gnomes," says Aunt Virtue, stepping back so she can study the picture for herself.

Aunt True nods in firm agreement. "Come now," she says. "I do believe they pushed the chaise lounge a bit to the left in the conservatory."

I watch them march down the hallway to the conservatory. I swallow trepidation and follow them. I love my aunts, of course I do, but sometimes I feel like, even though they've raised me from infancy, they have no idea what to make of me. They look at me sometimes like I'm not what they expected, but other times they look at me like I'm exactly what they expected. Either way, I feel like they're not sure how they feel about who I've turned out to be. I always feel loved, but there is usually an undercurrent of something like dread too. I have no idea why, but the dread has infected me. They are afraid for me, and to me it seems like more than the worry of other people's parents; it is genuine *fright*. So I always try not to say anything that might alarm them, but now I find that I just have to. There are too many questions welling up inside of me.

"How long have there been Stewarts in Boston?" I ask.

"Forever," answers Aunt True absently.

"*Look* at this chaise lounge," says Aunt Virtue.

"Oh, they have *definitely* been at this chaise lounge," agrees Aunt True.

I watch them nudge the chaise lounge a hairsbreadth to the left.

"Do you know anything about them?" I ask, trying to sound casual.

Suddenly, I am the center of both aunts' attention. They are still leaned over the chaise lounge but their gazes are sharp on me.

"Know anything about whom?" asks Aunt True shrewdly.

"The Stewarts who settled Boston," I clarify.

There is a long moment of silence. My aunts slowly straighten, still looking at me closely. I want to fidget. I feel like I have asked something I should never have asked, but I don't know why.

"What about them?" Aunt Virtue asks carefully.

What were their names? I want to ask. But somehow the words stick in my throat. I can't make myself say them. My aunts' dark eyes, full of love and that terrifying dread, are steady on me. I can see them willing me to drop the entire thing. But I *can't*. I can't drop *all* of it. There is so little I know about *myself*, and I feel like my aunts will never want me to ask any of the questions I have.

"What about my mother?" I persist almost desperately.

"What about her?" demands Aunt True, a challenge being flung to me. *Ask another question.*

"Who was she? Did you know her? Where did she come from? Why can't I find any other Blaxtons?"

"Have you been looking for them?" asks Aunt True.

"You need to stop looking for them," commands Aunt Virtue.

"Do you understand how hard it is for me to know *nothing* about her? She's my *mother*," I cry, trying to make them *see*.

"It means nothing," Aunt Virtue says staunchly. "She was never supposed to be here. She did not belong here. You are one of us: a Stewart of Boston. We who have been here from the beginning and will be here to the end. This is your home, we are yours, and you are ours. It matters not what anyone else may say, what words may be used on you. You are a Stewart of Boston. Remember that."

"I know that," I say. "I won't...run away. I'm not trying to—"

"Are you unhappy?" Aunt True asks me gently.

"No," I say honestly. "I'm not."

"Then forget about your mother," she says, still in that tender, loving tone of voice. She walks over to me and cups a hand on my cheek. "This is your life. *This.* This time, this place, this world." Her words are strangely firm, as if, by pronouncing them so clearly, she can make it be this way, make *me* be this way.

She turns back to Aunt Virtue, and they resume the minute adjustments of everything in the room, but I stand frozen, her words trembling in the air around me.

CHAPTER 3

School the next day feels unbearably long. It's so hard to concentrate on things like the Pythagorean theorem when I have decided that it's possible my aunts are immortal creatures. I meet up with Kelsey for American literature class. She is complaining because she lost a button on the brand-new cardigan she's wearing.

"Oh," I note. "I picked up a button this morning." I fish it out of my pocket, avoiding the old book pages occupying the same space, and hand it to her.

"Of course it's a perfect match," Kelsey sighs. "I don't know how you *do* that."

"I'm a good best friend," I tell her.

"That you are." Kelsey tucks the button into her own pocket. "You okay, by the way? You seemed quiet in Salem, but I thought you just weren't having a good time. But you don't seem yourself today either."

"I'm fine," I say.

But I'm not, of course.

I decide that I have to go see my father. I just have to. I spend a sleepless night worrying about all the questions in my head and knowing that my aunts will never answer them, but *somebody* has to. I know my aunts are convinced I should know who I am without knowing anything about my mother, but I feel like I just can't. How can I? And the fact that my aunts are so dead set against it makes me feel like I really have to know. I'm not usually such a brat, but in this case I can't help it. I just have to go see my father. He is not always lucid enough to answer questions like that—the poem about my name being a prime example—but I can at least give it a try.

The day is mostly sunny, although there is a chill in the air, and Ben is doing a brisk business in sweatshirts. I wait impatiently for him to give change to a customer. I haven't seen him glance my way, but as soon as he's done, he turns toward me, his pale eyes sharp.

"What's wrong?" He has obviously immediately seen my agitation.

"I'm going to see my father," I say.

Ben and I have never discussed anything about our family lives—Ben and I know both everything and nothing about each other—but he doesn't ask me anything about why my father is someone I have to visit. He just says, "Why?"

"Because I have so many questions, Ben. I don't have a mother—"

"Everyone has a mother," Ben interjects calmly. "You have a mother; you just don't *know* your mother."

It seems like a pointless distinction for him to be making

right now. "Fine," I agree. "Whatever. I don't know her. And no one will tell me anything about her. I have to ask my father. I have to *try* to ask my father. I have to know. I feel like I have to know. I need to hear the *words*."

Ben is silent for a moment. His eyes darken as the sun passes behind a cloud. He says carefully, "Do you think he'll tell you?"

"I don't know. But I have to try."

There is another long moment of silence. Ben's eyes search mine. I feel like he is asking me a question that I don't understand.

"What?" I say.

He just shakes his head, and it might be my imagination, me projecting my own emotional upheaval onto him, but I think he looks sad, and on impulse, I hug him. I have never done this before, and the awkwardness of having done it strikes me as soon as it happens, and I let go so quickly that I don't even have time to register how it feels. I am suddenly embarrassed, and I have no idea why I've done it—why am I constantly doing things without thinking?—and I have the fleeting impression that Ben looks surprised before I turn and flee to the subway station like a coward. I am almost relieved when the train predictably gets stuck underground for a little while; it gives my cheeks time to stop burning.

I take the Red Line all the way to the Alewife end, where there is a small, nondescript, charming-looking building that you would never know houses the less sane members of Boston's better families.

"Selkie." The nurse at the front desk smiles at me. I am on a first-name basis with everyone at this place. I have been coming here, after all, for sixteen years. "Where are your aunts?" She looks past me for them. I have never come alone before.

"Just me this time," I say confidently, as if this isn't unusual. "Is my dad around?" It's the most ridiculous question for me to ask. Where else would he be?

"Of course he's here," she answers, which highlights the absurdity of my question. "I'll have someone fetch him for you."

There's a little room where you meet with people. It feels like a pretty little sun porch, filled to the brim with too many flowery patterns on the furniture and the drapes, but you always know that people are watching—politely but close enough to intercede should anything happen. There's a grandfather clock in this room, but it always tells the right time. I find that odd and unsettling.

"Selkie," says Dad as he walks into the room to see me, and he holds his arms out for a hug, and I hug him back, and he smells vaguely of hospital, which he always does, but that is not a bad smell to me; that is my father's smell. "What brings you here? Where are your aunts?"

"They're home," I tell him truthfully. He is holding my hands in his and beaming at me, and I study him, just to make sure he's all right, the way I always do. "How are you?"

"I'm fine," he assures me. "So happy to see you."

"Good." I smile, and then I hesitate, trip over my errand, think maybe I should turn around and leave.

Dad notices. His smile turns quizzical. "Is there something wrong, Selkie?" His expression grows more concerned. "Aunt True and Aunt Virtue are all right, aren't they?"

"They're fine," I say. I clear my throat. "Dad. Can you tell me about Mom?"

He smiles the absently fond smile he has always smiled the few times he has spoken to me about her. "One day," he says, "I walked into my Back Bay apartment to find a blond woman asleep on my couch. The most beautiful woman I had ever seen."

I am frustrated. I have heard this all before. "But who was she?"

"The most beautiful woman I had ever seen," he says. "And she gave me you, and she told me to name you Selkie."

"Did you love her?" I ask.

"The most beautiful woman I had ever seen," he repeats vaguely, his gaze unfocused.

"Why did she leave me, Dad?" I try not to sound like I'm on the verge of tears.

"She couldn't stay in Boston, of course," he answers, and I am shocked because this is—*finally*—something new. I think of my aunts, saying that my mother hadn't belonged here.

"Why not?"

"And you were my *right*," Dad says fiercely, looking at me.

I blink, startled. "What does that mean?"

My father's gaze loses the unusual clarity it just had, softens. "Where are your aunts?" he asks.

"Home," I answer briefly, trying to get him back to his mood of revelations. "Didn't she love me?"

"Love you?" he says, as if the words hold no meaning for him, and I am disappointed. I have lost my window of lucidity.

I decide to just give one more question a shot. "I went to Salem," I start, reaching into my kangaroo pocket, closing my hand around the ancient pages.

"Salem," he repeats blankly.

"There was this book," I continue. "Well, books," I amend.

He looks at me, vaguely interested. "Books," he says. "Powerful things, books. All those words, trapped in writing."

It is so similar to what Will had said at the Which Museum that it gives me pause. I go on slowly. "Your name was in them—you, Aunt True, Aunt Virtue."

Dad's eyes sharpen. "What books?" he asks. "What books were they *exactly*?"

"I don't know," I stammer honestly, taken aback by his reaction. "I don't remember the names. But look—this is a list of the first settlers of Boston, and you're all listed." I pull it out, show it to him eagerly.

"We're an old family," he interjects, and he sounds saner

than I've ever heard him. He looks narrow eyed at the paper I have handed him.

"And then there was this portrait, Dad," I say, unfolding it, "this painting, in another book, and it's Aunt True and Aunt Virtue, I mean, look, It's *them*, but it's from 1760." I thrust it at him. "And there was this epic poem, and—"

"Blaxton," Dad cuts me off, and his voice is dangerously quiet. I have never heard him talk that way to me before, and for the first time, I might be scared of him but I think I am more confused.

"Mom?" I say, because she is the only Blaxton I've ever heard of. "What does she have to do with it?"

"Not your mother," he tells me, biting the words off. He drops the pages to the ground.

I stoop to pick them up, stuff them back in my pocket. "Then who—" I start, but he lunges for me suddenly, grabbing my hands in his, the grip iron tight. "You're hurting me," I manage, but my voice sounds so small, and I feel frozen.

"And if Blaxton's involved, then you've been talking to Benedict," he accuses, his voice slicing.

I look up into his face, and it is so contorted with fury that it doesn't even look like my dad anymore. "Who?" I stammer.

"Benedict Le Fay," he spits out.

"Faye…?" I echo vaguely, still thinking he must mean my mother somehow.

My father catches my chin painfully between his fingers. "What did you tell them?" he demands, and he is breathing quickly, sucking in his air through his teeth. "I knew they couldn't be trusted. It's like the old saying goes."

I should be terrified, I think, but I am still too stunned. "Who? What old saying?"

And then, suddenly, attendants are on my father, pulling him away from me. They are restraining him, apologizing to me, pushing him away from me, through the door, but I cannot hear what they are saying because all I know is that my father meets my eyes and shouts, thoroughly enraged, "Did you tell him your birth date?"

Then my father is gone, through the door; it slams shut behind him, and air whooshes out of me in a great rush, like I had not been breathing for hours beforehand, and maybe it is the fear finally hitting me, but I feel almost dizzy, and the nurse is there and she is comforting me, apologizing, asking if I'm okay, pushing a glass of water on me, and I take the water blindly but I don't drink it, and I clutch it, and I say, "I have to go home. I have to go home."

I take the water with me when I leave, but I don't realize that I'm carrying it until I reach the T station. I look down at it, clutched in my hand, and then I turn away from the T station door. I walk a few steps along the sidewalk. It is rush hour, and the people on the sidewalk are not delaying; they are hurrying toward their destinations, and they pay me no attention.

I turn my back to them, and I open my hand, and the glass tumbles to the sidewalk and shatters. Its water streams along the concrete, and shards of glass sparkle like diamonds around me, vicious and beautiful.

I lean down and pick up one and wrap it carefully in a tissue I find in my pocket and then put it in the pocket of my sweatshirt, beside the ancient pages.

I have no idea why.

By the time I reach Park Street, I am still dazed and shaken. Nothing makes sense. Nothing is any clearer. I feel like my life is composed entirely of other people's secrets, and that isn't fair—it's *my life*. I am dazed and shaken and I am *furious*.

I step off the subway train and dart around a guy who comes running in front of me out of nowhere. I go home and find my aunts at the dining room table.

"Really, gnomes and their taste for Napoleon brandy," Aunt Virtue is saying, and they both look up when I come in.

"Selkie," says Aunt True. "You're late for dinner."

"Where were you?" asks Aunt Virtue.

"I went to see Dad," I say, a little breathless still.

"Your father," says Aunt Virtue.

"Why didn't you tell us? We would have gone along," says Aunt True.

"Wait," says Aunt Virtue and frowns. "This isn't about your mother again, is it?"

"Oh, Selkie, is it?" says Aunt True. "We told you—"

"I know," I say. "I know you told me, and I'm sorry, but I couldn't help it, I just wanted to know—"

"You *can't* know, Selkie." Aunt True's tone is begging me. "You just *can't*. You cannot ask these questions; you cannot hear these words."

"Please," says Aunt Virtue.

"What will happen?" I ask. "I don't understand."

"We will lose you," says Aunt True. "We will lose you forever."

And I want to tell them that they will never lose me, that I will always love them, no matter who my mother is. But their wide, dark eyes look at me, full of fear, and I can think of nothing but trying to soothe them, trying to get things back to normal.

So I sit down and eat dinner.

It is that night, after dinner, almost bedtime, when I am trying and failing to do homework, that I make the connection that I should have made so much earlier. *Benedict*, my father had said, and I finally think of Ben. I had always assumed his name was Benjamin, but had he ever said that? No. He has always just been Ben. I don't even know his last name. *Benedict Le Fay*. Who I told my birth date to. The only person I've ever told.

It doesn't make sense to me, any of it. How can Ben be

involved? And what, exactly, is Ben involved with? There are so many odd things going on. Could he be connected to my mother? But how? When no one else in the universe seems to be? I think of the vandalized pages in the pocket of my sweatshirt—Stewarts throughout Boston history. Could Ben have something to do with that? Ben, who is as inextricably a part of Boston to me as the Common itself?

I look out my bedroom window. The Common's lazy paths are signaled to me by rows of lights along them, leading eventually to the brighter corner where Park Street T station sits. I stand there, torn. Is it madness to go look for Ben now? He is probably not there, not this late, but I feel compelled by the same need to find out *something* concrete that drove me to visit my father. My aunts don't want me to know, but I *have* to know. How am I supposed to make any decisions about my future when I know nothing at all about my past? When I don't really know who I *am*?

I make the decision. No harm in running down there. My aunts think I'm in bed. They won't think to look for me; they won't notice I'm gone. Anyway, they're in bed by now too.

I pull on my sweatshirt, check its pocket, all the strange things I'm randomly carrying around because I'm insane: pages ripped from old books, check; shard of glass wrapped in tissue, check. Then I slip past the grandfather clock on the landing—it chimes 6:15 as I pass—down to the front hall and out of the house.

I walk briskly down to Park Street. It is a damp, chilly night.

The air feels saturated with rain. I don't expect Ben to be out on a night like this, but he is there, just out of the circle of light from Park Street, standing on the grass. He is wearing jeans and a windbreaker, sweatshirt, *and* raincoat, and none of them match—bright orange sweatshirt, bright blue windbreaker, Kelly green raincoat, the colors clash and run together, and that is also not unusual for Ben. He is, however, without anything to sell, which is highly unusual for Ben. He is standing, the collar of his raincoat turned up against the rain in the air, hood over his head, his hands tucked into the pockets of his windbreaker, and he watches me approach, his eyes never leaving me. In this half-light, those distinctive eyes of his are the color of the rain beginning to fall around us, quicksilver, hinting flashes.

I walk over to him, but once there, I don't know what to say, how to begin. *What do you know about my mother? What do you know about* me?

Ben looks at me for a long moment, his expression unreadable, and I look back, and he talks first. "Don't say my name."

The only name he has ever told me is Ben, but I know that's not what he's talking about, and that makes me furious suddenly. Ben clearly knows so much more about me than he has ever let on, than I have ever told him, and I still know *nothing* about him. He doesn't even want me to know his *name*.

"Benedict Le Fay?" I ask scathingly. "*That* name?"

Ben winces like I'd reached out and slapped him, which is so overdramatic. All I did was snap his name.

"So that's your name, is it? A name you never told me? How do you know I know it now? Are you in constant contact with my father's nurses? And how does my father know your name, anyway? How do you *know* my father? Why does my *father* get to know your name and not me?" The questions trip out of my mouth in a tidal wave. Now that I've started asking things, I think I might never stop.

"Okay," says Ben, his eyes flickering around us as if he's scared I'm making a scene, attracting attention. "You clearly have a lot of questions, and you deserve answers—"

"I *deserve* answers?" Something about the phrase makes me even more furious than I already was, like the truth about my entire life is a treat he's giving me, a reward for good behavior. "How nice of you." My voice is dripping sarcasm. "Exactly how much do you know about me, Benedict Le Fay?" I fling his name at him, the only thing I've managed to learn about him.

He hisses in a breath. "Stop that," he commands harshly. "You need to stop that."

I am so sick of being ordered around. "Stop what? Saying your name? What is the big deal? I know *one thing* about you. Benedict Le Fay, Benedict Le Fay, Benedict Le Fay."

Ben staggers away from me as if I'd shoved him, although I haven't touched him. For the first time, confusion begins to thread through my anger. This upsets him *that much*?

"Benedict Le Fay," I say again, curious now.

Ben seems to gather himself enough to lunge forward and

grab my shoulders unexpectedly, the motion making his hood fall away from his head.

I gasp in surprise.

"Stop saying it like that. Please. Where did you *learn* that? You're going to—"

The skies above us open up suddenly, drowning out whatever he was going to say. He groans and drops my shoulders, hastily pulling his hood up again.

I feel so battered by strangeness I'm exhausted. "You need to tell me what's going on, Ben."

"Fine," he agrees. "Yes. But not here. We can't stay here."

"I'm not going anywhere," I tell him, annoyed.

"You don't have a choice."

"I'm not," I repeat very deliberately, "going anywhere. You're going to tell me what's going on. Right now."

"I can't," he snaps. "You said my name. Several times. Not nicely. And now it's pouring and I'm wet. So we do *not* have a choice. We are going. If we stay here, the world will end."

"I'm not going anywhere until you start making sense," I insist.

"Selkie," he bites out, "I am the only thing that has ever made your life make sense. Do you trust me?"

I hesitate. Only hours earlier, I would have said yes unequivocally. I study Ben's pale eyes, but I might as well try to interpret the mood of the puddles growing around us. "I don't know," I admit.

"Good answer," says Ben cryptically, which doesn't exactly

inspire confidence. "But I need you to now, just for a minute more, just the way you usually do, and come with me."

I search his face, his well-known features, the well-defined slope of his cheeks, the elegant curve of lips that I have given far too much thought to. I look over my shoulder. Beacon Street is nothing more than a row of impressionistic lights, looking very far away and unattainable to me.

"Please come," Ben begs me.

I look back at him.

"Please come *now*," he says. He is looking anxiously around him, and he is coiled up, poised to spring. "*Please*. I will explain everything to you, but there isn't time right now. We have to *go*." He looks back at me, pleading with me, and I realize that, up until this moment, Ben has never asked me for anything. I am still angry, but I am also struck by his nervous determination, so unlike him; he is normally so unflappable.

"Where?"

"The subway station," he says.

It sounds safe enough, I figure. It's late, but there are still people in the subway, and it's only a few feet away. "Okay," I say.

"Thank you," says Ben, heartfelt, and then he takes my hand, dashing to the cover the station represents. The raindrops are hard as they hit the cement, tiny explosions that reverberate and soak the cuffs of my jeans as I am pulled in Ben's wake, and then he tumbles through the station doors, pulling me after him, and he slams them shut behind us, and every single person around us in Park Street station, the people going in and out, the people going up and down, all vanish into thin air. The silence that falls is terrifying in this space that is made for the noise and bustle of a city.

I stare around myself in shock because there were *people* there; they were everywhere.

"Well," says Ben, and I realize that he is breathing much harder than the quick dash through the rain should have warranted. "We *just* made that. Let's not do that again in the future if we can avoid it."

I look at him, leaning against the door. "What have you done?"

"I haven't done anything. *You* did it. You said my name. A lot."

"And that made all the people in Park Street station disappear?"

"All the people in *Boston*," he corrects me, and he steps carefully away from the door. "If you open this door, we will be pulled out into the Nowhere, do you understand me? You cannot open the door. But you can look through the window."

I walk to the door, and I realize that Ben is standing very tensely, as if he expects me to throw the door open and that somehow we will be pulled out into some place called Nowhere and that will be very bad. I don't pull the door open. I put my face to the window. Outside is nothing but darkness. It is not just that the lights have gone out in Boston. It's that there are no lights to go out. There is *nothing*.

I step back in alarm. "I don't understand. Where did it go?"

"You broke my enchantment," says Ben simply, as if that makes sense.

I stare at him. "I what?"

"You broke my enchantment. You said my name, and you made it rain, and you broke it. And really I'm never going to hear the end of it, I must say."

"What are you talking about?" I demand, bewildered. "I didn't make it rain. I can't make it rain."

"Of course you can," Ben says, as if *I* am the crazy one.

"You're not making any sense." I am losing patience now. "Nobody has made any sense—"

"Ever in your life. You're just noticing it now."

"Ben," I say firmly, ignoring his flinch. "Tell me what's happening."

"What's happening right now? What we'd been waiting for, I suppose, although I didn't think it would happen quite this way. But you told me your birthday—that was the first break in the chain." Ben starts pacing, shaking rainwater out of his thick, dark hair with his hands, the droplets flying every-where. "Then you got into the Salem Which Museum, and Will gave you the books, and you started asking the right questions finally, and it was only a matter of time until you knew the right words, but I thought we'd be able to tell you everything very calmly. I think your aunts were planning an old-fashioned tea or something. I didn't think you'd be able to dissolve my enchantment. That's usually so much harder to do than you made it look just now."

"What are you talking about? Your enchantment?"

"Yes. You know. Your whole life and the way you were just normal enough to stay hidden and safe."

I stare at him, thinking he's lost his mind. "You're telling me that my whole life is nothing but an *enchantment*?"

Ben stops pacing and looks at me, quicksilver eyes serious. "Yes," he answers simply. "And you just broke it."

I continue to stare at him, silent, trying to comprehend this.

"I told you the world would end if you kept saying my name," says Ben.

CHAPTER 4

L et's go," says Ben, as if it's a typical evening out in Boston. He starts jogging down the stairs at Park Street, toward the subway.

"Wait. I don't understand," I say. I am tired of saying this, and I don't even think Ben hears me saying it anymore, if he ever did. I decide to avoid the doors with their terrifying black emptiness beyond and follow him. He leaps over the barrier. I halt, pull my T pass out of my pocket, and swipe the card. It beeps its approval, and the gates swing open.

Ben, who had been leaning over and frowning down the Green Line track to our left, turns at the noise, and he looks absolutely astonished. "Did you just *pay* to get in here?"

"Well, it's an unlimited pass," I say, "so, technically, I paid at the beginning of the month. What happened to everyone in my life? My father, my aunts, Kelsey?"

Ben looks blank. "What do you mean?"

"Were they all just figments of my imagination?"

"Of course not. They all exist. Everything you knew exists. It was just the perceived *normalcy* of you that was enchanted. I mean, who has the energy to enchant people into existence? Just getting you a timeline was very impressive work, let me tell you, not just anyone could have pulled that off. You should see the effort it takes just to keep that sweatshirt of yours intact." He nods toward my sweatshirt and starts walking away from me, toward the stairs leading down to the Red Line.

I don't follow him. I look down at my sweatshirt, my simple maroon-with-white-Boston hooded sweatshirt he gave me on my birthday. "This is an enchantment?" I say.

Ben stops walking, turns back toward me. "Yes. A protection. One I've managed to hang on to despite your attempts to weaken me as much as possible, and it would be nice if you would just leave that one alone, thank you very much. Come on." He holds his hand out, wiggling his fingers.

"No," I say. "Wait. Hang on. If everything I knew exists, what happened to it?"

"Oh, it's all still there. We just have to get back to it, which is what we're doing now. You just peeled off your layer and threw it away, so now I have to get us back to all the other layers."

"How?"

He gestures toward the stairs to the Red Line. "Have to go catch a train."

"The subway," I say flatly. "We're going to take the subway."

"Well, it isn't just a subway. It's never been just a subway. It connects the Thisworld and the Otherworld. You never noticed it because it was one of the layers I didn't let you see."

"You've been controlling what I see and don't see?"

"Yes. That was my job."

"Your job," I echo hollowly, my stomach sinking. There's so much about this that is unbelievable, but it's the idea that Ben was only friends with me because it was his *job* that hurts. "Who made it your job?"

"I promise we'll reveal everything after we get out of this mess you made and I get us back to Boston." He says it good-naturedly, with a smile, waggling his fingers at me in invitation.

The smile undoes me a bit. I am angry and confused and scared, but he is *Ben*, and he is smiling at me. He is *waggling* his *fingers* at me. How can Ben being adorable be *wrong*? I close my eyes, feeling overwhelmed.

"You're…confused," Ben says, and he sounds confused that I'm confused.

I open my eyes, disbelieving. "Yes, I'm confused. Listen to the things you're saying to me, Ben. That your 'job' is to make everything in my life a *lie—*"

"It was an enchantment," he corrects.

"That makes it more confusing, not less," I point out.

He regards me for a second. "I did *too* good a job with your enchantment," he concludes. "You really had no idea."

"Wasn't that the point?" I retort.

"Yes, but…" He looks at a bit of a loss, which I've never seen him look before. "Let's just get back to Boston, and then we can all tell you together."

"Who 'all'?"

"Your aunts, of course."

"So my aunts know all about this," I realize. "All about you."

"Yes."

"Why didn't you ever say anything?"

"Because not saying anything was basically the purpose of the enchantment."

"And my father knows too."

"Yes."

"So he'll help explain it too."

"Well. Not really."

"Why not?"

Ben looks at me like this is obvious. "Well, because he's insane."

For some reason, this surprises me. I thought, with all the craziness in the world around me, that surely, in the middle of all this, my father *must* now be considered sane. "Oh," I say and try to deal with this.

"Can we go now? We really should keep moving. We're on the wrong side of the boundary right now. I need to cross us back over."

I swallow and make my decision. None of this makes any sense, but I seem to be all alone in a deserted subway station with only Ben for help, and what else am I going to do? I take a deep breath and put my hand in his.

It feels like a momentous occasion. He threads his fingers through mine and gives my hand a little squeeze, and I feel breathless. I've been feeling that way for a while, given the pace at which things have been happening around me, but this is an entirely different sort of breathless.

"Thank you," he says to me, and his smile at me is warm and genuine, and everything is ridiculously confusing but I still feel flushed at that smile.

Ben starts walking, and I follow, and yes, I still have no idea what's going on, but Ben's holding my hand and could it be that that's really all I need to feel like things are moving in the right direction now? I hate the fact that that might be true, but I can't deny that I'm much more pleased right now than I was just the minute before.

"This is why my aunts didn't want me asking questions, isn't it?"

"Well, yes," Ben answers.

I want to ask him about my mother, but maybe it's better to wait until we're back with my aunts. We walk in silence down the staircase to the Red Line, stand on the platform, waiting patiently. Except that I've never been all alone on the Red Line platform before, it feels like a normal day. I stand with Ben's hand in mine—okay, not *completely* normal—and gaze down onto the tracks, waiting. And after a while, I realize something. "The rats all disappeared too?" Normally you can stand on the platform and watch the rats scurrying all over the tracks.

Ben laughs, and then he says, "You are delightful," and his voice is warm, and so I am warm. I am sure I have blushed bright pink with pleasure, and I wish it were dark so Ben wouldn't be able to see me.

"Why?" I ask.

"Because. All the many questions you could have asked me next, and what you ask me is about the disappearance of Boston's *rats*."

"If the rats were part of the enchantment, I could have done without them."

"Don't blame me for the rats; that's Will. He's obsessed with all creatures like that, rodents and reptiles and such."

"You mean Will from the Salem Which Museum?"

"I mean Will from the Salem Which Museum."

"He had an iguana."

"Not surprising," says Ben.

"So he's involved in this too?"

"It was all his idea."

"He was the one who gave me the books, the books with my aunts in them." I pause. In a world where Ben is talking seriously about enchantments, this seems like a perfectly normal question. "Are my aunts immortal?"

Ben hesitates. I look at his profile—since he's looking at the tracks, not at me—but his expression is unreadable. Eventually he responds, "You should wait and ask them that question. It won't be much longer."

Which means the answer has to be yes. I ponder that, trying to make that sound like something that could be true.

I decide to change the subject.

"So. The T connects…what did you say?"

"The Thisworld—the world where mostly humans

live—and the Otherworld—the world where mostly nonhumans live—two worlds, existing side by side, but only overlapping in certain places."

"And Boston is one of them?" This seems difficult to believe. Boston has never seemed especially magical to me, but maybe that's because I've been enchanted to think otherwise.

"Boston is one of them," confirms Ben. "Park Street station happens to be one of the busiest portals in the Otherworld. Haven't you ever noticed how people pop up here out of nowhere?"

I have, but I've always just dismissed that. More of my enchantment, I guess. "What's a portal?" I ask.

"A safe place to go when an enchantment is dissolving and a way to get from one enchantment to another—and one world to another. It would have been much easier for us to get back to Boston, though, if you hadn't named me a few times and then rained on me for good measure."

"Why?" I ask.

"Because then I could have just jumped us," Ben says. "I'm a traveler. We don't wait for *trains*." He says the word with disgust, like it's beneath him. Then he adds, "Normally. When I haven't been rained on and named. Not that I'm blaming you or anything." He winks at me.

"A traveler?" I say.

"Best traveler in the Otherworld," he proclaims proudly, then frowns. "Possibly only traveler in the Otherworld."

"Only?" I say, but suddenly there is a squealing of track up above us.

Ben jumps a mile.

"It's only a Green Line train coming," I tell him, because he looks terrified.

"Exactly," he says and abruptly leaps onto the Red Line tracks.

I blink in shock. "What are you doing?"

"Can't wait anymore. Come on."

"Come *where*?"

"With me."

"On the *tracks*?"

"*Yes*." Ben sounds exasperated. And also frightened. And the last time Ben sounded frightened, all of Boston winked out of existence around us, so I jump onto the tracks with Ben.

Now that I am on the tracks with him though, Ben hesitates.

"Ben?" I query.

"Nothing for it," he says. "Green Line train. We have to go." And he starts walking, looking grim.

"Why? What's a Green Line train?"

"Nothing good. Worse than the goblins, so this is the lesser of two evils."

"But we were just waiting for a train. Why wasn't the Red Line train bad?"

"Because only the Green Line is evil," Ben explains impatiently.

I catch up to what else he said. "Wait, goblins?"

"Yes. Watch out for them. Their talent is seduction, so be on the lookout."

All of this is making even less sense than everything else. "*What?*"

"Just think, you know, how you *don't* want to be seduced, and you'll be okay."

"What are you talking about?" I complain.

We had been walking at a brisk pace, but Ben stops suddenly. "Do you hear something?"

I do hear it. I look behind us. "A train."

"They jumped the tracks," breathes Ben, sounding terrified, and abruptly takes my hand again. He speaks directly in my ear, over the noise of the oncoming train. "Whatever happens, do *not* let go of my hand, do you hear me?"

He doesn't wait for me to reply, just takes off at a mad dash. He is running impossibly fast, and I am stumbling in his wake, but his hand stays in mine, and he keeps pulling me up. He does not ever look behind, at me or the train, but I keep looking behind obsessively, and the train is barreling down on us. I have no idea what Ben's plan is, but I am hoping he has one, and then, suddenly, the train disappears and the tracks disappear and it is blinding sunlight, and Ben tumbles to the ground of a grassy meadow, and I tumble right over him and, in my shock, let go of his hand, tumbling head over feet down a steep hill until I land with an unpleasant and painful splash in some kind of rocky brook.

I sit there for a second stupidly, winded and getting soaking wet, until I become aware that there is a rat looking at me across the brook.

And Ben said there wouldn't be rats, I think, which is the first thought I feel like I *can* think.

And then the rat says, in brusque, clipped, perfect English with not a hint of a ratly squeak, "My stars, what the hell are *you* doing here?"

CHAPTER 5

I do not answer the rat. It never occurs to me to question that the rat can talk—given the day I've had, that seems like the most normal thing to have happened in hours—but it does occur to me that I no longer understand the rules of my life, this life where saying a single name can cause all of Boston to wink out of existence around me. So I consider it wiser not to answer the rat, and anyway, I don't know what the hell I'm doing there, so I *can't* answer the question. Maybe the rat is a goblin like Ben warned me about? This seems preposterous, but no more preposterous than anything else, so I think, very firmly, *I do not want to be seduced.* Which I don't.

I scramble my way out of the brook, tumbling inelegantly into a patch of cheerful pink tulips. And then I take a second to catch my breath and try to get my bearings in this new world. First things first: *Where is Ben?*

I glance back at the hill I tumbled down, which is extremely steep, and think—hope—that Ben must be at the top of it. I pick myself up, dripping wet, and go to start climbing up the hill, and that is when the tulip grabs me.

It probably shouldn't be surprising, because I should

probably stop being surprised by anything at this point, but I let out a little cry as the tulips entwine themselves around me and pull me back down into them. I struggle, pulling tendrils of leaves off of me, and think that I never before really thought of tulips as being deadly, but their soft petals brushing against me are terrifying. I kick and flail and then think suddenly, slicing through my panic, *I do not want them to touch me.*

The tulips shrink back, and I scrabble away from them, breathing hard. I stare at them in disbelief, because they are back to looking like a typical clump of tulips, innocent and not at all murderous.

"What the *hell*," I say out loud, because I can't help it.

"Well," huffs the rat. "What did you expect? You trampled them on your way out of the brook. They had to defend themselves *somehow*."

I ignore him and start struggling my way up the hill. By the time I get to the top of it, I am exhausted and hot from the sun. I would love to take off my sweatshirt, but Ben had said it was an enchantment, and I've had enough of breaking enchantments for the time being.

Ben is sprawled spread eagle on his back in the middle of the meadow. The rat had leapt easily up the hill in front of me, and it is now sitting on Ben's chest, its nose up against his. It looks up at me as I finally reach them, its beady black eyes accusing.

"You've *killed* him," it says.

You know how people always say things like "my heart stopped"? It actually happens to me then, in that moment. "What?" I gasp and fall to my knees next to Ben and shake him. He is still and lifeless and does not react at all. "How…?"

"Hmph," says the rat, sounding disgusted, and jumps off Ben's chest.

I barely notice, because I am busy thinking, *Whatever happens, do not let go of my hand.* I look at my hand, and I look at Ben's, and I fit them together.

His eyes flutter open and squint into the sunshine above him. "Oh, good," he says drowsily and closes his eyes again. "We made it."

I barely have time to be relieved about this, never mind time to be curious about this, when Ben suddenly snaps his eyes open and sits straight up.

"We made it," he repeats, looking at me. "*Very* good." He startles me by releasing my hand and suddenly putting one of his hands on either side of my head and then, astonishingly, kissing my forehead exuberantly. "Very good," he says again and picks himself up lightly. "Let's go."

"Ben," I protest. I want to stop running around for a few minutes so he can answer my questions. I want to point out that he was apparently just *dead* and I revived him by holding his hand.

"Oh," Ben says flatly, and I realize he is talking to the rat. "You're here."

"Of course," snaps the rat. "Where else would I be? And

you brought her *here*?" says the rat. "Your mother was right: you are the *wrongest* creature in the Otherworld."

"I didn't have a choice," he tells the rat and then takes my hand and uses it to pull me up. "Come on, we have to go."

"Where *are* we?" I ask, because this is clearly not anywhere near Boston, where it had been damp, chilly nighttime, not sunny, hot daytime.

"Why didn't you have a choice?" asks the rat. It is now trotting along behind us as we walk through the meadow.

Ben answers the rat instead of me. "There was a Green Line train."

The rat gasps. I have never heard a rat gasp before. It is quite something. "A *Green Line train*," it says. "Benedict…"

"I know," Ben replies grimly.

"Wait. What do you know?" I ask. "Why is a Green Line train so bad?" By now, I am ready to scream with how little sense any of this makes.

"So you brought her *here*?" shrieks the rat.

"I was wet," grumbles Ben. "And she named me. A lot. This was the best I could manage. But it's fine. It's only a brief stop. We'll be on our way to Parsymeon in no time."

"She *named* you? How does she even know your name? How could you be so *clumsy*?" shouts the rat.

"I'm sorry," I say sweetly. "My father told me his name; it wasn't Ben's fault. And I don't mean to be rude, but who are you?"

The rat makes a noise I can only describe as, well, a squeal.

"The *impertinence!*" it exclaims. It is making such a huge deal, hopping around the grass in some sort of stricken dance, you'd think I was trying to kill it.

"Never ask for names," Ben tells me. "Too much power in a name, no one will give their name to you, and if you ask for it, they'll react like…well, like that." Ben nods his head vaguely toward the rat. "Anyway, he's my father."

This takes the cake for most ridiculous thing I've heard so far today. "Your father?" I echo.

"Sadly," sighs the rat.

"So." I study Ben, trying to find rodent features in a face that I have always personally considered quite handsome. "You're a…rat?" I venture.

Ben looks indignant. "Don't be silly," he says impatiently. "Do I look like a rat?"

"No. But then, what are you?"

"A faerie, of course," he answers. He is saying all this as if he would have expected me to know these answers already. Ben and I need to have a chat about things that are *obvious* and things that are *not*.

"But your father's a rat?"

"Why do you keep saying I'm a rat?" snaps the rat.

I stare at him, and we all stop walking.

"Because you look like a rat," Ben snaps back.

"I choose to personify as a rat," says the rat primly. "But I am clearly a *faerie*."

"And he thinks *I'm* the wrong one," mutters Ben.

I consider my next question because, after all, I can only ask one at a time. Ben says he is a faerie. What's the next thing you ask when the boy you're pretty sure you're in love with says he's a faerie? A thought occurs to me. I think of my historic books, of my aunts and my father, scattered throughout Boston's chronology. "So is…everyone a faerie?"

"That's a complicated question," Ben says awkwardly.

"How did I get *involved* with all this?" I'm not even sure I expect an answer to the question. I am asking it mostly of myself, but Ben answers.

"You were *born* involved." Ben resumes walking.

I follow, asking again, "Where are we?"

It's the rat who answers me. "It's his home."

"How did we get here?"

"He's a traveler." The rat actually sounds proud of this.

There's that word again. I look at Ben, and there is a trace of a smile on his face.

"What does that mean?" I ask.

"I can jump," Ben explains, "from place to place. Although it's harder for me when I'm wet, which is why we ended up here instead of Boston. Easier for me to lock on to the Otherworld than the Thisworld."

"And that's something faeries do? Jump?"

"No. Just me. It's something *travelers* do."

"You can't keep her here," the rat interrupts us.

"I know that. I told you: we're going to Parsymeon."

"I thought we were going to Boston," I say.

"Her mother is looking everywhere for her," says the rat.

I stop walking abruptly, rounding on him. "My *mother*?"

The rat ignores me. "She sent the Green Line after you; you barely made it *here*. How do you expect to hide the fay? You'll never be able to. The Seelie Court will arrive with a chiming of bells—"

Ben stops walking abruptly, turns, and picks up the rat by the scruff of its neck. It squirms in his grip and demands, a ratty squeak finally emerging in its voice, "Put me down! Put me down *this instant*, boy!"

"You insist on personifying yourself as a rat, then I will insist on treating you like one," Ben snaps. "And you're not helping. Stop. It." He punctuates the words with a little shake.

"You can't run from the entire Seelie Court. How will you do it?"

"Stop it," I shout. "Stop talking."

Ben looks at me. The rat, still dangling from Ben's hand, looks at me as well.

"What is he talking about?" I demand. "My mother is looking for me?"

Ben looks at a loss, which is really a terrifying thing to see. I feel cold. "How long have you known this?"

Ben says nothing, which is incriminating.

I stumble away from him. Suddenly I can't bear to be near him. "I've been trying to find her. You never said…*anything*—"

"Listen to me." Ben drops his father and makes a grab for me, but I dodge him. "You can't have her find you."

"Why not?" I demand.

"I'll tell you everything—*everything*, I promise, but not here. We have to get to Parsymeon."

"No." I shake my head. "I don't know what that is. You said we were going to Boston."

"That was before the Green Line train came. Parsymeon would be safest. It's a form of Boston; it's pre-Boston—"

"I don't care. Take me to Boston. Take me to my aunts."

The rat looks at Ben. "Well," he remarks, "you're in trouble, aren't you? The fay has spoken."

CHAPTER 6

B en takes a deep breath. I stand watching him, wary and stony, and terrified and furious.

"Fine," Ben says. "Boston. Take my hand."

I don't.

"I can't jump you if you're not touching me."

"Now, all of a sudden, you can jump us to Boston? You couldn't before?"

"I'm dry now," he snaps. "And I'm home. I'm more powerful when I'm at home."

"Boston," I say firmly. "My aunts."

"Yes," he agrees, sounding irritated.

I take the hand he's offering, and there's a moment when I'm looking straight into his unusual eyes, all blue and green in this land of meadow and sky, and then I blink and we are standing in Park Street again. It is *Park Street*, and people are dodging around us, everyday Boston people going about their lives, and Ben's eyes are a flat, slate gray in the damp and gloomy T station.

"*Do* be careful," an attractive man in a black suit snaps at Ben, and Ben dodges away from him, using our joined hands to pull us forward.

"Damn goblins," he mutters.

I try to turn my head to look back, saying, "*That* was a goblin?" but the man has already disappeared.

We emerge from the T station into Boston. It looks exactly the same as it always has. How can I possibly believe this crazy story about enchantments and faeries? Then I realize that someone is sitting on our stoop—someone who turns out to be Will from the Salem Which Museum. I stop and blink at him in astonishment. I feel Ben draw to a halt next to me.

"Hello," Will says to me pleasantly, as if it is perfectly expected that he should show up at my front door. He looks beyond me to Ben, and he smiles, looking amused.

"Benedict," he says. "You're looking *challenged*." He looks back at me. "Are you being challenging? Excellent, Benedict can always use a bit of that."

Ben crinkles his nose, looking annoyed. "I'm running away from the entire Seelie Court with the fay of the autumnal equinox; I am quite sufficiently challenged, thank you," he grumbles.

"Oh, stop being so melodramatic; everything's going according to plan," Will scolds him.

"What plan?" I demand hotly. I look between them. "Why do *you* have a plan about me? You don't even *know* me."

Will's face turns hard. "I have known you since you were *born*, my dear. I have known you since *before* that."

"Then how come I've never seen you before?"

"Because no one sees me unless I want them to," snaps Will.

"Oh," I say sarcastically. "Are you a special invisibility faerie?"

Will sputters a bit, starts to say something several times before cutting himself off in indignation.

I look at Ben, who is unexpectedly smiling, looking at me with eyes flashing silver with laughter, and for a moment, it's as if all this craziness never happened. It could be a moment between us on the Common, a shared joke, and I want to smile back at him and have everything be normal again.

"Will's a wizard," Ben says, and just like that, I am reminded that everything is as far from normal as *possible*.

I step around Will, heading for my front door.

"Oh," says Will, turning to keep me in his sight. "I thought we might talk first."

"First?" I echo.

"Before you go inside," he clarifies.

I am immediately suspicious. "No," I say firmly. "I am going to see my aunts."

But I don't have to say anything else. The door swings open and my aunts come barreling out, armed with a broom and a mop, and commence to enthusiastically whacking at Will.

CHAPTER 7

It takes Ben and me a while to break up the furious battle between my aunts and Will—longer than you'd think, considering that up until that moment I'd always thought my aunts to be too old to throw accurate right hooks (I am wrong about that, it turns out). Ben and I do a lot of dodging of blows, and we finally manage to shove everyone inside, and I call from the doorway to the passersby who have stopped to stare, "No worries! Got it covered!"

The squabbling struggle has now moved into our front foyer, and I finally manage to get my aunts into the front parlor and Will into the dining room, and I stand in the foyer that separates the two rooms and shout, "What is going *on*?"

"How dare you come into this house!" Aunt True spits across the foyer at Will. They are practically snarling with anger, my aunts, and I am truly terrified. What could possibly be happening here?

"It's too soon," Aunt True shouts at him. "It is far too soon."

"It isn't," Will replies. "It is Selkie's timeline, and Selkie's the one who decided it was time. She was the one who started using the right words, asking the right questions."

"Benedict manipulated her," Aunt True accuses, her voice low.

Ben barks unamused laughter. "Trust me, I share your opinion of the timing of this. Will is the one who gave her the pages."

"Then it's *your* fault," spits Aunt True. "*As usual.*"

"There's nothing that can be done now," says Will. "It's all begun. *She* was the one who revealed her birth date."

"I'm right here, you know," I point out. "And I have no idea what you're talking about, and that needs to stop right now. Someone needs to tell me what's going on. I want to know why you're in history books, and I want to know who my mother is and why she's looking for me and why, if she's looking for me, I can't let her *find* me. I want to know who Will is, and I want to know how Dad knows Ben and why Ben seems to think he's a faerie who's been enchanting me my whole life."

There is a moment of silence following my outburst.

Will turns to my aunts. "You didn't tell her *any* of this?" he asks in anguish.

"We didn't have time," Aunt Virtue sniffs.

Aunt True adds, "We didn't know she'd begun asking the right questions. Benedict whisked her off to the Otherworld as soon as the enchantment broke."

Aunt Virtue glares at him.

"She named me," Ben snaps. "A lot. And then I was wet. I've been only a step or two ahead of the Seelies this entire time. They sent a Green Line train after us at Park Street. If she were with anyone else, she'd already be named."

"A Green Line train?" echoes Will. "In *Boston*?"

"Well, we weren't in Boston, because we got stuck in the portal when the enchantment dissolved. I have to say, I would have appreciated a little *warning* about her naming power."

"No one is criticizing the thoroughly magnificent job you've done getting her here safe," says Will soothingly, and then, to me, "He really is very good at what he does." Back to Ben, "We're just saying that you could have done a much better job explaining all this when you were breaking the enchantment."

"I told you." Ben scowls. "I didn't break the enchantment."

"But how did she know your *name*?" asks Will.

"Dad told me," I answer, looking at my aunts.

Will makes a noise of disgust and throws up his hands. "I warned you about him. Now everything's spiraled out of control."

Ben crinkles his nose. "Exactly what I've been saying. But why should anyone listen to *me*? I'm just the one who's been keeping her safe all this time."

"*You*," shrieks Aunt Virtue. "Keeping her *safe*?"

"What's going on?" I shout, and they finally fall silent. "Ben says my mother is looking for me, but I can't have her find me. Tell me why."

My aunts look nervous. They wring their hands in concern.

And then Will suggests, "Maybe you should make some tea. You always did make exceptional tea—"

"What do you know about it, Will Blaxton?" Aunt True snaps at him. "You stopped coming for tea, remember?"

"Will you *never* get over that?" asks Will, sounding long-suffering.

"No, I won't get over that! You broke my heart! I was just a young girl!"

"You were four hundred years old!" Will retorts, voice rising again.

"But I was young in the ways of love!" Aunt True exclaims.

We're off topic again but off topic in a different sort of way. "Wait a second," I interject, looking between the two of them. "You two…"

"Not really," Will responds stiffly.

This causes Aunt True to burst into loud tears, burying her face in her hands, while Aunt Virtue rubs her back soothingly and shoots deadly glares at Will.

"Oh, for the love of…" says Will. "It was a *very* long time ago."

"The wound is still fresh," Aunt Virtue proclaims grandiosely. "The heart does not heal at the same rate as the rest of the body. But I would not expect you to know that, as you do not possess a heart at all."

Aunt True's wails begin anew.

Will looks very awkward and uncomfortable in the dining room doorway, an incongruous black eye making him look much more rakish than his professorial attire would have predicted. "True," he pleads across the foyer, "it was never going to work out, love. *You* know that. I'm a wizard, you're an ogre; these things don't work."

Aunt True sniffles and lifts up her head to look at him, hiccupping, her frazzled dark hair sticking out all around her head. "I know," she says, her voice very small and unlike her and, unexpectedly to me, *young*.

Will moves hesitantly across the hallway, like he is approaching a skittish horse. He reaches Aunt True, and she closes her hands into the sweater he is wearing and turns her head into his chest.

"There, there," he says and pats her head uncertainly. "Let's focus on your…" He glances at me and gestures lamely. "Whatever she is."

Apparently, these are the magic words of reconciliation. Aunt True straightens away from him and wipes her eyes and says, "Fine. I'll make tea."

CHAPTER 8

This whole thing is so strange, but everyone is behaving as if it's not. I sit, stunned, at the kitchen table while Will and my aunts make tea, chatting amiably about people with names that sound like faerie tales, as if there had been no odd scene at all, as if none of this was the very height of oddness. I am frustrated beyond belief—so frustrated I feel tongue-tied.

Ben comes to sit next to me. He seems uncomfortable, a bit fidgety, and I think how strange it is that he is in my house after all this time. He really does look like he's out of his natural habitat. I stare at him, my mind so full that it's blank.

He says to me, "There's something I've realized you need to know and probably don't know: nobody can force you to do anything."

I feel dazed and try to process this. It sounds like an after-school special, and unlike Ben, and I don't know how to react. "Okay," I decide slowly.

"No, I mean it. Nobody can make you do anything that you don't want to do. Just remember that if somebody tries to…hurt you or…just think, 'I don't want this,' and the charm will kick in, as long as you're wearing this." He reaches out, brushes his fingertips over the sleeve of my sweatshirt.

"My sweatshirt?"

He nods. "That's the talisman of the protective enchantment."

"That's the enchantment?" I ask.

He just looks at me solemnly. Why do I need a protective enchantment? Somehow, it's clear everyone thinks I'm in grave danger. Ben has been keeping me safe my entire life. I resent all the secrets and mysteries, everything I haven't been told, but everyone has been working so hard to keep me *safe*, it seems.

"Why does everyone think I'm in danger?" I ask.

Ben glances toward Will and my aunts. "It's…Your mother…"

"If you've known this all along, why didn't you tell me? Any of it?" I am numb with hurt. My entire life is in upheaval, but it's Ben's betrayal that hurts me the most. I can understand my aunts and father holding some deep, dark secret back on me—I'd suspected it for so long—but for *Ben* to be involved, Ben who I'd considered…well, so much more. Everything. Ben who has been more than a crush, Ben who I've been in love with—was it all just a lie? An enchantment, as he would call it?

"Tell you that your mother was looking for you, but I didn't want you to find her, I needed you to stay with us instead?"

"You didn't think I'd listen," I conclude.

"You didn't when your aunts begged you to drop it, did you?"

"But you would have been different," I say desperately. "You're *you*."

Ben looks at me for a second, then drops his eyes to the table. "I didn't know my mother either," he says, and I blink at the revelation. "I was trying to decide, if I heard that my mother was looking for me, whether my curiosity wouldn't…" He clears his throat.

I don't know what to say to that. I'd like to ask Ben more about his mother, but Ben's voice is reluctant, and I do not think he is eager to open the topic. And anyway, the focus now is on *my* mother. "You're going to explain everything to me now, right?"

My aunts set cups of tea carefully on the table—sugar, milk, a plate of cookies. I don't want any of this, but my aunts and Will set about preparing their tea as if nothing is happening. Will grabs two cookies and pops them in his mouth in quick succession.

Aunt True looks at Ben. "It's not going to rain inside. You can take off some of your layers," she says.

"Thank you, but it is *always* on the verge of raining here," he replies politely. "The very air is too moist for me to function correctly." He seems to reconsider his statement and adds, "Except in winter. It's not bad in the wintertime."

"Plus, it's an ogre house," says Will. "Benedict feels ogre magic like a scratchy wool sweater. The layers are protection." Will looks at me confidentially. "Water is Benedict's special affliction, especially if it's flowing. He doesn't work right if he's wet."

This would all be very fascinating to me, except… "Ogre house?" I echo and look at my aunts.

"How is it they have told you absolutely *nothing*?" Will demands in disbelief.

"It wasn't time," Aunt True says.

"It *was* time. She told Benedict her birth date."

"I agree with them," Ben interjects. "It wasn't time. We weren't ready."

"It was time, Benedict." Will turns his frown from him to me. "This is not a good idea," he announces.

"What isn't?" Aunt True asks.

"Benedict has a *soft spot* for her," Will flings out, sounding disgusted. "The two of you having a soft spot for her"— Will waggles his fingers at my aunts—"that we expected. But *Benedict* wasn't supposed to get *emotionally attached*." He drawls it mockingly.

I look at Ben, complete with a ridiculous little flutter in my heart.

Ben is scowling at Will. "I disagree with you about the issue of timing. We needed more time than this. You know we did."

"*You* needed more time; *you* weren't ready because of how you feel about her. But it was never for us to dictate the timing of things. It was for her." He indicates me. "She told you the date of her birth, Benedict. That was the omen."

"I've had enough," I interrupt abruptly, and everyone looks at me in surprise, as if they had forgotten that I was there and that I'm *angry*. "I want someone to explain to me what is going on here, and I want that explanation *now*. You tell me the story, or I let my mother find me and I hear it from her. Your choice."

There is a moment of silence.

"We might as well get settled," says Will wearily, taking another cookie. "We'll be here for a while. Now, my dear." He looks at me kindly. "What do you know about your birth?"

CHAPTER 9

One day my father walked into his Back Bay apartment to find a blond woman asleep on his couch," I say to Will.

"Yes." Will looks delighted by this story. "True enough." He looks at my aunts. "What a lovely, clever way to put it."

"Who is she?"

"Who?"

"The blond woman asleep on the couch."

"Your mother."

"I know *that*," I say impatiently. "But who is my mother?"

Will looks about to answer but Aunt True interjects, "Let *us* tell her." She looks at me and takes a deep breath. "Your mother is a *bean shìth* of the Seelie Court."

"I don't know what that means," I say.

"She's a faerie," says Aunt Virtue.

"Not just a faerie," says Will, "one of the most powerful ones. The Seelie Court rules the Otherworld."

"My mother is a faerie?"

"Yes," says Aunt True.

"A faerie *queen*," corrects Will.

I stare at him for a moment. Then I say skeptically, "You're telling me I'm a faerie princess?"

Ben chuckles—such a normal sound out of him that I am momentarily startled. I look at Ben, and he *grins* at me.

"Yes," he says, "he's telling you you're a faerie princess."

"Faye Blaxton is a faerie queen?" I clarify.

"That's not her name," says Will.

"What's her name?" I ask.

"Oh, no one knows." Will shakes his head. "No one will ever know. That is one of the most precious secrets, the names of the faeries in the Seelie Court. Names are powerful things."

"I know your names," I point out. I remember Ben, complaining about the way I was using his name.

"You know what I have told you to be my name, which is not quite the same thing," says Will. "As for Benedict, he has the misfortune not to be faerie royalty. Names of mere plebeian faeries are required to be revealed under faerie law. Must keep the population in line, you know."

"How does that keep the population in line?"

"Say a faerie's name the right way, you can dissolve his or her enchantments, weaken him or her."

I look at Ben. "That's what happened when I said your name."

Ben nods.

"What was this enchantment?" I demand.

"To keep you safe," says Aunt True.

"Safe from *what*? Why do I need to be kept alive? I don't get it. Why am I in danger of dying?"

"Not dying," Aunt True says somberly, anxiously. "Being killed."

"Being killed by who?"

Aunt True and Aunt Virtue wring their hands together fretfully.

Will explains, "The members of the Seelie Court do not have children. There was a prophecy, so many years ago that nobody can even estimate the age of this prophecy any longer—"

"Or just the other day," interjects Ben.

"Don't be confusing," complains Will.

Ben shrugs.

"A prophecy," Will continues firmly, "that there would be four fays born of the seasons and, according to the Seelie Court, that these four fays would be the reason that the Unseelie Court would rise and take power in the Otherworld."

"What's the Unseelie Court?" I ask.

"They're our greater of two evils," answers Ben grimly.

"Exactly. The Seelie Court may have its issues, but the Unseelie Court, well, no one wants *them* in power. Anyway, the four fays born of the seasons would be Seelies themselves. No other fays would have nearly enough power. So there was a prohibition on the Seelies creating children."

"But..." I begin.

"But here you are," Will agrees. "Your mother fell from the Otherworld. She was pushed. To this day, no one has ever caught the perpetrator, and the assumption is that it was someone from the Unseelie Court. She fell and your father found her, and he nursed her back to health—it is a *long* distance to fall. Your mother was in his debt, a dangerous place for a Seelie to be. She was desperate to be out of it. She asked him to name his payment." Will pauses. "And he named a child."

I am silent for a second. "Why would he do that?"

Will looks at my aunts, and I follow his lead.

Aunt True and Aunt Virtue exchange a look, and then Aunt Virtue starts speaking. "We are ogres, child. The last of the ogres—your father, True, me. We came here with Will years ago, here to this place. Safety from the Seelie Court, for all the creatures of the Otherworld who weren't faeries—it was Will's idea. The Seelie Court was always biased a bit in favor of their own kind."

"Yes, their cruelty toward faeries is slightly milder," agrees Will drily.

"So Will founded Parsymeon, an Otherworld place locked into the Thisworld for all the non-faeries to stand together, to weave our own protective enchantments, and together, all of us, we could keep faeries out."

"Parsymeon?" I say.

"Boston," says Ben. "Will insists on calling it Parsymeon, but it's Boston, centuries ago, before the Boston you knew. This is Will Blaxton, who founded Boston by planting apple trees on Beacon Hill, apple trees born of the apples of the Isle of Apples."

I stare at Will. "Boston was founded by a *wizard*?"

"Yes, as a home for supernatural creatures." Will sounds annoyed that I sound so dubious. "A new world—why should it only house Puritans? *I* named the place Parsymeon. But then the Puritans were dying in their stupid little settlement, and I felt bad, and I invited them here, and they renamed it Boston and they ruined the whole place."

"Blaxton," I realize. I look at Ben. "You called him Will Blaxton."

"It's where your mother's last name came from, yes," he confirms. "Surely you've realized by now where the Faye comes from. It isn't her *name*. It was simply the best we could do with the records."

"Faye like your last name?" I say to Ben.

"Yes," Will answers on Ben's behalf. "But it really just means *faerie*. Benedict's family happens to be a very old one."

"But not a royal one." Ben smiles tightly. "We have a bad habit of falling out of favor, we Le Fays."

"Anyway, Parsymeon is still supernatural today," continues Will, who is beaming like a proud father about this. "It has the highest concentration of supernatural beings anywhere in the Thisworld."

"But only two faeries," murmurs Ben.

"Well, wasn't that the *point*?" says Will. "Keep the Seelies out, keep all faeries out?"

"How did you get in?" I ask Ben.

"Special permission from the Witch and Ward Society," he replies. "I had to apply and everything. But you were to be kept safe, and they needed a faerie to do that, much as they hated to admit it."

I look at my aunts, connecting the dots. "Because you don't like faeries," I conclude.

"Faeries are flighty and capricious," says Aunt Virtue staunchly, "and you are *not* one. Not entirely. There is ogre in you."

"Ogre," I echo. "So I'm…half and half."

"Exactly," agrees Aunt Virtue.

Aunt True says, "We'd wanted a baby so very desperately for so very long. Centuries."

"Or minutes," murmurs Ben.

My aunt ignores him. "But how were we to get one without faerie magic? So your father asked your mother for a baby."

"I warned him not to," Will says. "I knew the prophecy. I knew the danger you would be in from the very beginning. And I knew there would be a price—the Seelies *always* extract a price. But Etherington would not be dissuaded."

"And your mother brought us a baby." Aunt Virtue smiles at me, her expression so soft and full of affection. "You. A beautiful little changeling, half-faerie, half-ogre."

"Which made you"—Aunt True's voice is hard—"only half ours."

"My mother named me," I realize.

"Of course she did," Will says. "Power over you."

"Is it a problem that everyone knows my name?"

"No one knows your *whole* name," Aunt True tells me.

"Your middle names are secret," Aunt Virtue adds.

"You should keep them that way," says Aunt True.

"Why?"

"In order to completely dissolve a faerie's powers," explains Will, "you would need to know all of the faerie's middle names. Faeries frequently have three or four middle names, to make them harder to dilute. Of course, give a faerie too many names, and they can't work under the weight of their burden, and you have the same effect as their name being known."

"I have a cousin with 302 middle names," muses Ben. "She's quite useless."

"So, know a faerie's whole name, dissolve all his powers. Know just a couple of his names…" I look at Ben.

"It weakens us. But it doesn't destroy us completely."

"That's why you couldn't hold the enchantment around me together anymore."

"Right. It was broken. And why I had such a difficult time jumping. I was wet *and* diluted."

"But," interjects Will softly, and he is staring at me, delight in his face, "not dissolved." He turns his look to Ben now. "Oh, it's very pretty work, Benedict. I would never have known it was there if we hadn't been discussing your enchantments."

"What?" I ask. I look from Ben to Will to my aunts in confusion.

Will is still smiling at Ben, looking a cross between proud and amused. "How much *energy* is that taking you, to keep that up? No wonder you're letting the Seelies get closer to you than usual and fretting about the moisture in the air."

Ben looks embarrassed. "It's not a big deal," he grumbles.

"*What?*" I demand.

"Benedict's still got you enchanted. It's a minor enchantment, but it's *very* well done, virtually undetectable—"

"The protective charm," I realize.

"Yes," says Will, eyes narrowed speculatively at Ben. "And what a very pretty thing it is too."

There is a moment of uncomfortable silence.

I venture finally, "If faeries aren't allowed into Boston, how did my mother manage to get here?"

"Ah," says Will. "That is a question we have never been able to answer. She was pushed through to Thisworld, but we don't really know how."

"And Ben got here because of the Witch and Ward Society. What's that?"

Will rolls his eyes. "Let's not talk about *them*. That's the problem with Boston these days—so much bureaucracy, so many societies and sewing circles, it's ridiculous."

"Will hates the Witch and Ward Society," says Ben, "but I've always found them quite reasonable to deal with."

"Well, they didn't steal *your* book, did they?" grumbles Will.

"I'd rather deal with them than the Sewing Circle," remarks Ben.

Will makes a noise of abject disgust.

"Who's that?" I ask.

"The Sewing Circle is the link between Boston and the Otherworld. The Witch and Ward, if they could, would close all borders entirely. The Sewing Circle insists on keeping Park Street open."

"The Witch and Ward has never understood that Boston's power is in *balance*," says Will. "Half-Thisworld, half-Otherworld. It must stay locked into overlapping to keep its power. Unlock the worlds, and the supernatural powers would cease to be augmented by the presence of the humans and the Seelies would be able to get in. Safety from exposure—I've never understood what's so *tricky* about that for them."

"Safety for everyone except faeries," remarks Ben. "Faeries you locked into the Otherworld, good riddance to them."

"Faeries caused the disturbance in the Otherworld in the first place," Will tells him.

"A few faeries. Was it our fault the Seelie Court happened to be composed of faeries?"

"How did you get involved?" I ask Ben.

"He found you," Aunt True answers, looking displeased. "Even here."

"Well, it's my job: locate faeries trapped in the Thisworld. It happens, you know. And I'm unusually good at Thisworld magic, so it falls to me to do it. So I snuck into Boston—"

"He *jumped*," says Aunt True, glaring. "Which strictly speaking isn't allowed. This is why the goblins tried to get rid of all the travelers."

Ben flickers a glare of displeasure at her but otherwise ignores her. "I jumped in, and there you were. And I knew what you were and I knew about the prophecy, so I knew you had to be protected.

"Ogre magic can only do so much to hide a faerie. Faerie blood is powerful. It calls to other faeries. As I explained to your aunts, if they wanted to hide you, they needed a faerie to cast the enchantment over you."

"You," I conclude.

"Yes."

"We didn't want to have to trust a faerie," says Aunt True.

"Never trust a faerie," adds Aunt Virtue.

"But we didn't have a choice, and of course, Will said Benedict was on our side."

"All faeries outside of the Seelie Court are on your side," says Ben. "Things are bad in the Otherworld. Faeries disappear all the time, named for no reason. Everyone exists in a state of terror, waiting…" Ben actually shudders. "All of you panicked when you shut us out of here."

"No, it was the only way for us to be sure to keep the Seelies out," retorts Aunt True. "Make sure there was no faerie blood allowed here at all."

"Well, there is faerie blood allowed here," replies Ben and gestures at me. "There she is."

"She is an ogre," Aunt Virtue proclaims grandly.

"Only half. She is only *half*-ogre. You cannot claim all of her."

"Maybe no one should claim me at all," I interrupt. "Maybe I'm just *me*. Why has no one considered that ever, in my entire life? I'm more than just a pawn in some stupid prophecy. So let me get this straight: to keep me safe, all of you decided an enchantment should be placed over me?"

"Yes," Aunt True says.

"And I wouldn't know who I was—*what* I was?"

"You *couldn't*," Aunt Virtue says desperately. "You couldn't know. We had to hide you from *everything*, even yourself, in order to hide you from *them*."

"Did it never occur to you that maybe I didn't want to be enchanted?"

"It was for your own good," Aunt True says.

"You don't understand," says Aunt Virtue. "Benedict was supposed to kill you. Immediately."

"What?" I exclaim.

"Long-standing order," replies Ben, not looking at me. "Kill any changelings I might find born of the Seelie Court."

"But you didn't."

Ben gives me a look that can only be described as disbelieving. "I don't kill *babies*, Selkie. That's a terrible thing to do. To take a baby's laugh out of the world is one of the most dangerous types of black magic that can be performed."

"It's true," says Will, "but what's mostly true is that the Seelie Court severely overestimated Benedict's loyalty." Will looks delighted by this.

Even Ben looks amused. "This is a common mistake when

it comes to me," he admits. "You were prophesied to save the Otherworld. I wasn't about to kill you."

"And we were desperate to keep you safe," says Aunt True, begging me to understand.

"They never wanted you to break the enchantment," says Will.

"That's why all of you tried to get me to stop asking questions," I conclude. "You never wanted me to find out who my mother is."

"It didn't matter. Eventually you told Benedict your birth date. That was the first link in the chain. There was nothing anyone could do after that. Prophecies will not be denied."

"As if prophecies function so cleanly," retorts Ben bitterly. "You know how prophecies work, overlapping and contradictory. There was nothing to say which prophecy was going to be the correct one."

"You used to be quite keen on it being *this* prophecy," says Will scathingly. "Saving the Otherworld, that's what you were all about. Now, the fay of the autumnal equinox turns out to be *her*, and you've changed your mind."

Ben crinkles his nose, looking displeased in the extreme.

I look at him, because there it is again, the implication that I am special to him, and I can't help it: I *want* to be special to him, even after everything.

There is a long silence.

I look at my aunts. "What do you think, about this

prophecy that I'm going to bring about the reign of this evil Unseelie Court, then—"

"That's just it," Will cuts me off. "You're not. I've studied the prophecies. You're going to bring about the downfall of both courts, Seelie and Unseelie. Peace will finally reign over the Otherworld."

"So," I summarize, "I'm a faerie princess who's apparently going to orchestrate a coup d'état."

"Yes," says Will brightly. "Make sense?"

"No," I say. "Not really. Not at all. So the Seelies want to kill me?"

"The Seelies. The Unseelies," Will responds cheerfully. "Lots of people want to kill *you*."

"You see?" says Aunt True to me desperately. "You see why we had to do what we did? We had to keep you *safe*."

I am silent for a long time, considering everything. This is all insane. I cannot believe I'm sitting in my kitchen, next to the boy I'm in love with (faerie), my aunts (ogres), and the owner of a museum in Salem (wizard). This has to be a dream, right? It must be a dream. I just can't understand how I ended up here, all because I wanted to know who my mother is.

"And what about my mother?" I ask.

Everyone exchanges a look.

It's Will who answers.

"She wants to kill you too."

CHAPTER 10

I am silent, stunned in the wake of this, the biggest revelation of them all. My mother wants to kill me—my mother, who I have longed for my entire life. It is no longer just that she abandoned me, that I have been suffering from neglect. Neglect would be *good*, benign—not, you know, *murderous*. It is no longer just the confirmation of my great fear that my mother might not love me. My mother doesn't want me to be *alive*.

How can this be *true*? I look at my aunts, mournful and silent, and I wonder. Would they lie to me about this? About *this*? Just to keep me with them?

Will is talking, something about what we should do now, but I can't even be bothered to translate the words. How can I think about moving on from *this*?

The house is suddenly suffocating.

"I need to go for a walk," I hear myself say.

"Outside?" asks Aunt Virtue fretfully.

"It's perfectly safe," says Will.

"She isn't hidden anymore," Aunt True points out. "The faeries can find her."

"But we're in Parsymeon," says Will, "the safest place she can be. Faeries can't get into Boston, remember? Well, nontraveler faeries, and so far as we know, there's only one of those, and he's right here already. And Seelies especially can't get in."

"I'm going outside," I reiterate, because I have to get out of here. I need to *breathe*. "I need some *air*."

I walk out into the foyer. The grandfather clock on the landing chimes six, and I pull open the front door and stand on the stoop. It is very late by now, and Beacon Street is as silent as it ever gets. Across the street looms the Common, normally my refuge when I need to think. But normally, I meet Ben there. Normally, it's being with Ben that I find so soothing. Normally, Ben seems to exist outside of all of the chaos of home and school. And now he doesn't. Now he seems to be the source of all of it. I lose all interest in taking a walk, in going to the Common, in *moving*. I sit heavily on the stoop. I want to talk to someone about this, but I have no one to talk to. I want to call Kelsey, but I'm not even sure if she still exists. I lean my forehead down to my knees and breathe.

I don't know how long I sit there before the door opens and closes, bringing with it briefly the sound of voices from inside the house. Ben sits down next to me. I don't look, but I know it is him.

"What if I didn't want you out here with me?" I ask, voice muffled by my knees.

"I wouldn't have been able to come out here," he replies.

Smug, I think, but don't correct him, because it's true. I don't really want to be *alone*; alone is how I feel—like I'm the only half-ogre, half-faerie princess prophesied to bring about a coup d'état in the whole wide world. Well, I probably am.

"They're arguing about the Sewing Circle. I had enough of that," he continues.

I say nothing. I have nothing to say about sewing circles. I have nothing to say about *any* of this. My mind is so full, it's a blank.

There is a moment of silence.

"Are you very upset with me?" Ben asks finally, sounding hesitant.

"I have no idea," I respond truthfully and then look at him for the first time. He looks like Ben, swaddled in layers, dark curls all unruly on his head. His unusual eyes are silver at the moment. *Faerie eyes,* I think. Are they faerie eyes? "How old are you?" I can't help asking.

He shakes his head. "We don't work that way. To some I'm ancient, to others very young. The same is true for you."

I can't make this make sense for me. "How old are you to *me*?"

"To you? To you I'm me."

It sounds like a riddle. "And what is that?"

He looks as if he's searching for the right word. "Perfect, wouldn't you say?" he decides finally, pinning me with a platinum stare.

"My entire life was a fiction *you* created for me," I point out helplessly. "And then you kept me there."

"You were protected," says Ben. "It wasn't a fiction; you were just protected. Did it feel like fiction? Did it not feel real?"

I can't answer that question. He must know how real it felt. If it hadn't felt real, I wouldn't feel like my heart was breaking at the moment, because I would have been in love with Ben the same way you might be in love with a famous actor. I wouldn't have been as desperately in love as I was.

"I didn't have a choice," Ben says when I stay silent.

"If what everyone is saying is true, you did have a choice," I point out.

"Do you think we're lying?"

"I don't know." I pause. "I think you're at least an expert in enchantment. I think, if you wanted to, you could get me to believe anything you like—even that I'm a faerie princess."

"I can't force you to believe anything that you don't want to believe, ironically *because* I'm an expert in enchantment."

"What do you mean?"

"Well, the protective enchantment—no one can force you to do anything."

"So you can't lie to me?"

"I can't lie to you, no. Well, not if you don't want me to."

"Do you think I do stupid things sometimes?"

"*Yes*," he says fervently.

I am uncertain if he would have lied to me there or not. But I guess it's the best I can do to test it.

I look at him for a long time. He studies me in return. I think of how, only hours earlier, he was just a boy on the

Common to me. Hours? Or was it lifetimes? Maybe this is what Ben means about faerie age being uncertain. Maybe time passes like this for faeries.

Thinking about everything we've been through this day (year? century?) reminds me. "You died," I say. "When we got to the meadow."

"Did you let go of my hand?" asks Ben, sounding unconcerned.

"I *fell*," I defend myself.

"I wasn't dead," he says. "I was resting. Jumps drain energy, and I was wet and diluted. I didn't have a lot to spare. It's how we ended up there instead of Boston in the first place, easier for me to lock on to my home world. Boston is tricky under the best of circumstances, all those barriers against faeries. I would have been fine; the recovery was just quicker if I could steal some energy from you."

"Some what?"

"Well, you, you're *drenched* in ability, but you don't know how to use it. In the meantime, I was wet and named, so I needed to borrow a bit of yours to get us enough charge to get out of Park Street."

"So you stole power from me by holding my hand?"

Ben crinkles his nose. "'Power' makes it sound so… 'Stealing' makes it sound so…"

"I didn't give you permission for that."

"You didn't tell me not to though. That's the key to my enchantment over you right now. No one needs *permission*. They just need to avoid outright refusal."

I frown. "Tricky," I accuse.

"Well." He flashes a bit of a smile. "Yes. I'm a faerie. And a good one."

"My aunts don't like you."

"No one really likes faeries except for faeries. I don't blame them entirely; faeries made it bad for ogres before there was Parsymeon. Your aunts want you to be all ogre. They wish your faerie blood would go away."

"And what do you wish?" I can't help but ask.

He looks at me, his gaze unerring, so intent that I think, wildly, for a moment, that he's about to kiss me.

"I don't even know who you *are*," I blurt out before Ben can even answer the question.

Ben looks at me for another long moment. "I am Benedict Le Fay," he tells me. "I am the best traveler in the Otherworld. And I am and always have been entirely at your service."

"Because I'm the…whatever you say, the fay of the autumnal equinox."

"Because you turned out to be *you*."

I swallow thickly. Half of me is so thrilled, I want to stand up and dance. The other half of me is *terrified*. The best traveler in the Otherworld is entirely at my service. I don't even know what that *means*. I eventually look away, clearing my throat, trying to find something less intense to talk about.

"People keep saying your name. Does it keep hurting you? Will calls you Benedict all the time, not even Ben."

"Oh, you have to have intent," says Ben. "Just saying a name isn't enough; you have to say the name with the proper—or improper, I suppose—intent."

"But I didn't even know there was an enchantment when I said your name," I point out, confused. "I had no intent to dissolve the enchantment."

"You were angry with me," he explains, his eyes still on me, reflecting starlight. "You intended to hurt me. Malicious intent, that's all it takes."

There is a moment of silence between us. "What happened to your mother?" I ask suddenly. I'm not sure why.

Ben looks away from me. "I don't know," he says, and I believe him.

"Your father mentioned her." I don't want to bring up the exact quote, about how wrong Ben was.

"He does that. He brings her up whenever he's trying to get me back into his idea of good behavior. But we don't know what happened to her, either one of us. One day she just…disappeared. That's what my father says, anyway. I don't know."

I study Ben's profile, which is tipped up in the direction of the moon and the stars. "Do you believe him?"

"Who else do I have to believe?" he asks with a shrug.

"What will happen to you?" I say after a second. "If my mother catches us."

Ben is silent for a very long time. "I don't know."

"You have an idea?"

"There's a reason why our names must be known under faerie law. When a member of the Seelie Court uses your whole name on you…I mean, other faeries can do it, and it isn't pleasant, but when it's a *Seelie*…"

"What happens?"

There is another long moment of silence. Ben clears his throat. "Well, I have never seen it done, but probably the mortal term for the outcome is *death*."

Apparently my mother is a homicidal maniac. *Great genes.* The shiver I've been suppressing fully rises. I lick my lips. "You shouldn't be here."

Ben looks at me in surprise. "Where else would I be?"

"I don't know. Somewhere else. If my mother catches me, she can't do anything to me, right? Because of your enchantment? But if she catches *you*…"

Ben shakes his head. "I won't leave you. Not now. Now, when your faerie blood's no longer hidden, when the Seelies can find you? No."

"But the Seelies can't get into Boston."

"The Seelies haven't been overly motivated before. They're very lazy. Now there's you. Who knows *what* will happen now? Armies could be mobilizing as we speak. And I can only protect you so far. The Seelies have a way of *making* you want the things they want."

"But—"

"*But* I was supposed to kill you. Years ago, centuries ago, or minutes ago, depending on which time you're keeping. I didn't. I'll be named just for that. It doesn't matter whether they find me with or without you."

"What if you....put up a new enchantment? Hide me again?"

"I can do that," Ben agrees. "But the prophecy is in motion. The enchantment would only be temporary."

"But it would buy us time," I say desperately. I want to forget about stupid faerie time; I've only just turned seventeen. I don't want to launch a coup d'état. I don't want to be stalked by homicidal faeries. I want to go back to my regular life—my aunts who love me, my father who I adore, Ben who I flirt with on the Common—and forget I ever wondered anything at all about my mother. I was going to try to get Ben to take me to the *prom*. That's how normal my life had been, and now it's *this*.

"You would have to forget all of this," Ben says. "And another enchantment—is that really what you want?"

He's right, and I know he's right—I don't want to be enchanted; I want to know the truth. I've always wanted to know the truth. I feel like I've been looking for it my entire life. I just wanted the truth to be something *happier*. I shake my head, unsure what else to say, not really trusting myself to speak, honestly.

Ben stares at me, his eyes now a washed-out periwinkle. "Selkie," he says. "I—"

I never hear what Ben is about to say, because at that moment, the air around us fills with the chiming of a million tiny bells.

CHAPTER 11

It doesn't seem like that should be a threatening sound, but I have time—barely—to register Ben's eyes going wide with obvious panic. And then he reaches for me, a hand on my arm, and then we are gone. We are in a world with suffocating heat, then a world so cold my lungs feel like they're freezing. We move through worlds so swiftly I can barely register them—worlds of day and worlds of night, worlds with winds that could knock me off my feet, worlds with snow drifting up to our waists. The weather does not have time to even affect me. We even skip through a world with driving rain, but I am touched by no more than a drop or two before we are at the next world. And then finally Ben stops. We hit a world of still darkness, and we stay long enough that I suck in oxygen, long enough that, now that the world has stopped whirling, I lose my balance and collapse against Ben's chest. He is still dressed in the multilayers he wears against the Boston rain, and they make a comfortable pillow, but he is breathing very quickly, even as he holds me up, and he says in my ear, "Can you stand? I need you to stand. We can't stay here. We have to jump again. I just have to warn him."

I make an effort to stand, managing to gasp, "What…?" but Ben dashes off before I can gather myself enough to form the question. I can hear him shouting, and it takes my ears a second to stop ringing and realize that he's shouting for his father. He comes back, and I say, "Did you find him?"

He is no longer breathing heavily. His voice is calm and even and harder than I have ever heard out of him before, so much so that I could almost think it isn't Ben at all in front of me. "No. They've already been here. Don't you see? This isn't night. They have torn the very sun from the sky."

I don't even have time to register this before Ben reaches out and pulls me roughly against him and says, "Close your eyes. You'll be less dizzy," and I am less dizzy when we finally stop, who knows how many worlds later.

Only slightly less though. When Ben lets go of me, I stagger a bit and finally decide it's easier to just sit on the ground. It's another meadow—this one of wildflowers—and it looks like a bright, cheerful world, only I am terrified.

"What happened? What was that?" I ask.

Ben is pacing, his hands in his dark hair, and he is muttering to himself.

"*Ben*," I say. "What happened to my aunts?"

"They're fine," he answers, distracted. "I'm sure they're fine. They were in the house—ogre magic in the walls of the house, tough to cross immediately. Stupid, *stupid*, for us to be outside, and no time to *think*; your enchantment couldn't protect you. You didn't have time to *think*—"

"What was that?" I ask again.

"Seelies," he says. "Lots of Seelies."

"Seelies…chime like that?"

Ben doesn't answer. I think of how close I might have been to my mother. Was she really trying to kill me? I think of what Ben had said, tearing the sun from the sky. What sort of beings would *do* something like that? I do not want to ask what had happened to his father.

"Can we go back to Boston now?" I just want to get back home, back to my aunts. This unfamiliar world is terrifying in its otherness.

"Shh," Ben snaps at me. "I have to think, let me think—" He cuts himself off, listening to something I can't hear, and something passes through his eyes, something I can't quite read but it is something knowing and something decisive, and he turns to me and pulls me up and closes his hands around my shoulders. "Listen to me."

"Ben—" I begin. I sense, instantly, that whatever he is doing now, I do not agree with it.

"Listen to me," he repeats more sharply. "Listen to me as you have never listened to anything in your life. This sweatshirt is your protection, do you hear me? As long as no one but you sees this sweatshirt, you are *safe*. Remember this about the sweatshirt. Remember how *important* this sweatshirt is."

"How would I forget?" I ask, bewildered. "You've already told me."

"Selkie Stewart, I am sorry for this."

I stare at him, wide-eyed. "Sorry for what?"

He leans forward and kisses me, very quickly and very chastely, and into the silence of my shock in the wake of this, he says, "Good-bye."

I fumble for the blaring alarm clock by my bed. Aunt Virtue is in my room, on her hands and knees, poking a broomstick under my dresser, no doubt looking for gnomes.

"Good morning, dear," she says without looking at me.

"Good morning," I respond and yawn.

"Did you sleep well?"

"Yeah." I swing myself out of bed and pause, looking at myself in the mirror over the dresser, in the old *Yankees Suck* T-shirt I have worn to bed every night for a while now. I have this tendency to wear the same T-shirt to bed until it is threadbare. "I had the strangest dream."

"About what?" asks Aunt Virtue absently, not sounding very interested.

"I'm not sure," I say. "Can't quite remember. But it was *very* complicated." I open my closet door and stand regarding my clothes for a second. "I think there was a rat involved," I decide finally and select a tweed skirt for the day.

CHAPTER 12

Mike is surprised when I kiss him impulsively, outside Cabot's Ice Cream where all the kids from school go.

"I didn't think you liked me," he says, regarding me quizzically, like I'm some sort of exotic species.

"You didn't?" I respond, just as quizzical, because I think I've been *obvious* about liking Mike. I have liked him forever. I cannot remember a time when I didn't like him.

Mike shakes his head, an indulgent gesture, and says, "You're something, Selkie Stewart. Just what, I don't know."

"A faerie princess, maybe," I say and giggle at my own joke.

Mike laughs at me and kisses me again, and it is only afterward, as he is drawing back, that I find myself confused.

"Your eyes are brown," I say.

"Yeah," he answers slowly, looking amused.

I am staring at his eyes, but I am not seeing them. I am seeing other eyes—pale eyes, eyes a color I can't place... I am frowning with the effort of this—it feels like it is just on the edge of my memory, odd, pale eyes, and a quick grin to go with them, a nose that crinkles, and... "I thought your eyes were..." I trail off, confused.

"They've always been brown," says Mike.

"Of course," I say. "Of course. I knew that." I smile, like I was joking.

But that night, after Mike drops me off and we name a time and place for our next date, I walk across Beacon Street to the Common and sit on a bench. There is someone who should be there who is not. I cannot shake this ridiculous feeling.

I decide maybe I am just missing my mother—it happens sometimes; I should really make an effort to look for her, something I want to do but have been procrastinating forever—and I go inside.

⁙

"Everything in your house is so old," says Kelsey. She is lying on my bed, and I am very painstakingly redoing my makeup for the umpteenth time, because I fail at mascara and because it has suddenly become very important to me that I not fail at mascara.

Sometimes, I don't know who I am now that I have started dating Mike.

"I mean," continues Kelsey, not minding that I'm barely paying attention, "*normal* people don't have houses like this."

"We *are* normal people," I say, slightly irritated, studying my reflection. Kelsey has dried and straightened my hair, on her insistence, even though it's naturally straight, and it looks like spun gold shot through with silvery streaks where it picks up the light. I am pleased with the outcome of my hair, less pleased with the outcome of my eye makeup; it looks harsh and abrupt in my pale face, seems to swallow my sky-blue eyes.

"What's up with that clock?" says Kelsey. "I find it creepy. When I got here, it was chiming eleven o'clock, and now it's chiming seven. I've only been here twenty minutes!"

"It's just broken," I say. "It's not *creepy*."

"It's just this *house*," says Kelsey. "It's like it's been here since, I don't know, since *before* Boston."

"You mean, when Boston was called Parsymeon?" I tuck my hair behind my ears, switch its part, experimenting.

"What?" says Kelsey quizzically.

"When Boston was called Parsymeon," I repeat. "*You* know."

"No, I don't know. Boston was called Parsymeon? When?"

"Before it was called Boston. How do you not know this? Didn't we learn that at school?"

"Uh, no," says Kelsey, staring at me like I've lost my mind. She changes the subject, like she doesn't want to go any deeper down *that* rabbit hole. "You should bring a sweatshirt. It'll be cold at the football game."

"Good thinking." I turn to my closet, which is a total mess because I am a complete and utter pack rat. I am always grabbing things and saving things for reasons that I can't explain. I stand on tiptoe to rummage through the shelf at the top on which my sweatshirts are stacked, trying to find one that I haven't worn a million times already this fall. I pause on a maroon one emblazoned with *Boston* across the front, like tourists would buy outside Park Street station. Where did I get *that* from? I wonder and tug at the one underneath it, a gray one from a downtown store. *Weird*, I think as I straighten. *I should give it away…*

I stop, halfway out my bedroom door, and look back toward the closet.

"Selkie?" asks Kelsey curiously, turning back to me.

I glance at her. She is halfway down the hallway, lit by the streetlight through the lavender panes of glass in the Palladian window above our front door.

I look back toward the closet. I am deep in thought. I can see the sleeve of the Boston sweatshirt, dangling off the shelf. *Remember how important this sweatshirt is*, someone says to me, someone I can't place, at some time I can't remember— but *someone* said that to me. Who was it? Who could it possibly have been? Who would tell me that a simple Boston sweatshirt was important?

I shake it off and turn back to Kelsey. "Nothing," I say. "Nothing." I shut off my light, and I follow her down the front staircase. The grandfather clock chimes one as we pass it.

The football game is a success. We win, and Mike throws a couple of touchdowns, and afterward we go out for ice cream, and Mike is sweet and cute and holds my hand and makes me laugh, and I am the envy of every girl at school, and I should be flushed and happy.

But all I can think of is the Boston sweatshirt. It's been *haunting* me. I cannot place where I got it. I feel like someone gave it to me, but I can't remember who. And I feel like the most important thing I will ever know in my life is the knowledge of *who gave me this sweatshirt*. It's driving me crazy that I can't remember.

As soon as I get home, I pull the sweatshirt off the shelf, and I stare at it for a long time. It looks like a normal sweatshirt. Why would it be important in any way? The thought that it might be important, tugging at the edge of my consciousness, feels like something that came from a dream. I try to remember if I've had a dream about this sweatshirt, but nothing rings a bell. I can think of nothing but that this is *important—so important.*

I pull the sweatshirt over my head—

It all rushes back to me, like someone has ducked my head in cold water, and I am gasping as it crashes over me—*everything*, my murderous mother, my ogre aunts, Will Blaxton of the Salem Which Museum, the sound of the chiming bells of the Seelie Court, and *Ben*. How could I have *forgotten*?

I get to my feet. The sweatshirt is warm around me, like the first hug I have had in a very long time. I go downstairs, and my aunts are sitting in the conservatory. They are knitting. They have been knitting a pair of socks for as long as I have been alive. They are each in charge of one sock, and by now the socks are so large they could fit the biggest giant to ever live. I wonder now how many centuries they have been knitting these socks. The yarn of them is a bright pink snowdrift around the twin dark spires of my aunts.

They are knitting automatically, their eyes darting about the room for the sight of the hated gnomes, and I march in and I say, "I remember everything."

"Everything what?" Aunt Virtue asks blandly.

"That you are ogres. That my mother is a faerie."

Aunt True laughs and says, "A likely story."

The two of them knit away.

"Where is Ben?" I ask.

They look at me. "Who?" they ask. I don't believe their act, not for a second. As unbelievable as it seems, I *know* somehow that my real life is this faerie tale I've been told. This strange, Ben-less world, where I'm dating Mike Summerton, must be an enchantment.

"Ben," I say. "Benedict. Benedict Le Fay. Where is he? What happened to him?"

My aunts look at me for a long moment then turn back to their socks.

"Forget about him," says Aunt Virtue. "Forget about all of it. You're not supposed to remember. Not yet, not now."

"But Ben *told* me to remember, I think. To remember this sweatshirt…What am I wearing?" I ask.

"Jeans," says Aunt Virtue.

"No, for a top."

My aunts peer at me.

"A green sweater," says Aunt True.

"No, no, it's very clearly a yellow sweater," says Aunt Virtue. They exchange a confused look.

I am relieved. If Ben's enchantment is still working, then I am safe. And that means Ben must be safe too, somewhere, because it would be his energy keeping the enchantment going.

"Where's Ben?" I ask again.

"Don't you understand?" demands Aunt True. "This is a different enchantment. An alternate enchanted Boston for you, one where you never even met Benedict."

"And it's not nearly as good as the first one was," says Aunt Virtue with a sigh. "Look how quickly you figured it out."

If I've figured it out, can my mother find me? If I've figured it out, are Ben's powers dissolving?

"What do you hear from the Otherworld?" I demand.

"We don't have contact with the Otherworld, Selkie," says Aunt True. "We're hiding you, darling. We need to keep as low profile as possible. We haven't even discussed anything with the Sewing Circle. We don't want *anyone* to know."

"Ben's disappeared," I say. "Ben was always here, and then I *forgot* about him."

"It's a different enchantment," Aunt True reiterates. "It's an enchantment where you never knew him."

"But I *do* know him."

"Because it isn't a very good enchantment," says Aunt Virtue.

"It was the best he could do," I realize, piecing together those last moments before I woke up in my bed and forgot that Ben had ever existed. "It was the best he could do in the time that he had: send me back here, erect another enchantment, but a messy one. He didn't have time to make it as good as the other one. Which means it's only a matter of time before my mother finds me."

"Let her come," says Aunt True, suddenly fierce. "We have our own ways. Ways faeries don't know. Let the faeries try to take an ogre out of Boston. See how the inhabitants of this land will rise up against them."

"And we'd like to have a chat with your mother," adds Aunt Virtue. "Can you imagine, killing your own precious child?"

"We will keep you safe, dear," Aunt Virtue promises me. "Forget about Benedict Le Fay. It is so like a faerie to not keep his promises. *We* will keep you safe. You are an ogre. Your faerie blood means nothing. We will find a way to keep you safe."

"Somehow," says Aunt True.

But they sound worried, frightened.

CHAPTER 13

I am too keyed up to sleep. I sit in my sweatshirt, stick my hands in the pocket, and find the bedraggled pages from the Salem Which Museum.

There is also a shard of glass in my sweatshirt pocket, wrapped in a tissue, and I remember breaking the glass and saving a shard, in a reality that never existed, a past I never had. I still have no idea what I'm going to do with this shard of glass, but, let's face it, I have no idea what's going on with most of my life.

I sit up all night on my bed, in my enchanted sweatshirt, thinking about my terrified aunts, about all the supernatural creatures in Boston, banding together to keep faeries out. *And what am I?* a small voice whispers inside of me. Would Boston accept me as the ogre my aunts say that I am? Or am I really a faerie princess? I find myself listening for chiming bells. The only bells I hear are the bells in the church at Park Street, and finally, it is morning.

I go down and eat breakfast as usual. My aunts say, "You cannot go to school. It isn't safe outside the house."

I stare. "So I'm just going to…stay inside for the rest of my life."

"Until the war is over," Aunt True says, which doesn't exactly inspire confidence.

There is a knock on the door—Kelsey, to walk to school with me.

"You cannot go," Aunt Virtue says firmly.

I scowl and go and answer the door.

"Hey," says Kelsey.

"I'm not going to school today."

"What? Why not?"

The answer to that question is incredibly complex. It involves prophecies and fake lives and who even knows if Kelsey is real? She could just be a figment of my imagination.

"Just…not going," I say and wonder if I should add, *Actually, I'm never going to be able to leave the house again.*

Kelsey looks at me with concern. "Are you okay?"

I am the opposite of okay. My aunts think my mother is actively trying to kill me. I don't want to think my aunts are lying, but I don't want to think my mother is trying to kill me. And the only person I could have talked to about this has enchanted himself out of my life history. And apparently, the plan for possibly *ever*—half-faerie, half-ogre, it's possible I'm immortal, I don't even know—is to just keep me locked away.

Suddenly I am angry. No one ever tells me the truth, it seems. No one ever gives me *choices*. I am so tired of being ordered around, of being a spectator in my life. It may be reckless, but I decide I am going to Salem and getting *answers.* If my mother finds me, I have Ben's enchantment on me—and the way I feel at this moment, just let her try anything with me.

Ben's enchantment, I think. *Ben has given me* choice. My aunts can't make me stay locked up because I don't want to stay locked up. I need answers, and I need to find Ben too.

"I need to go to Salem," I announce abruptly, decision made.

"Salem?" Kelsey echoes in confusion.

"Yeah."

"For what?"

I hesitate. "Do you remember I ducked into that museum while the rest of you hung out in Salem?"

"What? No. When?"

"When we went to Salem this year."

Kelsey looks at me for a moment, her green eyes quizzical. "We didn't go to Salem this year."

I should have expected that, but I don't know why it seems like the last straw of frustration. *Why is this my life, and who can I blame for it?* I want to scream.

"Of course we didn't," I say resignedly.

"Selkie, are you okay? You're acting weird. Actually, you've *been* acting weird for a little while now."

"If I told you what's going on with me, you'd never believe it," I tell her honestly.

"Of course I'd believe it. Don't be silly," she says comfortingly, and she is my best friend, and I *so* wish she could understand.

I shake my head. "No, never mind. It's nothing, really. I just…have to go to Salem."

"Then I'll go with you," Kelsey decides.

"No," I protest. "No, really, I don't want to—"

"I'm not letting you go alone. I'd never let you go on an adventure like this *alone*." Kelsey puts her hands on her hips. "We'll have to have some kind of catfight over it, maybe push each other in the fountain or something."

The idea is ridiculous. But so is the idea of Kelsey coming along with me.

"You know I'd beat you in a catfight, right?" continues Kelsey.

She probably would. "Kelsey…" I begin, but I can't come up with anything else to say. Finally I settle on, "I'm not sure it's safe."

Kelsey folds her arms and gives me A Look. "Oh," she says. "Then I am *definitely* going with you. What kind of friend would I be if I let you go by yourself to do something danger-ous? I'd miss out on all the fun!"

I'm a little sulky that Kelsey's won the argument and is tag-ging along with me, so we don't really talk until we get to Salem. It's Kelsey who breaks the silence.

"So," she asks. "What are we doing here?"

"I have to talk to this guy I know here," I answer. "His name is Will, and he owns a museum."

Kelsey doesn't ask me any more questions. She follows me as I walk the blocks to the street where I went to the Salem Which Museum.

And it isn't there.

I stand on the street, and I stare at where the museum should be—an alley between a souvenir shop on one side and a bank on the other. I am speechless and at a loss as to what to do. Maybe Will doesn't exist in this enchantment either, like Ben. Or maybe I am a crazy person and all of it—the empty Park Street station, the talking rat, the story about my heritage, Ben himself—was just an elaborate, vivid dream. For all I know, maybe I am in the same institution as my father right at this very minute, still in the throes of this terrible hallucination.

The harsh November wind tumbles up the street toward us, slamming into us. I huddle instinctively into my sweatshirt, tucking my hands into the pocket—and I close my hand around the shard of tissue-wrapped glass. The museum waves into existence, right where it's supposed to be, just the way it looked before. Kelsey utters a little squeak next to me, but none of the other people coming and going from the bank and the shop so much as look up.

"How did you *do* that?" breathes Kelsey, awe in her voice.

"I have no idea," I admit. "That's pretty much how it goes around me."

I step forward confidently and push open the door, and there I am again, in the Salem Which Museum. Will is sitting in the front room this time, reading, but he doesn't look surprised to see me. He closes his book, sets it aside, and frowns at me.

"Hello, Iggy," I say to the iguana wandering around by the front door. And then to Will, "Hi."

Will glances at Kelsey, then back to me. "Your aunts are furious and terrified. They've raised so much of an alarm, the goblins have completely shut down the subways."

"Good thing we didn't take the subway," I say.

"This isn't funny," snaps Will.

"I agree. Where is Ben?"

"It doesn't matter," says Will. And then, "Does it matter?"

"Of course it matters. He always matters. And he's made a mess of things. I was kissing Mike Summerton because of him."

"What?" says Kelsey.

"Who is Mike Summerton?" asks Will. "Not a goblin, is he? Goblins can be very seductive."

"He's not a *goblin*," I say.

"Goblins look just like any of us," says Will. "Just much more attractive."

"What are we talking about?" asks Kelsey in bewilderment.

Will and I ignore her.

"Where. Is. Ben?" I say.

"Do you know how rude it is to bring this up in mixed company?" Will sweeps a hand toward Kelsey.

"Kelsey," I start.

"No. No way." She shakes her head firmly. "I want to know what the hell everyone's talking about."

There is a moment of silence.

"Where's Ben?" I ask again.

Will is silent for a long moment. Then: "He's a special guest of the Seelie Court, or so I hear. And there isn't a prophecy without him; he's part of the prophecy, the one where we win, anyway."

I think of what Ben said would happen to him if the Seelies got him. "Is he…" I trail off, not sure what to say.

"Well, his enchantment's flickering, but it's holding, so I would imagine he's weakened but pretty much okay. He hasn't been named yet."

"Why not?"

Will's gaze is flat and unamused. "Oh, my dear, *that* should be obvious."

I bristle. "It isn't to me, so why don't you tell me?"

"The Seelie Court needs him to get to you."

"But if they named him, wouldn't the protective enchantment around me dissolve?"

"But you're here in Boston—a Boston that's been reinforced. The goblins are raising armies and the borders are more tightly closed. Can they get at you here? Yes. Of course. Eventually, I'm sure. But would you make it a whole lot easier on them if you went to them? Yes."

Well, there's nothing to be gained by walking into a trap. And yet…

"Ben's there because of me, isn't he? Because he could only save one of us, so he saved me, not himself."

"Don't think of it that way," says Will.

"How else should I think of it?"

"You shouldn't think of it at all. Ben didn't want you to."

"If I'm going to be the downfall of the Seelie Court, maybe I can bring it about now," I suggest.

"You're not going to be the downfall by yourself. We need the other three fays of the seasons."

"There are others?"

"Of course. Did you think you were all alone in this? None of us is ever as special as we think. You're just the autumn fay. There are three others, and the prophecy is firm that all four of you must be assembled."

"So where are they?"

"You are the only one we know about. And I've no idea how to find the rest. I've been reading every book I can think of, but I'm getting nowhere. Anyway, it doesn't matter. Even if we have all four fays, the prophecy requires a Le Fay, and there's only Ben left of the line, considering his mother hasn't been seen in centuries now—or a few minutes, depending on the time you're keeping."

I blink. "Did you know his mother?"

"Of course. Everyone knew his mother. She was the best enchantress in the Otherworld. Where do you think Benedict gets it from?"

"What happened to her?"

"No one knows the answer to that. Trust me, she's a dead end; we'll never find *her*. If we're going to find the other three fays, we need Benedict. It's what the prophecy says."

"If the prophecy says Ben's going to help us, then won't it just happen? He *has* to escape and help us; it's prophesied."

Will shakes his head. "That's not how prophecies work. Prophecies war, one against the other. Until the words are written down, the possible paths are manifold. We have one; the Seelies have another. The prophecy isn't that you *will* restore peace to the Otherworld. It's that it will never be done *without* you."

"Then we don't have a choice, do we? We have to go to the Seelie Court to rescue Ben."

"I would like you to tell me how you propose to waltz into the Seelie Court and waltz out with a prisoner."

I frown. "Well, first, you're going to help me."

"Even if I thought this foolhardy plan wasn't going to get all of us named immediately, I can't actually set foot in Tir na nOg, no non-faerie can, not without a silver bough, and nobody knows how to make one of those except the Seelies."

There is too much here for me to unpack. Will is using words that make absolutely no sense to me. "You need to start at the beginning."

"No," says Will. "I don't need to start anywhere. You are going straight home. I am not going to be responsible for getting the autumn fay killed."

"So that's it?" I say. "You're just going to let Ben be named?"

Will falters. "Benedict knew the risks." He must realize how lame that sounds, because he adds, "There's nothing I can do, Selkie. Nothing any of us can do. I'm sorry. But if Benedict's going to get out of Tir na nOg, he'll have to find some astonishing way to do it." There's a moment of silence. "He's an exceptionally talented faerie. He'll figure it out."

I am silent, thinking furiously, because I can't just leave Ben in there. I can't; he's there because of me in the first place.

A rabbit comes hopping into the room, and I look at it fully. "Does it talk?" I ask, thinking maybe it will be of help, the way the talking rat could have been in Ben's world.

"No, that's just Bunny," says Will.

"Not very original when it comes to names, are you?" drawls Kelsey sarcastically.

"Don't be silly. Those aren't their *real* names." Will glares at her, then turns back to me. "Now go home."

I'm not going to go home, I think. *The subways are links with the Otherworld. If I can figure out how they work, if I can just get to a subway…*

Will ushers us out the door. I am deep in thought, but I grab a button from his change-collecting bowl on the way out because you never know.

"Now what?" Kelsey asks when we find ourselves standing on a Salem street, with the Salem Which Museum disappeared behind us again.

"You should go home," I say. "Take the ferry, like we came."

"And what are you going to do?"

"I'm going to get on the T," I say grimly.

"Then I'll go with you."

"Not a good idea."

"Why not?"

"The T is...supernatural."

Kelsey lifts her eyebrows. "The *T* is? Supernaturally terrible at working, maybe."

"No, it really is."

"Then I've got to see this."

"Kelsey," I protest. I wish Ben's enchantment made me able to force people to do as I wish rather than just keeping them from forcing *me* to do things. It would make life so much easier. The enchantment he's left me with seems boring and stupid and useless at the moment.

So Kelsey and I walk to the T, which is in chaotic disarray because one of the lines has stopped running—probably the line I need to take to get to Tir na nOg. I wish I knew what to do to make the subway a portal to the Otherworld, but it seems just like the usual subway. Kelsey and I get on and it kicks into motion. I peer out the window, and I don't know what I'm looking for—maybe a glimpse of that bright, sunny world Ben transported us to? But all I see is the dark tunnel.

I turn away with a sigh. The man across the aisle, dressed in a dapper trench coat with a plaid scarf, reading a *Metro*, is looking at me. *Is* he looking at me? I feel paranoid and confused. I look away, then back at him quickly, and in that moment, reality flickers. It's the best way I can describe it. I am, for one brief moment, no longer in the T. I am in what seems like an expensive hotel lobby with clusters of fancy, uncomfortable seating and a fireplace. And then, before I can get my bearings and look around, I'm not. I'm just on the T, and it's squealing into Park Street.

"End of the line," the PA tells us. "Everyone off."

The man I thought was watching me gathers up his briefcase and exits the subway car.

"But this *isn't* the end of the line," I point out, bewildered.

Kelsey shrugs. "Something must be going on."

We find out what once we're back on the platform.

"Fire on the tracks," someone comments. "No trains past Park Street."

Park Street is a mess at the best of times; now it is a teeming mass of irritated humanity. The air sounds like complaints and annoyance. And it's pointless to stand here, jostled and crowded, unable to *get* anywhere. I wish I knew what to do. I curse Will for not helping me.

Someone says to me, "You should get out of here." A man, tall and dark, with brilliant blue eyes.

I shrink away from him instinctively and do just that, taking Kelsey with me.

And when we get aboveground, Will is there, looking very unamused. "You," he says, "are an *enormous* amount of trouble."

"How did you find us?" I grumble, annoyed.

"The goblins control the subways. You don't think the goblins know when the autumn fay gets on?"

"And then you beat us here?" I demand.

"I came express. The king of the goblins is a friend. Now what do you think you're up to?"

"For someone who won't help me," I retort, "you're awfully concerned with where I go."

"Look," he says, "I don't know what to make of the prophecy now that Ben's gone—reading prophecies isn't, strictly speaking, my specialty—but I'm not going to lose the one fay we've found. You are, right now, the one glimmer of hope we have in taking back the Otherworld. So, like it or not, I'm keeping you safe. And surely you've noticed by now that that's getting harder to do, that the walls between the worlds are breaking down. We're scrambling to reinforce them, but it would be easier for all of us if you would just *stay put*."

"Okay," Kelsey interrupts. "I've had enough. Finally. I mean, I think I've been pretty patient so far, but what the *hell* is going on here?"

Will looks at her. "Who *are* you, anyway?"

Kelsey opens her mouth, but I cut her off. "Don't tell him. Names have power, and he's a wizard, and not one I'm sure I trust."

Will looks highly indignant. "Not *trust* me? Not trust *me*? I have kept you alive your entire life, child!"

"Ben's kept me alive," I point out. "Ben and my aunts and my father. All I know is that from the moment I've met you, I've barely had two seconds strung together where my life isn't in danger. So the verdict's still out on you."

"Trusting a faerie over a wizard," grumbles Will. "It's easy to tell *you* are new to the Otherworld."

"This is what I'm talking about," says Kelsey, frustrated. "Faeries? Wizards? What is going *on*?"

"Humans don't get involved in Otherworld politics," Will snaps at her.

"Huh?" says Kelsey eloquently, staring at him.

"Your friend here," says Will, sweeping a hand toward me, "is half-ogre, half-faerie-princess. There's a dangerous prophecy that she is going to overthrow the ruling faerie government and restore peace to the Otherworld, which is why her mother wants her dead. Everything clear now?"

Kelsey blinks at Will then looks at me in amazement. "He is *insane*," she hisses at me, obviously worried about Will's state of mind.

"Possibly," I agree awkwardly. "But he's not *wrong*."

She stares at me.

"You're going home," Will says. "Both of you. To your separate homes."

"No, definitely not," says Kelsey. "Either Selkie is surrounded by crazy people, or you're all totally sane and this is *true*. Either way, do you think I'd leave her alone?"

I have never in my life loved Kelsey as much as I do at that moment. I mean, I've always known that she is pretty much the best friend you could ever ask for, that she is the definition of loyal, that she will stand by you through thick and thin, but I never really stopped to consider if she would stand by me if I found out I was some kind of faerie princess harbinger of death or something. I mean, who would consider such a thing? But there she is, just outside Park Street station, as if this is totally within the realm of what you sign up for when you become friends with someone.

I bury her in a sudden, fierce hug.

Will sighs. "Fine," he says. Then again, more firmly and sounding more annoyed, "*Fine*. I will let your aunts deal with you."

He says this like it's a threat, but I've had seventeen years now of dealing with my aunts. I'm confident that things are shifting my way.

We walk toward Beacon Street together. The wind sweeps over the Common in the way that only wind over the Common can—like a sentient being that fiercely battles your desire to reach your destination. Will shudders deeper into the threadbare coat he has pulled on, but though I feel it raw against my cheeks, the wind halts at my sweatshirt, draws up short at the barrier of enchantment so much more perplexing than wool.

If Ben could market these sweatshirts, he'd make a fortune.

Will makes a little noise of disgust, a tiny *hmph*, as we reach the edge of the Common opposite my house, and I look at him.

"It's just, well, *predictable*, isn't it? I was thinking that the other day. Looks exactly the same as it did in 1632."

"Houses weren't built like this in 1632," I tell Will.

"How do you know how enchanted houses were built in 1632?" he demands.

"This house is enchanted?" says Kelsey.

"Got the lavender windowpanes. That's how you know a house in Boston is an enchanted house."

"I knew it!" exclaims Kelsey triumphantly. "I always knew there was something weird about this house." She pauses. "So, the lavender windowpanes, huh? I thought that was just a chemical reaction, a bad batch of glass."

Will gives her a withering look. "That's never been replicated? Ever? Really? It's actually been replicated lots and lots, just not by humans. It's goblin glass."

My aunts open the door as we're crossing Beacon Street, their voices tumbling over each other.

"How *dare* you leave?"

"Where have you been?"

"With the Seelies wanting to capture you."

"And *kill* you."

"And the locks breaking."

"And the walls crumbling down."

"And you leave this *house*?"

They finally fall silent. They both look at Kelsey.

"And what is *she* doing here?" Aunt True demands.

"Hi," says Kelsey innocently.

"Your…whatever she is," sputters Will, "has it in her head to rescue Benedict at the Seelie Court."

This strikes my aunts momentarily dumb. They look at me in horror.

"*Selkie*," says Aunt True.

"The *Seelie Court*?" says Aunt Virtue. "You can't go to the Seelie Court."

"Could we possibly go inside to discuss this?" asks Will with strained politeness.

"No one was supposed to be outside today at all," Aunt True sniffs with a pointed look at me, and then she ushers all of us inside, including Kelsey.

On the landing, the grandfather clock chimes seven.

CHAPTER 14

It's an argument—more of an argument than I have ever had before with my aunts. I can tell that their desperation stems from fear for me, but I am growing progressively more frustrated that they won't listen to me.

"It's a silly infatuation," Aunt Virtue tells me.

And maybe, on other days, even I have been worried that it might be a silly infatuation, but it *doesn't matter*. I cannot possibly pretend not to be responsible for his current predicament. "I *owe* him," I say. "Every second I am breathing is a debt to him. Even if I hated him, I'd have to go to the Seelie Court. I am…" I struggle for the word.

Aunt Virtue blinks and wheels backward, looking at me in horror, as if that is the worst thing I could ever have said.

Aunt True gasps. "*Selkie*," she says in a low voice. "Stop it. Stop it right now."

"It's too late," says Will. "Honor bound. She's an indebted faerie. The Threader will be here any minute to seal her fate."

"She is *not*!" Aunt True cries. "Don't say such things! She is an *ogre*."

"She was only ever half that," Will says gently. "The faerie part of her is just as strong, and she's gotten her honor tangled up. If you don't let her fix it, her power will leak from her and eventually she'll just drift away. Faeries and their odd, non-sensical sense of *honor*, you know how they are."

Aunt True is clutching her teacup so tightly that her knuckles are white and I think it might break. "Will she drift away? Maybe she'll just lose the faerie part of her. Maybe she just won't be the fay anymore," she whispers. "And what do we care about the fay of the autumnal equinox? Let her just be *ours*, forget about the rest of it."

"Is that a risk you want to take?" Will asks.

There is a long silence. I don't really understand what's happening here, what they're saying, but I know that I can see the path I need to take. I see it clearer than I've ever seen anything else.

"Can I say something?" I venture.

Everyone just looks at me expectantly.

I take a deep breath and try to gather my thoughts. "I didn't mean to ask for this, this prophecy, and…all this. I should have listened when you told me to stop asking questions about my mother. But I'm the one who brought us here, and I'm the one who has to fix it. This is *my* life, my parents, my friends; I can't have you hide it from me, take it from me. You have to let me be *me*. Ogre, faerie, whatever I am, just let me be *me*. Surely it will all work out."

Aunt True and Aunt Virtue stare at me fearfully.

"Do you really think you will *live* to see the fulfillment

of the prophecy?" asks Aunt True finally, her voice swamped with sorrow.

"We cannot protect you in the Seelie Court, child," inserts Aunt Virtue, looking incredibly sad. "No one can."

"The Seelies block the magic of others," adds Will. "They always have. You cannot reach into the Seelie Court from outside it; you will have to be on the inside. And none of our enchantments will work in there," Will continues. "I could try to cast something over you, but my magic will break as soon as you reach the Seelie Court. Without a silver bough, only faerie magic works inside the Seelie Court."

"Good thing I'm a faerie then, isn't it?" I say, and my aunts both make identical little strangled sounds, and I realize what I've said. "Oh." I blink at them, feeling confused and a little lost. "I meant…" What did I mean? *Am* I a faerie? Is that how I've started thinking of myself? What about the ogre part of me? Where did that go?

"The Sewing Circle will be here any minute," Aunt Virtue cuts me off stiffly.

"Who are they?" I ask.

"A bunch of old bats," mutters Will.

"In the old days, when all things were easier, the Sewing Circle kept track of faerie obligations," explains Aunt Virtue, as if she is reading it from an encyclopedia. She seems to have detached herself from the conversation. "The Sewing Circles wove them into the tapestries. There are fewer Sewing Circles these days."

"Why?" I figure I need to know everything I can possibly know about the Otherworld.

"Faeries don't really interact with other faeries anymore," explains Will. "Easier to keep your head down and not get involved with each other. You never know when the Seelies might come calling, when a betrayal might happen. Easier not to get into any obligations in the first place."

There is a sudden flapping noise from the fireplace.

"And here they come," says Will grimly.

Kelsey, wide-eyed, shifts on the couch as far away as she can get, as the room abruptly fills with bats, streaming from our chimney. They settle on every free surface they can find. I have never seen a bat close up before; I never knew they could *frown* so effectively.

"They're literally *old bats*," murmurs Kelsey, as if this is the thing pushing this entire day over the edge into full-fledged absurdity. And I tend to agree with her.

There is a knock on our front door. I look at my aunts.

"Well," says Aunt Virtue calmly. "It's you who have called her. Go and answer it."

Why not? I go to the front door and open it on one of those tour guides who dress in colonial garb and escort tourists around the city. Her dress is rust colored, striking against her dark skin, and her hair is topped by a scrap of cheap, white cotton edged in cheap, white lace and hoping to approximate a bonnet. She is holding a basket that she thrusts into my hands, and I take it automatically. Looking down into it, I realize it is full to the brim with pincushions and spools of thread.

"Well," she says cheerfully. "Let's get started."

CHAPTER 15

The woman immediately moves past me, confidently striding in the direction of the conservatory. Still clutching her basket of sewing supplies, I hurry after her, eager not to miss anything.

She takes my seat, which is the only one not covered with bats, and gestures for her basket. I hand it over and then stand and look about me for somewhere to sit that has not already been monopolized by the bevy of bats. Kelsey moves a tiny amount, disturbing a bat who turns a glare on her, but it is enough for me to squeeze in next to her.

"Now then," says the woman calmly. "Who is the honor-bound faerie?" She is carefully threading a needle as she speaks.

I look at my aunts, who aren't looking at me. Aunt True is worrying at a nail and looking at the floor. Aunt Virtue is watching the bats lined up on our mantelpiece. I look at Will, who is frowning magnificently at the woman who has entered. Nobody seems to be giving me any guidance, and I have no idea what to do.

The woman stops threading her needle and looks up

expectantly. Her dark eyes scan the room and land on me. It is as if she did not see me at all when I opened the door for her. She stares at me, transfixed. She replaces the needle and thread slowly into her basket and then breathes, "*Oh*." Extending a hand toward me, she then commands, "Come here, child."

My aunts still aren't looking at me, so I look at Will, uncertain. There is one thing I am sure of—in the hierarchy of people from the Otherworld I trust, Will ranks above this strange woman.

Will nods at me, although he still looks grim, and not knowing what else to do, I stand up and walk slowly over to her.

"Oh *my*," she exclaims, taking my hand in hers and squeezing gently. "I had been wondering how an honor-bound faerie had gotten into Boston. It's been ages since my services were needed. So you're what all the fuss has been about. You're the fay of the autumnal equinox. Aren't you *lovely*? But where is Benedict Le Fay? Sulking now that his enchantment has been broken? How came you to break his enchantment, child?" she asks me kindly and curiously.

"His name," I answer truthfully.

"Do *you* know Benedict Le Fay's full name?" she asks sharply.

I suspect that, if I did, there is nothing this woman would stop at to extract it from me. But I am able to truthfully answer, "No."

"You broke his enchantment with how many of his names?"

"Just the two," I respond, confused. "Well, three, I guess, depending on what, exactly, *Le* is."

"Two names," she muses. "You broke a Le Fay enchantment with just two names. That is some clever naming. That talent must be strong with you." She takes a deep breath and lets it out again. "Now. What have you gone and gotten yourself honor-bound about?"

I hesitate, unsure.

"Well, go on," the Threader urges. "*You* called me here."

"I didn't," I say uncertainly.

"Yes. You did. An honor-bound faerie. I am here to weave your obligation into the tapestry, to record it forever. Or at least the next few minutes, depending on the time you're keeping."

I stare at her. "What tapestry?" I ask, still uncertain.

She stares back at me, as if we are in identical stages of shock over the other. "*The* tapestry," she insists, which isn't exactly helpful.

I look at my aunts for guidance. Something about this woman, this unknown tapestry, this obligation talk makes me uncomfortable.

"But she isn't actually a faerie," Aunt Virtue interjects pleadingly. "Surely that means—"

"But she is a faerie. I wouldn't have been called here if she was not."

"She is only *half*-faerie," Aunt True adds desperately.

"Nevertheless, it is a full obligation." The Threader acts as if the conversation is now closed, and my aunts, looking dejected, don't fight anymore, so maybe it is closed. She looks at me expectantly.

I swallow.

Will says, "Oh, you might as well get it over with. *You're* the one who was so set on going in the first place."

I lick my lips. This is apparently my cue to plead my case. "Ben's in the faerie prison, whatever it's called. And he's there because of me. It's my fault. So I have to go save him."

The woman's eyebrows flicker upward. "Tir na nOg?" she asks. "Are you talking about Tir na nOg?"

"Yes," I say, recognizing the strange phrase.

The woman continues to look dubious. "You've gone and gotten yourself honor-bound over saving someone from Tir na nOg?"

"I can get in," I say stubbornly. "They want me there. They'll let me in. They'll probably have a welcoming committee waiting for me."

"Oh, they'll have a committee," mutters Will dryly. "The adjective used to describe it might not be 'welcoming.'"

"There will be no trouble getting *in*, child. They will send a Green Line train for you, of course. The trouble will be getting *out*."

"A Green Line train?" I echo. "Like the subway?"

"Yes."

I am thinking hard. So I just have to get on the Green Line and it will take me to the faerie prison. This seems unlikely, but everything that's happened to me recently seems unlikely, and who am I to argue with the idea that there's a faerie prison at the end of the Green Line? The Green Line *is* strange.

"The problem is once you're *there*," says Will. "No one's ever escaped Tir na nOg."

"Except for Benedict Le Fay's mother," remarks the Threader.

"Ben's mother?" I say sharply.

"Oh, that's a literal faerie tale," says Will. "There was never any evidence that she escaped; she hasn't been seen since. The only people who get out of Tir na nOg are *mad*."

"Mad?" I echo.

"They're *insane*, Selkie. Did you never wonder what drove your father to insanity? That's what contact with a Seelie can do, even without being imprisoned by them. That is the price they can exact. They steal who you are, what makes you *you*. Think of how much worse it is in their court."

I stare at Will, and I think of my father. It is one thing for my mother to apparently want to kill me. It is another thing for my mother to be holding Ben hostage in some kind of unpleasant circumstance in order to entrap me. But somehow, it is more than I can bear to think of her driving my poor father into madness, a man whose dearest wish was a *child*, a man I have never had an unsupervised visit with because of *her*.

"I'm a Seelie," I point out, and I try to sound firm about it, but I can hear the tremble in my voice. "*I* don't drive people mad."

"You're only half-Seelie," Will counters dryly. "It's the ogre in you that *they'll* drive mad."

"This is all pointless," inserts the Threader suddenly. "They'll name her as soon as they see her."

"And I'll die," I finish and try to wrap my mind around that. I feel very detached from it somehow. Maybe this is the only way you can face the looming circumstance of your death, by detaching from it so that it feels like it would happen to someone else.

"Faeries don't really die," the Threader corrects me. "They drift. They drift into dandelions and bumblebees, into the ringing of distant bells you can't pinpoint, into the sparkle of the sun on the sea. They drift until there is nothing left of them."

She says all of this matter-of-factly, but it sends a terrible shiver of foreboding down my spine.

"As they drift, they are mad," inserts Aunt Virtue, staring off into the distance, caught up in a recollection. "It is a terrible, awful thing to see."

"I saw one once," adds Aunt True, her voice no louder than a whisper. "Before we came here. I will never forget it." Looking horrified, she shudders.

"They won't name me," I promise them with a confidence I don't feel. Why wouldn't they name me? Why wouldn't they name me before I could get anywhere near Ben? For a moment, I think that Will is right and this is the foolhardiest thing I could ever do. And then the next moment, I think of Ben, of the quickness of his smile, of the light in his pale eyes whenever he looked at me. I think of Ben, covering me in a sweatshirt of protection and sending me away and begging me to remember him. I think of Ben, scared and alone in some terrible prison because he wanted to *keep me safe*. I look at my aunts and take a deep breath and say again, "They won't name me."

My aunts look at me with dark eyes wide with sadness.

"Wait a moment though," says the Threader thoughtfully. "I understand that you feel you are honor bound, but your life is not entirely your own, is it?"

I look at her sharply. "Yes," I retort. "Of course it is. Who else's would it be?"

"Well, it's ours," she answers simply. "All of ours. You are the fay of the autumnal equinox. There's a prophecy about you. You have a duty to fulfill the prophecy."

"But it's *my* prophecy. The things *I* do—like save Ben—will fulfill the prophecy."

The Threader gives me a coolly mocking look. "You really think prophecies are so simple? So straightforward? Do you know how many strands of thread weave in and out of each other over the Thisworld and the Otherworld? More than any mere faerie could count. All of the threads of all of the beings and all of the threads of all of the choices they make and fail to make, and you must follow those threads, must see them woven together in exactly the right way for any prophecy to come to pass. Prophecies are merely one way of reading the stars. Do you think that a prophecy as important as this one truly depends on the headstrong, stubborn decisions of some small slip of a girl?"

I look at her for one silent moment, and then I answer, simply, "Yes."

"You will not go to Tir na nOg," says the Threader sharply.

"I thought you were supposed to be weaving my obligations into your tapestry," I point out hotly. "This is my obligation."

"I weave the obligations of faeries that have nothing to do with me. But do you think I am *compelled* to do so? Do you really think I exercise no control over how the tapestry is woven? Do you truly believe that I have no *power*? I, who have survived this long? How dare you?" She draws herself up. "I am the Threader. If I say you will not do something, you will not."

"How could you stop me?" I demand recklessly.

"With my thread, of course," she replies, and then she does something I don't expect. She catches up a threaded needle in her hand and lunges at me with it. I think her intention was to prick the skin on the back of my hand. *I don't want her to touch me*, I think. The needle gets within a hairsbreadth of me and will go no farther.

Absolute silence falls over the room. I had flinched at the Threader's movement, but now I stand very still, staring at the needle poised over my skin. The Threader is also staring at it. Everyone is. The Threader withdraws her hand and tries again, plunging the needle toward my skin. Again, it stops a hairsbreadth away from me, and I can see the Threader's fingers around the needle quivering with the effort of trying to pierce through Ben's enchantment.

The Threader snaps. She flings the needle across the room, the thread unraveling out of it, clearly in a towering temper. She screams to the sky in frustration, and the scream rises and rises in pitch, and the bats around her take flight, flapping wildly around the room. The very walls around us seem to tremble. Everything is chaos, and in the middle of the whole thing, I know I have to make a break for it. Through the flurry of the bats, I dart over to my aunts and kiss each of their cheeks.

"But—" says Aunt True feebly.

"Be back before you know it," I promise breathlessly, and then, for reasons I can't explain, I stoop and pick up the threaded needle and pocket it before dashing out of the room. Things in the kangaroo pocket of my sweatshirt seem to be important when you least expect them to be, and I don't have time to stop for any other supplies.

The Threader is still shrieking her displeasure. "Come back here! Come back here immediately!"

I duck through the swirl of bats, battering them away from my face, and tug open the door. She can't make me go back, I think. Ben's enchantment is coming in handy after all.

"Selkie!" I hear Kelsey call, and I hesitate on the doorstep, guilty, and then shout back to her, "I have to go!" before darting across Beacon Street and onto the Common. I weave around the tourists and get to the subway station. It is still in chaos from the fire on the tracks, annoyed commuters complaining loudly to the world at large about the incompetence of the subway system. I get to the turnstile and swipe my card through, and everyone around me disappears.

The silence is terrifying. I look around the suddenly empty subway station and try not to panic. All of this stillness is far more panic-inducing than the teeming crowds had been. I am used to the press of people—the subway station is in its natural element then. Here, now, I feel completely lost. And for the first time since I got it into my head to rescue Ben, I suddenly fully comprehend why nobody wanted me to do this: because I have no idea what I'm doing and will probably get myself killed.

I take a deep breath. I can't turn back now. Ben is depending on me. I swallow and am just about to push through the turnstile when the door to the subway station opens.

I whirl, startled now at the idea that someone else is here with me. And it's Kelsey. "Bats," she announces dramatically. "I had *bats* in my *hair*."

"What are you doing here?" I ask her.

She is looking at the eerily empty subway station. "Where is everyone?"

"You're not supposed to be here," I tell her.

"Well, I'm here. Your aunts are so devastated that they're sobbing, and the wizard and the sewing lady are busy arguing about some love affair they had a few centuries ago, and do you realize that I think we've both hit our heads and are having some kind of shared hallucination?"

I look at Kelsey, such an anchor of normality in the craziness that has been my life, and she has been for as long as I've known her. I feel like crying suddenly. Just the other day, we were in class complaining about the impossibility of pre-calculus, and now I'm going to save my faerie quasi-boyfriend from a faerie prison where he's been put by my mother, who also wants to kill me. "I'm in love with him," I say, because it's the first thing I can think of to say, because I feel like it might explain everything, because I've never admitted it out loud before. "He's some kind of weird enchanting faerie, and I have no idea if I can trust him, but it doesn't matter because I'm in love with him."

"You've never even mentioned him," Kelsey points out, which is fair.

"I know. I'd forgotten him. And then when I knew him, I… My life is a mess." I give up trying to explain it.

"So I gathered."

A train squeals ominously into the station. A Green Line train. I look at it and say, "That's for me."

"I'll go with you," Kelsey says immediately.

"You can't," I tell her. "You *can't*. This is all so crazy, and I'm already being selfish and breaking my aunts' hearts, and I never even said good-bye to my father, and I can't be the reason anything happens to you. I can't. Please, Kelsey."

Kelsey looks at me for a long moment and then pulls me into a fierce hug. "Don't cry," she commands, even though she sounds on the verge of it herself. "This is a stupid thing to cry about. I'll see you in school tomorrow, and then afterward you'll introduce me to this boyfriend you've been keeping a secret."

"We'll be recovered from our shared hallucination in time for school tomorrow?" I ask, a weak joke.

"Yes," Kelsey says and hugs me a bit tighter. "Absolutely."

I cling a little bit to Kelsey, trying to freeze-frame the feeling of being here with someone who likes me and loves me and wishes me no harm and only good things. I have a feeling I'm going to need to remember what that's like.

Then I turn and take a deep breath and push through the turnstile and walk up to the train, whose doors slide open with a chiming of bells.

I am just about to get on the train, just about to put my foot on the first step, when the subway station door bangs open. I look back, and Kelsey looks up the stairs behind her in surprise, and then Will comes jogging down the stairs.

"Wait," he commands me and pushes through the turnstile. "Wait, wait, wait."

I set my jaw. "I'm going," I tell him.

"Fine. Yes. I can see that. Anyway, they've sent a train for you, so you'll never outrun it at this point."

"Ben outran a Green Line train."

"He's the best traveler in the Otherworld; *he* can do that. If you're determined to go and do this stupid thing, then there's something you need to know. You are…extraordinarily good at naming."

I stare at him. "What does that mean?"

"You broke Benedict's enchantment with just two of his names. Snapped it in two. That takes power, Selkie. That takes an extraordinary amount of power, to do something like that to a Le Fay enchantment with only two of his names. There is power in your name; it's thrumming through it. When you get to Benedict, make him use that power. Tell him to stop being noble about it and use it. Make him say your name. It's your Seelie blood, and it might be your only chance to get out of there, using the Seelie blood against them."

"I'm only half-Seelie," I remind Will.

And Will, to my disbelief, actually smiles. "True. And your ogre blood will get you the rest of the way out. You're absolutely insane, you know, but you also just broke the Threader's thread for you, completely unthreaded her needle, and I've never seen anyone do that before. So maybe you *can* do this, fay of the autumnal equinox. Maybe this is your prophecy." Will looks at me, really looks at me, and I feel like he's trying to read something, like the future is written in my eyes if he could only look closely enough. Maybe it is to Will. "I hope it is," he says softly, almost to himself. "I really, truly, genuinely do."

And I do feel like he means it. Will and I may have had our differences, but I'm glad that he came here to tell me this before I set off. I feel like I really needed to hear it. "Thanks," I say.

"You are a Stewart of Beacon Hill," Will tells me. "Remember that: *you are not one of them.* They'll try to make you forget who you are; they will try to erase your past and your future: *do not let them*."

I nod because Will's right. What else can I do? I can only remember who I am: Selkie Stewart of Beacon Hill, daughter of Etherington and niece of True and Virtue, and I am only half of anything and maybe that's the point.

"Words are important," Will says gravely. "The most important things there are. Remember that. Don't let them make you forget that."

He says that words are important, but all I can do in response is nod mutely. And then he nods mutely back and takes a step away, as if he doesn't want to accidentally trip onto the train with me or something. I glance at Kelsey, who gives me a little wave, and then I make myself move forward. I mount the steps into the car and sit on one of the seats. The doors close, bells chiming, and the train jerks into motion.

I am on my way to save Ben. I am also about to meet my mother.

CHAPTER 16

The train squeals along, and it seems like I am just on a conventional T in a conventional tunnel, except that we never hit Boylston. The train goes and goes, and I watch the tunnel pass by my window. I have my hands pulled back, hidden in the sleeves of my enchanted sweatshirt. In my pocket are tattered pages from old books, a piece of glass wrapped in a tissue, a button from the Salem Which Museum, and a threaded needle. I have no idea what I intend to do with these items, but they are all I have brought in terms of weapons, and I don't even know if they *are* weapons. I have these and the power of my name. Words: the most important things, according to Will. I don't even know what that *means*.

Maybe I won't need any weapons. Maybe there won't be any fight. Maybe my mother will be wonderful; maybe she'll hug me and tell me how much she's missed me. And then I'll say, *Can't we all just get along, all of us, the faeries and the Seelies and the ogres in Boston?* And my mother will say, *Of course, this has all just been a huge misunderstanding.* And I'll have a regular family. And Ben.

While I am indulging in this fantasy, the train suddenly bursts out into sunlight. One minute there is a tunnel, and the next minute there is sky. Just *sky*. Lots and lots of sky. And there, in the distance, dimly, some land that I cannot really perceive. It's like looking too hard at it makes it dissolve into blurs.

The train stops. Its doors open, chiming at me. I swallow thickly and exit, carefully stepping out on the narrow strip of land that lies between the train and the sky. It is a canyon, I can see now—a vast chasm of red rock, stretching to my right and to my left and below me, as if it is the only thing that exists.

"Are you crossing Mag Mell?" asks a voice behind me.

I whirl around, startled. The train has soundlessly disappeared, and there is a little girl watching me from a few feet away. She is an extremely beautiful little girl, her black hair pin straight and pulled back with a large pink bow. She is dressed in the sort of frilly pink lace dress that can only be described as a princess dress. And she is eating an enormous lollipop.

"What's Mag Mell?" I ask.

She nods in a vague way that seems to indicate the canyon and takes a slurp of her lollipop and says, "So? Are you crossing it?"

"I'm trying to get to Tir na nOg," I tell her.

She looks at me like I'm stupid. "That's the only reason you'd cross Mag Mell," she informs me.

"Oh," I say awkwardly, because I *feel* stupid. How did I

ever think that I would come here and save Ben and that this would all somehow *work*?

She studies me for a second, and I wonder what she's thinking, if she's thinking, *Who is this complete idiot who has shown up here and wants to get into a prison?*

What she says is, "Seventeen fusel."

"Seventeen what?" I echo.

"Seventeen fusel," she repeats impatiently. "For the train fare."

"I…But I paid at Park Street," I inform her, because I can think of nothing else to say.

"Well, that was stupid of you, wasn't it? Paying *before* it takes you anywhere? How'd you know the train'd go anywhere at all?"

I think about that for a moment. "Good point, actually."

"So. Seventeen fusel." *Slurp.*

"I don't know what a fusel is," I admit.

Her eyes narrow. And one foot, encased in a pink Mary Jane topped with an absurdly huge bow, begins tapping against the wildflower-strewn grass underneath it. "Well," she says. "You are stupid *and* useless." And she turns on her heel and stomps off, bows flouncing.

I watch her go, thinking that I'm off to a great start here in the Otherworld. And then I turn my attention to the vast canyon that I'm somehow supposed to be crossing. I bet Ben could just jump us across it, but I have no idea if I can do that sort of thing and how to go about it if I could. I stand there with my hands in the pocket of my sweatshirt, fingering my feeble weapons and trying to determine if one of them could come in handy. Maybe if I threw one of them into the canyon, it would turn out to be magical and a bridge would suddenly form?

And then I realize that there is something drifting across the canyon toward me. A hot air balloon, gaily colored and whimsical looking, trailing fluttering flags after it. I watch it as it gets bigger and bigger and then drifts to a landing right next to me—and then keeps skidding across the grass, thudding up great chunks of turf, and I find that my heart is in my throat because I'm convinced it's going to go tumbling right over the edge and I have no idea if it will be able to regain flight once that happens, until it finally comes to a swaying stop and a head peers over the top of the basket.

It's a boy, roughly my age, with a shock of untidy red-orange hair that he has squashed underneath a newsboy cap. His face is heavily freckled, his eyes are wide and green, and he looks at me and says sadly, "I wish I could tell you to run, but you wouldn't get anywhere anyhow."

I ignore this uplifting remark, refusing to let myself be afraid. "Can you take me across…" I wave my arm toward the empty space of the air occupying the canyon. "That, to the prison?"

"Of course I can," he replies. "That's my *job*."

"Oh," I say and walk over to the basket. It's tall, and I can tell it's going to be awkward to get in. I reach for the top of the basket, and he reaches over to grab at me, and somehow together we get me over the top and into the basket with only a minimum of inappropriate groping, until we fall in a heap at the bottom of the basket.

"You're quite graceful, aren't you?" he says good-naturedly.

I try to ignore him, but I'm sure I blush as I roll off of him. He sits at the bottom of the basket and looks at me as I stand, leaning against the side. I can see now that he's dressed in white pants with pink pinstripes and a loud, electric blue, Hawaiian-print shirt. He must really like color.

He just sits there staring at me for so long that I grow uncomfortable. "Shouldn't we…get going?"

"Oh, don't worry. They'll make sure we get back there. I like to see how long I can stay here, just…*breathing*. It's hard to breathe over there." He looks around himself wistfully, looking so forlorn that I feel awful for him.

"You don't get to come over here often?" I guess.

"Often enough, but it's always just to pick people up and then ferry them back over, and that's not…I mean, that's never…" He shudders a bit. "Well." He looks at me, suddenly smiling brightly. "Let's talk about something else."

"Okay," I say slowly, a bit startled by the abrupt change in his demeanor. But then I don't know what else to talk about. *I'm going to go to Tir na nOg, find one of the prisoners, and escape* doesn't exactly seem like a good way to start a conversation.

I must look blank, because he offers up a topic of conversation. "For instance, I have just discovered that I have lost a button." He indicates his loud Hawaiian shirt, where there is indeed a button missing.

"Oh." I blink and realize, "A button." I reach into my sweatshirt pocket and pull out the button I took from the Salem Which Museum. It, of course, matches the shirt perfectly.

He takes it in delight. "Thank you!" And then, "I am Safford. And I am very pleased to meet you. You're very useful!"

Yes, in lots of different ways, apparently, I think sardonically. But there is another thing I'm curious about. "You just told me your name," I note.

"Yes. Well, I'm required to, aren't I? Required to tell my name to the passengers I ferry across Mag Mell."

"What happens if you don't?"

"What always happens in the Otherworld when you do something the Seelies don't like?"

"Not good things?" I guess.

"One way of putting it," agrees Safford. "You came here by Green Line train."

"Yes," I say. "Doesn't everyone?"

"Not many people crossing worlds these days. The borders are closed, you know."

He is looking at me very sharply, studying me, and I don't want him to ask what's so special about me; I don't want to get into half-ogreness and fay-of-the-autumnal-equinox-ness.

"Is it going to be a problem that I don't have any...fusel?" I blurt out to keep Safford from asking anything more about my journey from the Thisworld. I wonder if any of the items in my kangaroo pocket can qualify as fusel.

"Fusel?" he echoes blankly.

"That little girl asked me for seventeen fusel." I indicate vaguely where I'd had the conversation with the little girl, who is no longer in sight.

"Oh," says Safford. "Dark hair, lots of bows?"

I nod.

"She's just an extortionist, that one. You can't blame her though. Her parents were named when she was just a little girl. That left her and her little brother, who's a tiny little thing, not much talent of his own. She's devoted to him, and it's up to her to keep food in their mouths." Safford shrugs.

Now I feel terrible about not having any fusel to give to the little girl. "What did her parents do?" I ask.

"Oh, you know." Safford makes a vague gesture. "A little bit of this, a little bit of that."

"No, I mean to get named."

Safford looks at me. "You ask that as if there's a *reason* for being named."

"There…Oh…" I trail off stupidly, absorbing that. I guess I had been thinking that there would be a reason for being named, like Ben was in danger of it because he had helped me. And I was in danger of it because I was *me*. But I guess there doesn't have to be a reason; I guess it could just be something that…*happens*, like a car accident or a plane crash.

"Like me," Safford continues, "forced constantly to either ferry faeries across to their namings or to provide my name to faeries who won't be named and can then use it against me. And what have I done? I have no idea. One day they just…came and got me and brought me here. I don't know. I guess what I did was *exist*." He looks so bitter, and so extremely sad, that I shudder.

And at that moment, the hot air balloon lifts into the air and out over the canyon.

"Lovely view, isn't it?" says Safford dully.

I look at the ground a dizzying distance below me and silently disagree with him—strongly. I've never thought of myself as being afraid of heights, but I guess now I know that I should never go skydiving. Nice to know these things; self-discovery is good.

Feeling giddy and thinking maybe I'm on the verge of hysterics, I turn away from the lovely view and sink to the floor of the basket. "This is my first time in one of these," I say, trying to explain my sudden weak insanity.

"Really?" Safford looks shocked.

The basket is rocking gently as we waft over the canyon, and I wish it would stop swaying. I can't tell if the thing is actually making me motion sick or if finally the prospect of what I'm doing is making me nauseated. "We don't really travel by these where I come from," I tell him.

"What's it like, in that world?" He sounds genuinely curious.

"I don't know," I say helplessly. I can't think of how to describe *home*. I am coming up utterly devoid of words. "It doesn't have many hot air balloons."

"I've always wanted to see it. I always wanted to be a traveler, bouncing between the worlds like that."

I think of Ben, my dizzy nausea receding suddenly. I should have thought of this so much earlier. "Did you ferry Ben across? Benedict Le Fay," I clarify.

"No, he didn't come by Green Line train." Safford's eyes are hooded and dark, and the tone of his voice matches them.

Bad topic, I think. *Never mind.* "*Lovely* day," I say like an idiot. Safford looks at me and smiles sadly.

I swallow thickly and think that this might be the last normal conversation I have for a while, so I should maybe make the most of it. "So you'll take me right to Tir na nOg?"

"Yes," he responds. "When we land, we'll be at the fortress where the Court receives its guests."

"And the prison?"

"And the prison. And then, beyond that, is the Isle of Apples."

"And what's that?"

"Oh, no one knows *that*. No one but the Seelies themselves."

"Well, it sounds like an island of apple orchards," I suggest feebly.

"Do you think so?" muses Safford. "Huh."

He does not look as if he is teasing me. I wonder if the words *isle* and *apples* mean something different in the Otherworld or if it's just that nothing makes much sense here.

The balloon lands gently on a patch of dead grass. In front of me, rising up to the sky, is an impossibly huge expanse of cliff face with regular windows carved into it. It is the least welcoming thing I have ever seen. And everything is utterly silent and lifeless. Nothing moves.

Safford breaks the silence, making me jump. "Here we are," he announces needlessly. "And now, your name, if you please."

I look at him, feeling vaguely panicked by the idea. I have already internalized the Otherworld idea that my name should be a precious secret.

"It's required," he informs me, not unkindly.

"Selkie," I say.

He shakes his head. "Not enough."

"Selkie Stewart," I respond.

He smiles at me almost pityingly. "You can try to hide your full name. You'll never succeed. They'll pull it out of you. Anyway." He clears his throat and raises his voice. "Selkie Stewart," he shouts to the cliff face, and it echoes back at us, up and down the canyon.

Nothing happens. I push my hands into my pocket and try not to shiver uncontrollably.

"That's it then. It was truly an honor to meet you."

I look at the cliff face for a moment longer.

"You've got to get out of the basket now," he prompts me. "There isn't any going back, you know."

"Oh." I hadn't even realized I was still in the basket. I scramble my way out of it, trying to look dignified while I do it.

"See you," Safford says to me. "Maybe. I hope." He looks

like he's about to say more, then seems to change his mind with a brisk little shake of his head.

The hot air balloon lifts up. I watch it dip and bob its way into the air over the canyon, and I wonder where it's going, and then there is a noise behind me, bolts being thrown, locks being unlocked.

I turn back to the cliff face, realizing that the bottom of it contains a pair of enormous doors. They are carved directly into the rock, and they swing open to reveal an entourage of strangely shaped creatures: some are tall, some are short, some are round, some are long, some walk on two legs, and some walk on four legs, but they are all covered in so much gleaming copper armor that I cannot even begin to guess at what they might be under all of that. Each of them has small, chiming bells lining its armor—they chime with every step they take.

Then the entourage parts, forming two lines. They all regard me, a few of them snuffling and snorting and some pawing the ground. I wonder what I am supposed to do and venture a step forward. Nobody makes a move to stop me, so I assume that this is permitted. I keep walking, gaining speed and confidence with each step. Nothing, so far, is happening. I realize at that moment that I expected Seelies to descend upon me immediately, furiously attempting to kill me. Or hug me. Or *something*, at least. Anything.

The rock doors slam shut behind me, not even waiting for my entourage to follow me in. It is very dark with them closed, and I can feel some dust tumble from the ceiling at the force of their slamming. I wonder if this cliff face structure is safe. Of all the things to worry about, I am worried that an enchanted prison might collapse in on me.

I move forward hesitantly, hands out in front of me so that I don't bump into anything. It is terrifying not to be able to *see*. I could encounter anything. Anything could encounter me. I feel a panic rising within me, and I fight it down. It takes me six steps—I am counting, in case I need to find my way to the doors again quickly, although I doubt they will open for me—and then I cross a threshold I cannot see, and there is bright, fierce sunshine. I have never thought sunshine could be angry before, but this sunshine is.

I am in something that could be either a garden or a great hall. The floor beneath my feet is marble, but lush plants seem to be sprouting from it. There are gilded walls, but there is no ceiling, instead just the furious sunshine, so bright that the sky is washed white with it and I can barely keep my eyes open. There are fountains, water splashing through them, catching the light, reflecting it in such a way that it is painful to look in their direction.

I want to stop to get my bearings, but I feel I am being watched, so I keep moving instead, with the idea in my head that it is important to convey an aura of confidence. I continue to walk, my sneakers squeaking against the marble. The huge green leaves of the plants on either side of me brush against my face, tickling my cheeks.

I am slowly growing used to the brightness of the light, enough so that I can tell that I am approaching the end of the garden room, whatever it is. A large number of things shaped like people are waiting there, all of them looking at me. They grow more distinct as I reach them. They are taller than regular humans, slender and lithe, with a grace that strikes me as lethal. If you encountered them, you might call them beautiful—just before they slit your throat. Their coloring is so washed-out as to be practically nonexistent. They look so pale they could be dead, their eyes seem disconcertingly colorless, and their hair is white, bright, gleaming. I draw to a slow halt in front of them.

"So," says one of them coldly. This particular one is a woman, and she is dressed in a green that matches the plants of the garden room. Her white hair is tightly pulled back except for a few ringlets that are intricately arranged around the delicate gold circle sitting atop her head. "The fay of the autumnal equinox comes to the Seelie Court. Welcome, Selkie Stewart," she hisses at me.

I am unprepared for how that feels. It is almost like someone has reached out and punched me in the stomach. I try not to let it show, but it is a huge effort not to double over with the sudden, breath-stealing *pain* of it. I don't know how well I conceal my reaction, but it is surely not well enough. I had hopes for a friendly welcome. This is not it.

"Now, now," says another voice. "Naming already. Where's the sport in that?" Another faerie is moving toward us, from the left, and I blink through the dazed spots that the naming caused to dance in front of my eyes. This one has left her hair loose, and it floats about her like a cloud as she moves, as if she is moving through a body of water that the rest of us can't see. The golden circle on her head is a bit thicker and not quite as pretty, and her dress is a deep, dark rose color. As she moves, bells chime, and I realize that they are sewn into every crevice of her long, bell sleeves and her trailing skirt. She moves forward, directly upon me, and gazes down at me.

I can never decide what color Ben's eyes are. They are blue or green or gray or all three or none of the three, but Ben's eyes are not at all like this. This woman's eyes are completely translucent. It is as if looking into her irises will show you the back of her head. It is unsettling, but I force myself to meet her gaze.

Her mouth—pale, colorless lips—twists into a smile that is the opposite of a smile. And then she says sweetly, "Selkie. Is this any way to greet your mother?"

CHAPTER 17

S he doesn't wait for a response from me, which is a good thing because I don't know how to respond. She turns in a graceful whirl, skirt and hair flying about her and bells bouncing in a merry jingle. "I shall take care of this," she proclaims, and just like that, we are alone in the garden room. "Excellent. Now." She turns back to me. "I imagine that you, half *ogre*, are not enjoying the sunlight."

"It's fine," I lie, but really, it is giving me the most terrible headache. But I don't like the way she said *ogre*. I honestly don't like any of this.

"Ah, you are a natural liar." My mother smiles. "Strong faerie blood in you. Stronger than most changelings. That was predicted. I should have expected it. Come. I can show you to your room." She whirls again. She moves as if she is not moving at all, and I wonder if that's how she is moving or if the naming and sunlight have made me confused. She seems to be moving impossibly quickly. I feel like I am running just to keep up, and I cannot tell what we are passing. I am going to be hopelessly lost, I realize, which must be the point.

"My room?" I echo, trying not to sound like I'm panting for breath.

"Well, of course. What *did* you expect? We are extremely courteous to our guests here. In fact." She stops abruptly, and I almost tumble right into her, catching myself at the last minute. She turns to me, and her eyes are glowing with excitement, and this makes me uneasy. "We have a guest who I suspect you are *most* interested in."

I know immediately she is referring to Ben. "Who?" I ask breezily.

Her smile grows wider. "*Such* a faerie," she murmurs. "I really wasn't prepared for..." And then, "Perhaps you would like to see him first? Before your room? Indeed, yes, I think so."

Just like that, she turns again, whirling in a completely different direction this time, and I am back to running to keep up, and then she draws to another abrupt halt. We are standing in an open doorway. There is no door, no lock and key, but I realize immediately why there isn't: because there is a smallish circle of stone on which Ben is lazily lounging, and it is completely surrounded by a small moat, the water tossing about in a tempest of rapids. Ben is in the very middle of the circle of stone, and I can see why, because the outer edges of it are wet with water that has been thrown up by the current of the moat. He is still dressed in the layers he'd been wearing when we got separated, and I wonder that they have given him this protection from the water. Then again, if Will is to be believed, the object *was* to keep him alive enough to lure me in.

"Benedict," announces my mother grandly, entering the room.

Ben flinches so minutely that, if I hadn't been watching for it, I wouldn't have noticed it. All of my hopes that I can find some way to get out of this that will leave me with a mother *and* Ben fall to pieces in that moment. "Good morning," he says in reply. "Afternoon. Evening. Whichever it is." He waves a hand in the air negligently, which I would imagine is the equivalent of a shrug had he been standing. He is staring fixedly up at the ceiling, looking very deep in thought about something.

"Look who I have brought, Benedict." He flinches again. "A visitor just for you!"

It is a moment before he reacts, turning his head slowly to look at me. Then he sighs, closes his eyes briefly, and then looks back at the ceiling.

"Oh, come now, Benedict!" *Flinch.* "Is that any way to greet the creature you valued greater than your own well-being?" My mother's voice is cold as ice now.

I can see Ben's eyes close again. Then he sits up, drawing his knees up, propping an elbow on them, his chin on his fist, and regards me carefully. "Hi," he says to me finally.

I have no idea what to say to him. I stand there and realize that somehow, I had not been prepared for the sight of Ben *trapped*. Will was right: I had been thinking that I would find Ben and he would have an idea and we would get out of this mess. Or that there wouldn't be a mess, that my mother would see me and gather me up in a surfeit of maternal affection. I sit and look at Ben, looking thinner and paler than I can ever remember seeing him before, and I wonder how much longer he has, and I realize that I am going to have to do all of this myself. I'd like to tell him not to worry, that I *will* figure it out, but at the moment, I can barely think straight long enough to even say hi back to him. I wonder whether I should tell him to use the power of my name like Will said, blurt the directive out to him, and get him to say it. But even if that works amazingly well and gets Ben to feel much better, what will it have truly accomplished? He would still be imprisoned by the moat. All the success might do is cause my mother to never let me see Ben again. No, I decide. I need to get a better handle on what's going on here before we use the power of my name.

"Well, go on," my mother urges me. "Answer him. Benedict"—*flinch*—"is an extremely reticent guest, you know. We cannot draw him out on any of the usual conversational topics."

"It's true," Ben tells me. "I am appallingly ill educated on the cantos of Spenser."

My mother laughs in delight. "He is a wit, our Benedict"—*flinch*—"isn't he?"

"This was a trap, you know," Ben informs me.

I shrug at him.

He crinkles his nose at me.

I am relieved to see the nose crinkle. He is okay enough to be annoyed with me. Maybe that gives me enough time to come up with a plan.

I look at the rushing water of the moat around him.

"Oh," says my mother, clearly catching the direction of my eyes. "It is so very deep. Not that it really needs to be; it could be the merest trickle of water, and it would deter Benedict." *Flinch.* She looks at Ben, her anti-smile frozen upon her face. "It is a drawback of yours, isn't it, my dear?"

Ben sends her an anti-smile of his own.

"Well." My mother turns to me. "Now you see. He is quite well. We should dress for dinner." She looks back at Ben. "We shall visit again later." She pauses, relishing the moment, and I can see Ben tense, much as I know he is trying to hide it. "Benedict Le Fay," she says lightly, almost playfully, and I can hear it tear the breath out of him. She nods her head, pleased, and sweeps out of the room.

I do not want to delay following her; I do not want to give her the opening to say Ben's name anymore, so I scurry after her with just a glance in his direction. He is very still, his eyes closed, and it is only as I leave that I hear him take a ragged breath.

CHAPTER 18

The room my mother takes me to is very large. The floor is stone, but it's covered in thick, furry rugs. There are wide openings that look out over an ocean, windows without glass, and I wonder what side of the building I am on or if the view is just an enchanted view, nothing like what actually exists out the window. There is a large four-poster bed, hung with tapestries that are trimmed with tiny bells. There is also a large white armoire, intricately carved with abstract swirls, and my mother throws it open. Inside, lined up, are a number of the flowing dresses that all the female faeries seem to be dressed in, all of them covered in tiny bells.

"You will dress for dinner," my mother informs me.

"No, I won't," I respond. It is nice, this act of teenage rebellion. I've never gotten to be an obnoxious teenager to my mother before. And I didn't want to start things off this way, but if she would just *smile* at me, *really* smile, be *nice* to me, just a *little*...

"Yes," she retorts icily. "You will."

"No, I won't."

She looks mystified by this, and I wonder if she is

encountering the resistance of Ben's enchantment. She narrows her eyes and walks over to me, and I wonder if the enchantment is holding or if she will remark upon it. But she doesn't so much as glance at my sweatshirt, so I'm thinking Ben, however many times his name has been used against him, is managing to maintain it for me.

"You will come to dinner," she spits out finally.

"Yes," I agree, because I don't want to get ordered around, but, well, as unpleasant as she's been, this is my *mother*, and I do want to get to know her—even if it's to get to know her so I can get the fantasy out of my head that she might actually love me.

She looks momentarily baffled by me, and I am pleased to have had that effect, and then she sweeps angrily from the room. Faeries don't stomp, I assume, but she comes as close to it as she can.

I stand in my room and wonder how I will know when it is time for dinner. I wonder if I am allowed to eat at the Seelie Court. I think of the myth where Persephone eats the pomegranate seeds and is condemned to be tied to the Underworld always. I wonder if it will be like that, and if so, why Will didn't warn me.

I walk over to the open window—a bit dangerous but maybe easier to escape from. Tir na nOg seems to be an endless maze. I cannot figure out how anything connects. Maybe my pane-less window is our best bet. But the window leads down to a sheer cliff face. I cannot even see any other windows from my viewpoint. And there stretches the ocean. It is calm, smooth as glass, and a long way out I can see the outline of an island.

It doesn't matter. Even if I had some way to get Ben to my room and then both of us out this window, there is no way Ben could deal with all that water, especially not in the state he's in at the moment. We need to go out the way I came in and hope for a way across the canyon but I just have no idea how to find it again.

It's enchanted, clearly—enchanted to be a labyrinth, to be impossible to escape. I would have to break the enchantment, but how am I ever going to learn the name of a member of the Seelie Court? And would one name even be enough? Would I need all of their names? The Threader and Will had been impressed with my ability to break Ben's enchantment with only two of his names. I think of my sweatshirt. Clearly, my mother is not breaking all of his enchantments with merely two of his names. But even if I am unusually talented in naming magic, as Will told me I was, I doubt that breaking the enchantment over this place is similar at all to breaking Ben's enchantment. Surely the faerie prison from which no one has ever escaped isn't going to be dissolved by my saying a word or two, no matter how powerful Will might claim words are.

My door is flung open, and my mother floats in. "It is time for dinner," she announces with a sweetness that makes me shiver.

Dinner with my mother—something I have fantasized about my entire life.

In my fantasies, it didn't go like this. I do not even try to keep track of the twists and turns my mother takes on her way to dinner. All I know is that eventually we are back in what I am sure is the same garden room as before, only now a huge table occupies its center, at which sit the colorless faeries of the Seelie Court. The entourage of odd creatures in copper armor is lined against the gilded walls, and I can feel their eyes on me.

The sun is no longer fiercely bright. In fact, it appears to be twilight. The air is gloomy around me, breezes sighing heavily and lifting strands of white hair to tousle.

"You never told me: what should I call you?" I say to my mother.

Her discomfiting eyes turn upon me. "You can call me Mother," she says, and then, with one of those smiles I find chilling, "Don't ask such stupid questions."

Dinner seems to already be in full swing when we get there. The Seelies are loud and raucous. Frankly, if I didn't know better, I'd say they were drunk. Then I notice all of the red wine flowing freely into copper goblets and I think, *Yep, they are definitely tipsy.*

"Here is a seat for you, Selkie," says my mother sweetly, putting just a bit of power into my name, enough for me to feel the pinch.

I refuse to let her see that it hurt, giving her a tight smile in response. *Pretty much an anti-smile.* I wonder if I inherited that ability from my mother.

I sit and look at the food in front of me. It is almost like food I recognize but slightly skewed. For instance, it *looks* like a bunch of grapes, but when I try one, it tastes like pork. All of the foods are like that. But I realize I am ravenous, and I fill my plate. I wonder if Ben is getting enough to eat, and slip a roll that tastes like cotton candy into the pocket of my enchanted sweatshirt. I don't know how I'm going to get it to him, but at least I have it if the opportunity presents itself.

I want to gather the courage to say something to my mother, strike up a conversation, but I can't think of any good openings. *Why did you abandon me as a baby? How come you've never once gotten in touch with me? Do you really want me dead? Do you love me at all?* None of these seem appropriate for casual dinner-table conversation, but when you have questions like these flitting through your head, how can you possibly talk about anything else? *Nice night, isn't it?* seems absurd. And my mother isn't helping. She just sits and eats silently next to me. And then there's Ben to worry about, and I can't think about him either. Well, it's irresistible, actually; I can't *not* think about him, but I have no idea how I'm going to get him out, and maybe my aunts and Will and the Threader were all right and this was all an enormous mistake.

"Is this seat taken?" says a pleasant voice, and I glance without much interest at the woman who has spoken. And then I look closer—because she is not like the other Seelies. Her hair is chestnut brown, and she is not dressed in something that's dripping with tiny bells. And she has brown eyes. Amazingly *normal* chocolate-brown eyes.

I am so relieved to see normal eyes I could cry. "No," I say hastily, because no one had sat next to me, obviously trying to avoid me at all costs.

"Pleasant evening, isn't it?" she asks as she sits elegantly. Everything about her would be old-fashioned in Boston: a towering, intricate hairstyle; a long pink silk dress with puffy sleeves. And her manners seem vaguely old-fashioned too, something lost-world elegant in the way she snaps a napkin out of thin air and lays it over her lap.

"This is Selkie Stewart," introduces my mother, taking vicious pleasure in using my full name.

My hand clenches involuntarily around my fork, and I have to close my eyes for a minute at the flinching pain, but luckily I'm facing the new guest so my mother doesn't have the satisfaction.

"Selkie, this is Augusta Gregory."

I am sure that my mother has just named her, given the sardonic look the woman sends to her, but the woman just says graciously, "Gussie. Please. So." She reaches for a copper goblet and takes a sip. "A new visitor. We don't get many here. Liven up the dinner conversation, no?"

"Too many visitors," complains the Seelie across from me. He looks like all the other faeries do, only his white curls are cropped shorter than the women wear their hair. His golden circle is tipped on his head, evidence of exactly how much he's had to drink. His pale, faerie eyes glow at me in the light that flickers from enchanted candles set in the middle of the table. "You'd think it was the old days again, Threaders flitting people back and forth as if *they* were the ones in charge." He looks suddenly thoughtful. "I can't remember what happened to the Threaders, but whatever it was, they deserved it."

"It doesn't matter," says my mother. "It's in the past."

"Yes," he agrees. "That's right." The male faerie pushes his plate away and leans back. A pipe appears from somewhere, and he sticks it in his mouth. Smoke drifts out of it, glowing hazy silver in the darkness around his head. I can't help but blink at it in surprise. It shouldn't surprise me—I'm in a faerie prison, after all—but *still.*

"What are you smoking?" I hear myself ask, and I didn't even mean to ask it, but I can't resist, because that smoke is beautiful and dazzling and *fascinating.*

"Stardust," he answers me. "What else?"

CHAPTER 19

I am sitting by my glassless window when my mother arrives the following morning. At least, it seems as if it's morning—I watched the sun rise—but time seems to move oddly here. It *should* be morning, surely enough time has passed for it to be morning, but at the same time, I feel like it's only been a few minutes since my mother left me in my room, a cool kiss on my cheek that wasn't the least bit comforting. I haven't slept. I miss my aunts. I wonder what I'm doing here, why I wanted so desperately to meet this mother I have who is so distant and terrifying. I was so stupid to be asking questions about her. Such an idiot. I wish I could talk to Ben. I would feel better if I could talk to Ben. Ben always makes me feel better. I wonder if it's as simple as asking my mother if I can. I guess it's worth a try.

"Can I see Ben?" I ask.

"Who is Ben?" she asks and then realizes, "Oh, Benedict? Clever of him, of course, not to give you his real full name." Her eyebrows flicker upward, as if she is surprised. "But I thought you'd have forgotten him by now," she says vaguely. "But, of course. If you wish."

She leads the way. I follow slowly. I am tired of feeling lost. What can she do to me? She cannot force me to go faster.

She keeps rounding back, impatient and complaining, but I persist in my steady pace, memorizing the path. I want to know how to find Ben on my own.

We arrive, finally, at Ben's cell. He is lounging on his back again, frowning up at the ceiling. I want to ask him what he's thinking so hard about, but it doesn't seem like the right thing to say right now. Maybe later. Maybe when I get Ben out of here, I'll ask him what he was thinking so hard about this whole time. This will be after I shout at him for getting himself into this predicament in the first place. And possibly after I kiss him too.

"Good morning, Benedict," sing-songs my mother, and the flinch is far more evident this time. "Selkie wished to come see you, didn't you, dear?"

The pinch from her saying my name is almost familiar now.

Ben turns his head to look at me briefly, his expression inscrutable, and then looks back toward the ceiling.

"Well, Selkie?" continues my mother. The pinch is more severe the second time, like I am already more sensitive. I wonder how Ben has been standing this. "Did you have anything in particular you wished to discuss with him?"

I have a million things I wish to discuss with him. I want to tell him I'm so hopelessly confused that I don't know what to do. I want to say that I feel like I don't know who I am anymore. I want to tell him how badly I want to go back to my birthday, when we sat on the Common on a golden autumn day and I loved him so much it hurt, thought he might love me back. But I don't want to say this in front of my mother. Honestly, I'm not sure I want to say it out loud in front of anyone at all, including Ben. It's almost embarrassing enough to be thinking it just to myself.

"Hi," is what I manage, and even though it's just one word, I feel, when Ben looks at me with his moonbeam/sunbeam eyes, that he can hear everything I'm thinking in it.

Ben opens his mouth then closes it. There is an expression in his eyes, almost a faltering. He finally says, "Hi. Pretty morning, isn't it?"

It is, actually. There is a single window, high in his cell, and the sunlight coming through it is so bright it feels almost pink.

My mother is looking curiously between us. Then she reaches out casually, trailing a finger in the rapids of the moat before splashing Ben. Ben gasps, sitting up and moving as far away from her as he can get without being splashed by the spray of the moat on the far side of the circle, drawing his knees up to make himself less of a target.

I flinch in solidarity with him and say, before I can help it, "Stop. He doesn't like water; he doesn't like being wet."

"Obviously," agrees my mother. "None of the Le Fays ever could bear to be wet. Isn't that right? Benedict Le Fay?"

Ben squeezes his eyes shut, and I can almost see him rocking with the wave of his name coupled with the splash he just received. My mother looks at me and says his name again.

I watch him rest his forehead against his knees and breathe quickly, sucking in rapid breaths.

"Stop it," I say. "Can't you stop it?"

My mother looks at me evenly. "Interesting," she says. "Don't you find that interesting, Benedict Le Fay?"

Ben winces with pain.

"Obviously I could stop it," my mother says flatly.

Ben hisses, and I look from my mother to him. A thin, fine, persistent drizzle has materialized over Ben. He may still have layers on, but he is still going to be soaked eventually.

"Time for breakfast," my mother says to me.

I pause, at a loss, as she walks out of the cell. I look at Ben, whose teeth are chattering.

"I don't know what to do," I blurt out.

"Just keep breathing," Ben says, as if that's helpful.

I wish I could shake him in frustration.

"Selkie!" my mother calls to me, a pinch in the name.

I toss Ben the roll I saved from dinner the night before, which he catches reflexively, looking surprised.

"That's not really very useful advice," I inform him quickly, keeping my voice down.

"Better you keep breathing than stop breathing," he replies.

Words to live by, I suppose dryly, as my mother calls me again.

"Go," says Ben solemnly. "Best way to keep breathing."

"I'll be back," I promise him.

"Just keep breathing," Ben repeats.

CHAPTER 20

After breakfast, I am sitting in the overly bright garden room, my thoughts going around in circles, when Gussie suddenly appears next to me.

"Well now," she says and sits next to me with a smile. "So good to have someone else here to talk to."

I look at her, and I wonder what her deal is. She seems friendly enough, but I don't know if I should trust anyone. *Never trust a faerie*, I have been told, and I am *surrounded* by them now.

She seems to read my suspicious mind. "They would tell you I'm a guest. Which I suppose is true because, like you, I can wander around here a bit. Unlike Benedict."

Ben's name has me sitting up and blinking. "What do you know about Ben?"

"That he doesn't like water," Gussie says simply, as if that's anything at all that I care about right now. Gussie is looking pointedly at the Seelies drifting all around us. "We can't talk right now."

This is frustrating. We're in a *Seelie prison*. Where are we ever going to be able to talk? "Then when *can* we talk?" I demand.

"I've been here longer than you have," she says cryptically. "I know my way around here."

"This place is a maze."

"Not if you look at it the right way."

This woman talks entirely in riddles, and I find it incredibly annoying. I wish she didn't seem like my only chance to get Ben and me out of here.

I look around at the Seelies and notice for the first time other faeries in among the Seelies, flickering through them. They are insubstantial, almost like ghost faeries, like I can only see them out of the corner of my eye, not head on. They could almost be a trick of the eye, a hallucination. I feel like I could be losing my mind, but it always seems to turn out that everything that makes me feel like I'm insane is actually true.

I try to tilt my head just so to catch glimpses of their unsteady outlines. If I look too closely, they seem to just dissolve into dust motes. But it doesn't matter that I feel like I can only sense seeing them, because now that I've become aware of them, I can *feel* them. There is something achingly melancholic and sorrowful about them, and I want to somehow break through to where they are and yank them back into fullness.

Gussie seems to know what I'm doing. "Ah," she says. "You've spotted them, have you?"

"What *are* they?" I cannot make the question louder than a breath.

"Named faeries," Gussie says. "That's what happens when a faerie is named. They dissolve like that."

"Are they…" I can't think of how to formulate the thought I want to say next. "Where are they?"

"They're here. With us. Just dissolved so that they can't get through. I've always thought they must feel dreadfully lonely."

I can't help but ask, "Why?"

"Because," she answers. "Can't you hear them crying?"

And now that she says it, I feel like I can, a long, low murmur of heartbroken sobbing. I blink in surprise. "Why didn't I hear that before?"

"Do you think the Seelies want to hear that all the time? They buffer it, naturally."

"Then why can I hear it now?" Even as I say it, the sound vanishes.

"Because I dropped the barrier for us," says Gussie.

I look over at her, and I want to ask who she is exactly.

Then my mother suddenly appears with an armful of yarn. She looks at Gussie with narrow eyes and says, "Time for you to be leaving, isn't it, Lady Gregory?"

Gussie inclines her head with a cool smile and rises. She gives me a look just before she leaves, but I have no idea what the look is supposed to mean. I wish people would stop assuming that I know what I'm doing.

My mother sits next to me and says gaily, "Don't you think it's time we got to know each other better?"

I blink at her. "Why?"

She is fluffing at the pile of yarn on her lap. "Oh, you know."

She looks at me, those unnerving colorless eyes directly on me. "We are fellow Seelies."

What we actually are is mother and daughter, but she doesn't seem to care about that.

"I am not entirely Seelie," I remind her.

"Oh, yes, you are," she says confidently and turns her attention to the yarn on her lap, winding it randomly around her fingers. I have no idea what she's doing with it. "The longer you stay here, the more that will be true. All memory of ugly things will fade for you. That's the charm of the Seelie Court. We don't allow ugly things to exist *here*. Ugliness is ferreted out and destroyed. So it will be with you, inside of you."

I feel cold. "What do you mean? I'll just…forget?" That was what Will warned me of, after all, that they would try to make me forget who I am.

"Eventually. But it *will* be better that way. It was better when I'd forgotten you. Then Benedict Le Fay's enchantment broke, and we all remembered you are that damnable prophecy, and it was pleasanter before."

"You *forgot* about me?" I am horrified by this.

My mother continues twirling her yarn. "Of course. Why wouldn't I? So unpleasant. Why would I wish to remember? Memories are terrible things, my dear. We would all do better to be rid of them. Mortals don't realize this. People like Will Blaxton, constantly scribbling words in books. *Histories.* Do you know the dangerous power of words on paper, freezing the memories, making them *there*, fixed points, keeping track of time? One should never try to keep track of time. It is so dangerous, so insidious. Keeping track of it is not the way time *works*. You were born a century ago—or was it weeks ago? See? So difficult to tell, and so much better that way."

I think of my aunts, talking of flighty faeries. I think of how desperately all of Boston clings to its sense of history, how you can't walk two steps without hitting a plaque or a tablet or a statue or a marker or *something*, words freezing the history into place. Was that Will's doing? All the supernatural creatures of Boston, violently reacting against the Seelies' campaign to eliminate history, memory, time? I think of Beacon Hill, frozen in time, standing strong against those who would tear it down, make it new, *forget* it. My hand closes around the battered pages of history in my sweatshirt pocket. Words and pictures, my aunts and father—how could I forget them?

"There's a prophecy about you," my mother continues. "I'm sure you've been told. But not one prophecy. No one ever has *one* prophecy. A web of prophecies. This is the one where you claim your blood right, stay a Seelie. You will lead us to the other three fays of the seasons, and our reign will be cemented forever. That is what the prophecy says: that we will never fall, ever, as long as the fay of the autumnal equinox remains here with us." My mother's eyes shine as she says this.

I stare at her, because this is not like any prophecy I have heard. Did everyone else have it wrong, thinking that I would overthrow the Seelie Court? When my mother thinks that I will help it reign forever? What does "a web of prophecies" even mean? What is the point of a prophecy if there are other prophecies competing against it? I am so endlessly confused.

So I ask the only thing I can think to ask. "And what about Ben?"

"Oh, we can name him if you like," she says negligently, frowning at the yarn on her lap, still twirling it this way and that. It still just looks like a random pile of yarn to me. "I've only refrained as a gesture of good will." She glances up at me with one of her anti-smiles. "My dear."

"I don't want him rained on. I don't want him wet. I don't want him *imprisoned*."

"Oh, well, that must be so. He is far too talented, and his memory is too long. Benedict does not have a cooperative nature. It is a failing that afflicts all the faeries in his line. Unfortunate, really. You'll see. You'll come around." My mother twists at her yarn and I sit, freezing in the bright, angry sunlight.

That night, after my mother leaves me in my room, I count carefully to one thousand and open my door.

I move through the dark hallways, using the route I'd memorized that morning and repeated to myself all day. I am not entirely sure it will work, that it won't be enchanted away from me, but then I have reached Ben's cell. I wonder if I was successful in memorizing the route or if this is Ben's enchantment: I didn't want to lose my way, so I didn't. Could it be that easy?

The moat is still rushing around Ben, and the rain is still falling over him. Moonlight is slanting through the window, and I can see from its glow that he is curled into a ball, back to me, huddled into his layers as much as he can be.

I clutch the blanket I've brought for him and take a running leap over the moat, just making it. It may be a deep moat, but thankfully it isn't an especially wide one.

"Ben," I hiss at him, spreading the blanket over him quickly. I crouch in front of him. His collars are pulled up over his face as much as they can be, and he is completely unresponsive.

I take a deep breath and lay on my side facing him, reaching for his hand under the blanket and sliding my hand into it. *Please let this work*, I think desperately, watching him.

It is not instantaneous, the way it was on his home world, what seems like oh-so-long ago—literally a separate lifetime ago. But I wait, patient, counting in my head, wondering how high I will count before I give up, and then, finally, he stirs. I want to weep with relief. When his eyes flutter open and focus on me, I think it is eminently possible that I am going to.

"Selkie," he says blurrily, closing his eyes again.

"Say my name again," I tell him. "Will said it would help."

"Selkie," he says, more clearly this time. "Selkie Stewart."

"There you go," I praise him with false gaiety.

He is shivering violently now. "I'm so wet," he says, teeth chattering. "I'm so, *so* wet."

"I know." I sit up, wringing rain out of his hair. "What can I do, Ben? Tell me what to do." I am so tired of feeling helpless, but I feel desperately out of my depth. I wish I'd thought to bring an umbrella.

He pulls at me feebly. "Dry," he says. "You're dry." He slurs the sentence together.

I'm not really dry, but I suppose, to him, I feel like a day in the desert. I get the gist of what he is trying to do, cuddling close to him, and he buries his face against my neck, leaving me covered with rain, but hopefully leaving himself drier. He is still shivering in my arms, but he does sigh with relief. "Say my name again," I tell him, pulling the blanket up over both our heads.

"Selkie Stewart," he says against my skin. "Selkie Stewart, Selkie Stewart, Selkie Stewart." He is shivering less now, and he is holding me more tightly, and that is a relief, that he is no longer limp. "Oh, Selkie Stewart," he says. "It was *so* silly of you to come."

"I'm so sorry," I choke out. "I didn't mean to make it worse."

"You haven't made it worse. It's almost exactly the same. Except now you come and bring me blankets. Selkie Stewart. I'm *so* happy to see you."

It is absurd, because we have never been in more dire straits, but those words warm me all the way down to my toes. I close my eyes and think how I love him, how I *must* get him out of here, keep him safe, the way he kept me safe for however long it was in this world without time. "Likewise," I manage to tell him, combing his damp hair away from my mouth.

He hums contentedly into my neck. I can feel his wet eyelashes brushing raindrops against my skin. I hold him, absently patting him dry with the blanket as much as I can without dislodging him. His breaths are evening out, which is a relief, as I suspect they'd been ragged since we left him that morning.

"I'm going to get you out of here," I promise him.

"Are you?" He sounds amused. "Do you have a *plan*? How very ogre of you."

"Well. Not really," I admit.

"Then it's a good thing I do, isn't it?"

"Oh, thank goodness," I say, relieved. "What is it?"

"Well, it's not an especially good one. It involves continuing to breathe."

"That is a *terrible* plan, Ben."

"It's a pretty good plan for a faerie, I'll have you know. We're not exactly natural *planners*. And I'm so *wet*, I'm always *so wet*. If you can keep bringing me blankets, I might be able to get dry enough to *think* one of these days, and then maybe I can…Maybe I can…" He falls silent for a second. "No one's ever escaped Tir na nOg, Selkie."

I consider, in that moment, telling him about his mother, that she was rumored to have been the only faerie to ever escape Tir na nOg, but I'm not sure that's the best information to impart at this moment, when I need him focused on escaping, not his mother. "Don't talk like that," I tell him.

"There has to be a way, I just can't put the pieces together. If I could just get *dry*…"

"All right," I say soothingly, brushing at his hair. I have never touched his hair before today. I have always *wanted* to, of course, but I have never done it. It is lovely hair, soft and thick, and I wish it wasn't wet. It seems, somehow, not like Ben's hair like this. "Tell me the pieces; I'll put them together for you."

"We can use Safford," he says. "You met Safford?"

"With the hot air balloon?"

"Yes. He's my cousin. Not that they know that or they'd never…He remembers…He remembers…We can use Safford, he'll help, as much as he can, but I don't know how… We'd have to get me over this moat, and I can't…I can't…"

"You could jump it, Ben. It's not that wide."

He is shivering again, and I can tell it is at just the idea of doing it. "I can't," he says. "I can't."

"All right," I say. "Shhh. All right. We'll figure out a way to get you over this moat. Ben, I swear to you, I'll get you dry."

He stops shivering and chuckles against me. "I'm supposed to be protecting you, you know. We've got this all mixed up."

"This is going to even our debt," I tell him. "After this, you're on your own."

I am joking, and luckily, he realizes it. He laughs, full-fledged, and cuddles me closer.

"What about your enchantment? I don't *want* you to be imprisoned."

"It doesn't work that way. It protects *you*, not me. I don't have enough energy to protect both of us."

"Is it taking up a lot of your energy, my enchantment?"

"Forget about it, Selkie."

"If you can only protect one of us, you should—"

"Can you not waste the energy I have left fighting with me? Be nice to me."

"I'm always nice to you," I say. "I just think—"

"No," he says, his voice stony and stubborn, and it's actually good to hear him momentarily energetic, even if it is an energy being channeled into disagreeing with me. "I will fight you on this until I have no fight left in me, and only then will you win this argument."

Because those aren't exactly circumstances under which I want to win, I let silence fall, thinking.

"So there's Safford," I muse eventually. "And maybe I could figure out how to make a silver bough?" It's the only thing I can think of, the only vague plan I have, the idea that maybe I could get someone in to help us.

"How would you ever find out how to make a silver bough? Only Seelies know how to—Oh." He cuts himself off. "Yes. Seelie blood. Of course."

There is an awkward silence. I feel like remembering I'm a Seelie has made Ben uneasy.

"I'm still me," I assure him. "Look. I'm still me."

"Yes," agrees Ben. "But they make you forget. That's what they do. They make you forget—"

"I'm not going to forget," I vow.

Ben takes a deep breath, lays his head back down, no longer buried in my neck but tipped against mine, so that our foreheads touch comfortingly. "A silver bough," he says after a moment. "That means we could get someone else in. We could work with that. We could…Maybe we could do this… If you could figure out…But, really, how *would* you…"

I think about the moat. How can I get him over the water…?

"Ben," I say abruptly.

He jumps, and I realize he'd fallen asleep. "What?" he whispers, tense, and I think that he must assume I've woken him because someone is coming.

"I don't think anyone knows I'm here," I assure him.

"Oh, of course they know you're here," he snaps at me. "How do you think you even got here?"

"I don't know, I thought maybe your enchantment…I wanted to find you…"

"It's not about what you *want*. It's about what you *don't* want. People can't make you do what you don't want to do."

"I didn't want to be lost."

"Not being lost doesn't necessarily mean finding me."

"Yes," I insist. "It does."

"You could find me and still be lost," he points out.

"I wouldn't be lost anymore, because I'd be with you."

Ben looks at me for a long moment, his expression as

inscrutable as always, and I wonder if I've gone too far, said too much, and I want to take it back. But when he eventually speaks, what he says is, "They're just waiting for you to forget. That's all it is. They're waiting for your Seelie blood to kick in, and you'll forget Boston and your aunts, and *me*."

"But I won't forget. I have ogre blood," I remind him. "You can't forget that I'm *not* going to forget, okay? Can they hear what we're saying?" I have no idea how faerie magic really works.

"No. Not unless they're here in the room with us, and they're not."

I find his hand and squeeze it. "Ben, whenever it snowed in Boston, it didn't bother you."

"Oh," he says. "Snow isn't really wet. Not until it melts. But as long as it was *snow*, no, that doesn't bother me."

"So if we could freeze the moat…" I suggest. I shift so I can see him under our blanket.

"I could walk over the ice," he realizes. He looks at me, and even in the darkness, I can tell how relieved he is. "I could walk over the ice!" he exclaims. "Selkie, you're *brilliant*."

"Glad you finally recognized it," I tell him lightly.

"Oh, I recognized it ages ago. I just kept it to myself," he rejoins. "Now we just have to figure out how to freeze the moat."

He says it like it's a simple problem. I decide to let him think it is. Anyway, I am thinking of other things.

"Do all faeries work that way?" I muse.

"Work what way?"

"Well, not all faeries are bothered by water. Clearly my mother isn't."

"No," he replies. "Some are, some aren't."

"Like an allergy."

"If you like."

"Don't the Seelies have anything like that? Anything at all?"

"It's church bells," says Ben. "Everyone knows that. Seelies love chiming bells, but church bells weaken them. But I'd like to see you try to get a church bell over Mag Mell. The Seelies would name you immediately."

Not if they don't know, I think.

CHAPTER 21

B en wakes me. I do not know how long I have been sleeping, but it is still dark in the cell; I can tell even through the blanket.

"You have to go," he says, sounding heavy to admit it. "If they find you here in the morning…They know you're here, but I'd rather not…You have to go."

I know he's right. I sigh and look at Ben, hesitant, trying to think what to say in farewell. Ben is staring intently at my sweatshirt.

"What?" I ask and look down at it. "Is there something wrong with it?"

"No." He shakes his head, and then he smiles at me. "Just thinking again how…You remembered."

"Of course I remembered," I tell him.

"I wasn't sure you would. I hoped, of course, but I wasn't sure."

I think of how much I missed him, even when I *didn't* remember—of how the Common felt empty, of how I longed for his unusual pale eyes. "Don't be silly," I say. "How could I not remember *you*? I will never forget you. I will always remember you."

There is a very nice moment when we lay there under our blanket and smile at each other, and I wish we'd done things like this when our lives were relatively normal.

"Promise me you won't leave me again," I say.

A shadow passes over his face. "Selkie," he starts.

"No." I shake my head vehemently. "You won't leave me, and I won't leave you. From now on, we do this prophecy thing—or we don't do it—together."

He is silent for a long time.

"Ben," I say worryingly.

He winces.

"Oh," I realize. "Sorry, I didn't mean—it's frustrating. How can I keep from naming you every time I say your name?"

"I told you," says Ben, "it's about intent."

"I didn't *mean* to hurt you then."

"Maybe not, but you were displeased with me, and you're actually a very good namer who doesn't quite have control over it yet, so…"

"I'm sorry," I say, meaning it. I may have been miffed at him but that's very different from wanting to cause him pain, and I wish my naming power would understand that.

"It's fine," says Ben. "It has some advantages. When you say my name like you like me, it's actually very nice."

"Is it?"

He nods. "I discovered that last night. That's not true of most namers—or at least, none I've met. Maybe I've just never met any who liked me." He shrugs, looking unconcerned about this.

"Maybe it's my ogre blood," I suggest.

"Perhaps," he allows.

I look across at him for a moment. Our blanket is saturated by now, sopping wet and heavy over us. Ben is not dry—far from it—but he's drier than he was. He looks bedraggled and exhausted, but he is still *Ben*. Ben, Ben, my Ben, who got himself locked up in this terrible prison just to keep me safe.

"Ben," I say, and what I mean is *I love you*. He blinks, so slowly that it's more like he closes his eyes for a moment. I hesitate, but it seems appropriate to our current coziness to reach out and brush his tangled hair off his forehead. "Ben, Ben, Ben," I repeat softly, trying to make sure that I'm saying it like I like him, like I *love* him. I want my tone to be *dripping* with love for him. I want him to be more drenched by my love than he currently is by the water all around us. I want him to realize what it is I'm saying in asking him to promise.

"Yes," he says, his voice sounding husky and his gaze very intent. "That's much better."

"Is it?" I can't get my voice to be louder than a whisper. My hand is still resting in his hair. I feel it would be awkward to withdraw it now.

"I promise," he says, and then he breaks the moment, pulling away slightly

I gather myself, moving my hand away from his hair, and then roll out from underneath the blanket, getting to my feet. Ben stands beside me, sweeping the blanket off of himself and handing it to me. He winces a bit as the drizzle spits at his cheeks.

"Keep it," I say.

"No, you need to take it. I don't want them to find it here."

I know he is probably right, but I am loath to take it. Ben looks severely miserable in the wetness attacking him now.

I reluctantly gather the blanket into my arms. "You should say my name a couple more times," I say. "It would do you good."

He shakes his head. "Not really. Unless you think we'll be escaping today. I'd rather save it until I truly need it. It can get diluted if you use it too often. Anyway, you just helped, saying my name the way you just did."

"Ah," I say, a little embarrassed. I watch Ben give the rain a glum look before futilely pulling up his collars and adjusting his coats. Then he sends me a falsely cheerful smile. "When we get out of here," I promise him, "we can go to some world that's never even heard of the concept of water."

"You won't last there very long," he points out.

"I'll bring some water bottles." I shrug.

He laughs and then abruptly turns serious. "Listen to me," he says and closes his hands around my shoulders. "You are *you*. You are not one of them. Don't think of yourself that way. Don't let them trick you into thinking that way."

"I won't," I promise.

His faerie eyes, bright silver-blue in the darkness, flicker over my face for a moment. Then he drops his hands from my shoulders. "Be careful. Keep breathing."

I nod, then lean up and quickly kiss his cheek before I can overthink it. Then, because I know I am blushing, I quickly take my running leap over the moat.

When I look back at him, he is standing hunched into his coats, looking awful. I send him a little wave, feeling a bit like an idiot. I think he flickers a small smile back at me, but I can't quite be sure.

⟨image: small decorative flourish⟩

I am soaking wet when I get back to my room. And what I find when I get there is Gussie, sitting perched on the windowsill. She looks at me, dripping onto the floor, and lifts an eyebrow.

"Well," she remarks, "I was wondering where you'd gone. And now I know. The Le Fays have always hated water. His mother was the same way."

I want to tell her to get out of my room, because I don't want to *deal* with all of this for a little while. I just want to collapse and not *think* so hard. But she mentioned Ben's mother, and I find myself saying, irresistibly, "Did you know her?"

"Oh, yes. She was the best enchantress of the day. Everyone in the Otherworld knew her. Which was precisely why the Seelies imprisoned her. The Seelies like powerful faeries, you know. They drink up the power, make it their own. They like having power around them; they get a bit drunk off of it. It's why I'm here and why you're here. But Benedict's mother was…not easily amenable. To anything. Headstrong. Seelies hate that."

"So they named her?" I conclude, feeling cold on Ben's behalf. I want to hear what she says in response to that.

"Oh, no, she escaped."

"Escaped?" *So she* did *escape*, I think. "She escaped from here? From Tir na nOg?" I want to clarify. I want to know everything about this story. If she was the only faerie to escape, then I want to know how she did it. And so I say, "How?"

Gussie lifts both eyebrows this time. "If I knew that, do you think I'd still be here?"

"How long have you been here?"

"Time doesn't exist here. Haven't you noticed? How long have *you* been here?"

I know exactly how long I've been here. I open my mouth to say. And then realize that I have no idea. Has it been two nights? Or just one? Or maybe more? Surely I was in Boston just the other day. Wasn't I? But it seems so far away. I can feel my face screwing up with effort as I think about this.

"See? They make you forget. It's what they do."

"But…I haven't forgotten. I won't forget."

"Not yet. You're stubborn. But it will come. I don't remember where I came from anymore. I had a house once. I think I did. I don't remember where it was. I'm not a faerie, you know. But I can't remember what I *am*." Gussie looks thoughtful for a moment. "They call me 'Lady Gregory' sometimes, and I think that maybe that means something? I don't know."

Gussie looks so bewildered that I can't stand it. I don't know much about her, but so far, as long as I have been here, she has seemed to be pulled together, to know what's going on. I realize at that moment that I'd been depending on her to know what to do—to give me guidance.

"I need to make a silver bough," I say desperately.

She looks at me sadly. "For what? Who will you give it to? Even if you could make one."

She has a good point. And I don't know. I falter. Who do I know who I could give the silver bough to?

"Anyway, you need glass to make a silver bough. And they don't allow any glass at the Seelie Court, haven't you noticed? They hate silver boughs. You need a Threader too, because you need a Threader needle. And all the Threaders...I don't remember what happened to the Threaders."

I think of the glass in my kangaroo pocket, of the Threader needle I grabbed on my way out of...the house...on...I can't think of the name of the street, and for a second, panic rises inside of me. Then I press it down. I say, "If I had glass and a Threader needle, what then?"

"You'd need a drop of Seelie blood."

And I am half-Seelie. I look across at Gussie and I say,

curiously, "How do you know this? I thought only Seelies knew how to make silver boughs."

Gussie looks confused. "I...don't remember, now that you mention it." She makes a frustrated sound. "Oh, it's so annoying, because there are things that I feel like I've been clinging to all along. Like you. You're important—the visitor who would come to the Seelie Court. The fay of the autumnal equinox. As long as you are here, they will draw power from you. You will make them more powerful than they have ever been. That's what they say, isn't it?"

"That's not the prophecy I heard," I point out.

"As if there's only one prophecy about anything. As if there is only one choice for you to make. You are surrounded by choices, child. You can do as you wish, and each choice brings with it its consequences. Now you are here though, and the choices have disappeared. They have won. You are their prize."

"But I'm prophesied to—"

"Didn't you just hear me?" she interrupts me sharply. "That's not how it works. You were supposed to bring peace, you and the other three fays of the seasons, if you'd met each other, if you'd joined each other. But separately, the prophecy was always that you would fall to the side of the Seelies. It is in your blood. There was no guarantee it would all turn out to be the prophecy we wanted. How foolish everyone is. How foolish. How foolish." She suddenly brings up her hands and covers her face with them, as if in agony. "It all went wrong, and you are here, and it is all over. It is all over."

I don't know what to say. I don't know what to *do*. I want to say it's not true, that I have not shifted the prophecy, but I think of how much my aunts and the Threader didn't want me to come here, and maybe it's true—maybe I've ruined everything forever.

"But why does it have to be me? Aren't there four fays of the seasons? Where are the rest?"

"They're still hidden, of course. You're the only one who has asked the right questions. So far."

Well, I'm tired of it just being me. I want the rest of them to be put into the same impossible situations I'm finding myself in. "Hidden where?"

"No one knows that, of course, except the faerie who hid them."

"And who was that?"

"You would need the book to know that."

"What book?"

"*A Pickle for the Knowing Ones.*"

Well, now she isn't even making any sense at all. I give up entirely on this pointless topic of conversation.

"I don't want to be part of a prophecy," I hear myself say. "I just want to be *me*. I don't want all these consequences hanging off of everything I do."

Gussie lifts her head out of her hands and looks at me. "And now you sound just like a Seelie," she remarks. "Let the past be in the past. No consequences, so no regrets. No memory to remember any of it."

Gussie leaves after condemning me as sounding like a Seelie, and with that ringing through my head, I peel off my clothing and spread it out as best I can on one of the fluffy carpets, hoping that it will dry off. Then I put Ben's sweatshirt back on, because I don't dare take it off for more than a few moments, and crawl into bed. The sky is just beginning to lighten from black to navy. I have time—I think, because it's so hard to tell with the way time moves here—before my mother comes to get me, but I don't know what to do with this time. I feel that I need to figure out the rest of our plan. I can make a silver bough, I think, if Gussie's instructions on that point are correct, but what good will that do me? She's right that I don't know what to do with the silver bough once I make it. And I'd been so excited about getting the silver bough. So had Ben. And we had neither of us thought through the fact that we're still stuck in here with a silver bough. It doesn't let *us* leave; it just lets other people come in.

The plan—or the lack of a plan—whirls itself around and around in my head until I feel like I am going mad. There is nothing I can do, nothing I can think of; I cannot think of it any longer. I turn my head into my pillow and wish desperately to just stop thinking about all of these things, for just a little while. It would be such a relief to just quiet my brain and stop *thinking*.

CHAPTER 22

Y ou changed," says my mother when she glides into my room that morning.

"My clothes have seen better days," I tell her. My clothes do not seem to be drying, and I wonder if the rain falling on Ben is enchanted to be even wetter than normal rain. I have bundled them up, in all their guilty drippingness, and stuck them under the bed, and I've pulled on one of the jingle-bell lined Seelie dresses I found in my room's armoire. And I've topped it all off with the sweatshirt, of course, which seems to be drying better than the rest, maybe because it's enchanted. But my mother shouldn't be able to see the sweatshirt. My mother should just see my jingle-bell dress.

My mother smiles, but it is as chilly as her smiles always are. "Look at you," she announces. "You look more like a proper Seelie already. Ready to take your rightful place."

I follow her as she dashes down corridors. The route is a different one and unfamiliar, but we emerge into the same central bright room. I am convinced the walls themselves move here.

I sit in the room and pick at breakfast. I do not think

about planning my escape. I am exhausted by the idea. I just need a break from it. I need to think about other things for a little while.

Gussie arrives at breakfast and sits next to me. She seems subdued, and I wonder if she is thinking of the things she said to me last night or this morning, or however time is moving here. Her hands shake as she reaches for a copper goblet to drink from.

I watch them in concern. "You okay?"

"Fine," she whispers, although she's so pale that even her lips are white. "I'm fine."

I glance at my mother, who is busy pulling yarn out of the air, behind which is the uneven flash of one of the named faeries, drifting away through madness. I look back at Gussie and lower my voice. "Have some water."

"I said too much last night," she says, her eyes darting nervously around the room. "I *remembered* too much last night." She puts her fingers up to her temples and closes her eyes as if she has a terrible headache. "I haven't remembered so much in ages. I shouldn't have…I shouldn't have…"

"Yes," I agree. "It makes your head hurt, doesn't it? Just stop for a little while. Give yourself a break."

Gussie looks over at me. "A break."

And then there is a commotion at the other end of the room. I turn to see what's happening, and what's happening is that two bear-like animals dressed in copper armor are carrying in two wriggling, screaming bundles. A murmur goes up from the Seelies all around us. Excitement. Something happening!

I am caught up in it too. Everything here had felt stifled and stalled and stuck, but now there is something actually happening. I follow the knot of Seelies instinctively, walking over to where the bear-creatures drop the bundles to the ground.

One is a little boy. He cannot be more than three or four. He sits on the hard marble floor and sobs. And the other is… the little girl who asked me for the fusel when I first arrived in the Otherworld. She kneels next to the little boy and pulls him up against her protectively, and I think of Safford, telling me about the little brother she was devoted to.

The little girl is also crying hysterically, but she is speaking, looking up at the Seelies all around her. "Please no," she is begging. "Please. I said to take me instead. Please."

"Foolish child," my mother rebukes her coldly. "You thought we would *bargain*?"

"Please," cries the little girl, cuddling her brother in more tightly. "*Please*."

"What is his name?" asks my mother of the little girl.

When she doesn't immediately answer, my mother leans forward and tips the little girl's head up, not unkindly. And she says, "Tell me his name."

And the little girl does. I blink in surprise, but she says in a dull monotone, "Trevor Suddington Lamp North."

My mother smiles and nods. "And what is your name?"

"Milla Doenna Nimble North."

My mother straightens and steps back, and the little girl flinches, and suddenly she is sobbing hysterically again, and I realize that my mother must have enchanted the answers out of her.

And then my mother says, very slowly and with a great deal of intent, intent that I can feel in the shiver of the air, "Trevor Suddington Lamp North."

And where there was a little boy being hugged by a little girl, there is nothing, suddenly, but a pile of dandelion fluff and a flash in the air that might make you look twice. There is a wail, not just from the little girl but from *underneath* the air somehow, and I think of the murmur of sobbing from all the mad, flimsy faeries in the corners of my eye. Their grief is a roar that threatens to overwhelm me.

My mother looks at the little girl, curled into a ball, because the dandelion fluff that had been her brother is gone, has drifted off into the air, is floating all around us, barely visible. She is sobbing as if her heart has broken.

My mother says, almost casually, "Milla Doenna Nimble North."

And there is no more sobbing from the little girl because there is no more little girl. There is a slant of dust motes in the air, dancing in the sunlight. And underneath, for just a moment, I can hear the pulsing crying of all the other named faeries.

There is, meanwhile, a murmur of pleasure from the Seelies,

and I can understand why, because I can feel it too, a charge in the air, like a buzzing jolt of electricity. Power, suddenly, all around, tangible, and I feel like if I leaned into it, it would feel *fantastic*. But I don't lean into it. I am holding myself so stiffly that I feel like I could shatter. My hands, I realize, are clenched into tight fists by my sides.

My mother turns and smiles at me, her translucent eyes lit up with a cruel and terrible delight that makes me feel ill. "Isn't it *delicious*?" she says to me.

"What did they do?" I ask.

My mother blinks at me, obviously confused. "'Do'?" she echoes.

"Why were they named?"

My mother makes a little shrug. "Why not?"

I can feel my heart pounding in my ears the remainder of the interminable day. Or the day goes by in a blink. I can't tell. Time is different here. It doesn't work right. It's both too fast and too slow all at once, and I can't explain it, but for some period of time that I can't determine after the naming, I sit, frozen and trying not to seem frozen. My mother is looking at me suspiciously, and I try to relax. Because I *was* relaxed earlier. I had stopped thinking about Ben, stopped worrying about a plan to escape. I had told myself I was taking a break, but *I had started to forget*. I had just been sitting in the bright, central room, relaxed, telling Gussie to relax. I was *becoming a Seelie*, just like Gussie had said, and that would have been that prophecy fulfilled, the Seelies would have cemented power, they would have been in power forever, naming innocent faeries who had done nothing just because they could.

And I know my mother had relaxed upon seeing me relaxed. I don't want to signal in any way that I am now back to thinking about the other prophecy, the one where I escape and I destroy this court.

I think of all the things that people have told me about the Seelie Court. I *remember*. I remember the little girl whose parents had been stolen and who was just trying so desperately to protect her little brother. I remember Safford, condemned for no reason. I remember Ben, wet and shivering and dependent on me to find our way out of here. I remember my aunts, trembling in Boston, terrified to *live* because of the threat of the Seelies hanging over us. I remember my father, driven mad by my mother for the crime of wanting a baby.

And I remember all the faeries I haven't met, all the creatures dwelling in the Otherworld just trying to go about normal lives, trying to *live*, the way Ben's father had been in his sunny, meadow world. How many more of them are there out there? And does it really all depend on me getting out of here, to give them their lives, to let them love and laugh and do as they please, to let them go where they wish and see the things they wish to see and protect their little brothers and adore their little daughters?

If it is all depending on *me*, on *my choice*, then I have to make it. I have to make the right one.

When I get to my room, I go to my windowless window. I stare out at the ocean. I close my hands around the history book pages in my sweatshirt pocket. I don't want to forget, I am not going to forget. *Words have power*, I think, so I say it out loud, to the sea and the sky.

"I am Selkie Stewart," I say firmly. "I am not Seelie. I am not ogre. I am simply *me*. Selkie Stewart of Boston."

It happens then, something flying toward me, at first just a dark speck against the sky, and then it gets closer and closer.

It's a bat.

It lands right on my windowsill and sits there, frowning at me and, granted, my acquaintance with bats is a severely limited one, but I have only met one type of bat that looks this grouchy.

Could the Sewing Circle reach me here? They're connected to the Otherworld, I know, but could a bat get through to Tir na nOg? Is a bat a faerie? Maybe a bat's not *not* a faerie? And maybe that's enough? My head hurts.

I kneel next to the windowsill and stare intently at the bat, as if it is going to start talking. It would be very convenient if it turned out to be a talking bat. But it just keeps on frowning at me, stubbornly silent.

"Are you from the Boston Sewing Circle?" I whisper.

The bat blinks at me. *Maybe it's Morse code or something.*

Too bad I don't know Morse code. I should have grabbed a Morse code dictionary to put in my pocket to take on this trip with me. You have to know a lot of random stuff to have a successful adventure, I think, and then wonder vaguely if I'm on the verge of becoming completely hysterical.

"Can you get a message out of here for me?" I ask, still keeping my voice to a whisper.

The bat blinks again.

I chew on my lower lip and consider. It's the best chance I have, I decide. Maybe this is some kind of Seelie bat. Maybe nothing is going to happen. But maybe it *is* from the Boston Sewing Circle. On the other hand, can I even trust the Boston Sewing Circle? The Threader and I didn't part on the best of terms. But I don't know what else to do, what my other options might be.

I scramble to my feet and tear toward the desk in the room, wondering if it will have mundane things in it like paper and pen. It does, even if the pen is a feather pen that has to be dipped in an inkwell. Good enough. My luck is holding. Maybe this is part of the prophecy kicking into gear.

I frown at the lantern perched on top of the desk, wondering how it works, wanting to be able to see better as I try to make a silver bough. I lean forward, intending to feel around for a switch of some sort, but it flares into light with a noise like the striking of a match as soon as I touch it.

Convenient, I think, and then I pull out of my pocket the shard of glass wrapped in tissue and the threaded needle. *Well. Here goes nothing.*

I need a Threader needle, a piece of glass, and my blood, I think. I unwrap the glass and position my finger over it, and then I carefully prick my finger with the needle. A droplet of blood wells up at the tip of my finger and then drops to the glass. And the glass glows white-hot. I half expect it to be hot to the touch when I reach out to smear the blood along it. It is not, but it seems to drink in my blood, and its glow fades to a faint throb. With any luck, I have just made a silver bough. Although it still just looks like a piece of broken glass. Maybe "silver bough" is meant figuratively. Metaphorically. Poetically.

I dip the pen in the inkwell and press it to the paper. *This is a silver bough*, I write. I feel like that needs to be explained; I wouldn't know what to make of this package if I received it. I certainly would never guess that this piece of nondescript broken glass is a silver bough. *Come to Tir na nOg right away. Bring a church bell. —Selkie.*

It takes an excruciatingly long time to write these few sentences. I do not know how people dealt with having to dip their pens in ink all the time. And it keeps leaving huge blobs of ink all over the place. But finally, I finish the note. I make sure it's legible through the inkblots then carefully fold it around the piece of glass, making it as secure as I can. Then I write on the front, very clearly, in all caps, *TRUE STEWART. VIRTUE STEWART. ETHERINGTON STEWART. WILLIAM BLAXTON. C/O BOSTON / PARSYMEON.* I underline all of it, just to make sure.

I walk over to the bat. "This needs to go to my aunts. Or Will Blaxton. Whoever you can find. And if you can't find one of them, then my father. But it would be better with my aunts or Will Blaxton." I enunciate exaggeratedly. The bat looks offended at this. But then again, the bat always looks vaguely offended. I pierce through the piece of paper with the Threader's needle and use the string to tie it around the bat's leg. The bat stands patiently until I am done, and then I remind it, "The Stewarts of Boston. Or Parsymeon. Whatever. They're ogres. Or William Blaxton. He's a wizard. I think."

If a bat could huff with indignation, this bat would. But it simply takes flight, and I watch it, until the moment when it seems to disappear into the sky—hopefully flying into the world where there is Boston.

Maybe help is on the way. I curl up on the windowsill and look at the outline of the island on the horizon.

CHAPTER 23

Dawn comes again, another night done. I don't dare tempt fate by seeking out Ben again. I want my mother to think I am forgetting, relaxing, becoming a Seelie. I want her to think it is her prophecy coming true. I go to eat breakfast, but this time I am determined not to relax, determined not to forget. I make myself keep thinking of Ben, keep thinking of my plan. If I have sent a silver bough to Boston, then someone will be coming, and I need to be prepared. I need to be ready.

Gussie sits next to me. She still looks pale and tired and drawn. The display of naming the day before—or the hour before, because who knows how time is moving?—helped neither of us.

I am on the verge of saying something supportive when my mother screams. And when I say she screams, I mean she *screams*, a shriek rising up above us, expanding, feeling as if it is sucking all of the air out of the room.

My mother lunges at me. She is contorted with fury, shaking with it, the gold circle on her tipped at a seasick angle, her hair flying out around her head, and I shrink back from her automatically.

"*Who did you send a message to?*" she bellows at me.

"W-what?" I stammer, scrambling away from her.

"You sent a message!" I can feel all of the members of the Seelie Court staring at the two of us but with only a mild sort of interest, as if they are finally relieved to have a diversion. "A bat from the Boston Sewing Circle managed to escape the Seelie Court with a message! I know it was you! *Who did you send it to? What did it say?*" She reaches forward to grab me, and I recoil, and she hits a barrier.

At least, that's what it looks like. Like there's an invisible wall between her and me, and she cannot reach me behind it. Her eyes widen in shock. She claws at the invisible wall, letting out another scream of frustrated fury.

Ben's enchantment, I realize. Still holding.

We stare at each other, and I smile for the first time in a very long time. The light in the room fades. Pandemonium breaks out. The Seelies start stampeding over each other, shrieking in obvious terror. My mother stares up at the sky, face even whiter than usual. I look up as well, but all I see is a fluffy white cloud, drifting in front of the sun, bathing us in momentary shade.

My mother whirls from me, dashing away.

Fear is a sudden, cold, hard knot in my stomach. Where is she going? I stumble forward, grabbing at my mother, reaching for anything, just one of the tiny bells on the hem of her dress, just to catch her and slow her, but she is, of course, far too quick. I am running full-speed and can barely keep her in my sight, and I need to keep her in my sight. I am aware if I

lose her, I will never be able to find her in the enchanted labyrinth of hallways and then I won't know what she is doing.
"Stop!" I shout, breathless. I do not expect her to listen to
me, but I cannot just do *nothing*.

I run into the cell just as my mother draws to a halt in front
of Ben. Ben is standing up and facing her, and I think that he
must have sensed something is going on. He looks wary but
also a bit befuddled. Then my mother raises her hand and
shouts, "Benedict Will o' the Wisp Celador Le Fay!"

It seems that it happens in slow motion. Ben's eyes widen
in obvious shock, and he wheels backward, losing his balance
entirely. For a moment, I think he is going to tip into the
moat, but I react without knowing I am going to. I am still
running hard enough to make the leap over the moat easily,
and my fist closes into the layers he is wearing and tugs him
back just before he falls.

He meets my eyes for a split second, and he looks thoroughly stunned. I am not even sure he recognizes me.
He tips forward and staggers, and he is too heavy for me
to hold up, and he falls to his hands and knees, and he
is coughing violently, choking, and I stand frozen, staring down at him at my feet, too cold and horrified, and
anyway, what else can I do? She has just named him, and I
am going to watch him dissolve, drift into madness, right
here in front of me.

And then the most amazing thing happens. Ben stops
coughing. He takes one wheezing breath and then another

deeper one. I look from him to my mother, confused and uncertain. Is something else supposed to happen?

My mother stares at him. "You have a hidden name," she whispers. And then she shouts it. "*You have a hidden name!*"

Ben lifts his head up. He is breathing heavily, but he is clearly recovering. It shows in his eyes, which are very bright, gleaming, a clear, crystal blue. And he smiles at my mother, a smile that is more like a smirk, a smile that is full of victory and smugness and pride. "She was the best enchantress in the Otherworld," he says. "Did you really think she wouldn't find a way to protect her only child?"

My mother's eyes darken, flash with fury, like an entire thunderstorm is going on in her head. "*Tell me what it is!*" she screams at Ben.

"That doesn't seem likely to happen," remarks Ben, "does it?"

With another exclamation of rage, she flings her arm through the air, and I am knocked off-balance by an enormous wave of water that sweeps onto the stone where I am standing. I catch myself before I tumble, but Ben crumples, gasping for breath, and I realize instantly that it is far too much water for him after all of those names.

"Stop it," I shout at my mother, kneeling in front of him to try to absorb most of the second wave rising up over us, trying futilely to keep it from breaking over him.

"Selkie," he gasps. "I can't…I can't…" His eyes are on my sweatshirt, and I realize instantly what he's trying to tell me.

The waves stop. In fact, the water in the moat stops

moving at all. The only sound in the room is Ben's terrible, tearing breathing.

I look from Ben to my mother. Her eyes are riveted on my sweatshirt. She can see it. His enchantment is broken.

She smiles. "Benedict," she croons at him, and he actually groans out loud in reaction. "I've been going too easy on you. I thought you were fading rather quickly. Your mother lasted much longer. What a pretty little enchantment. It's a pity you don't use your power for good, it really is. Ah, well. Benedict Will o' the Wisp Celador Le Fay, you were the last of a once great and noble line."

Ben does not respond. He is curled onto his side, shuddering with every breath he takes. She waves a hand, and it begins pouring onto us. Ben curls into a tighter ball. I kneel next to him, not sure what to do, not sure when help will arrive, not sure if anyone ever got my message, if anyone is even coming.

"Leave him," says my mother. "And come with me. Face me without an enchantment. He cannot help you now."

I know he can't. And I know it's up to me. I need to think of *something*.

I leap over the moat, and for the first time, I realize that I'm crying.

"Come along," says my mother, her hand encircling my wrist, pulling me along.

"Can't you make it less cold in there for him?" I beg through my tears. "Can't you make it warmer for him? He hates being cold; he hates it so much, *please*." It is not difficult to pretend to be hysterical—I think that I pretty much am. But I am hoping beyond hope that my mother will take the bait here. It is the best I can do, get her to think that maybe snow would be worse for Ben than rain. I have no idea if Ben can recover from an almost-full naming and a thorough soaking, but I've got to give him a fighting chance, and getting rid of the rain is the only thing I can think of.

"As if you are in a position to make requests!" scoffs my mother, flinging me into my room. We got here very quickly. Apparently, the drama of a long route to and fro no longer suits my mother. "Do you really think that Boston will be closed to us forever? Do you think, now that we have you here, with your power leaking into the air, that we will not be able to penetrate through their defenses? We'll get through, and we will get your precious aunts and your precious father, and we will destroy *all* of them. Everyone you love, everyone you *remember*. And that will teach you the danger of *remembering*." The door slams shut behind her.

I turn, unsure what I am going to do, just wanting to pace. But I cannot move. I take a step and then can move no farther. Something is preventing me from getting to the rest of the room. She's imprisoned me.

I sit in the tiny amount of space I have been allowed, and I refuse to cry.

I hate it in the Otherworld. That is what I decide after a lot of sitting on the floor feeling sorry for myself. If I had been kidnapped in real life, regular life, normal life, *Boston* life, I would at least have had some vague ideas of what to do. I could try to get to a phone to call 911, or I could scream and shout and surely someone walking by would hear me. I know to walk with my house key clutched like a weapon between my fingers, and that if you are locked in the trunk of a car, you should try to kick out the taillight.

But I have no idea what to do when you are trapped by invisible faerie walls in a faerie prison in the Otherworld, where the odds of someone on your side finding you in this enchanted labyrinth of a place seem impossibly small, where you do not even know if screaming will be of any help. And when everyone you've never met is somehow also depending on you. Nothing I've lived while trapped in Ben's enchantment has prepared me for this. *And*, I am well aware, I don't just have to get myself out of here, but Ben as well, and I have no idea what condition Ben will be in once I find my way back to him. I am not even entirely sure there will be a Ben any longer, but I try not to let myself dwell on that. I find myself wishing for Gussie to come and find me, but I don't know what Gussie is really capable of doing. If Gussie could help, wouldn't she have escaped long ago, the way she'd said? And Gussie said the prophecy was *mine*, *my* choices. For reasons that I don't understand, I am the most important person here, and *I* have to make the decisions; *I* have to get Ben and me out of Tir na nOg and find a way to save everyone. I try to think about productive things, to systematically go over everything I know about faeries. I need to dissolve this enchantment around me, but I only know how to dissolve an enchantment using my unusually good naming power, and I don't know my mother's name—

I lift up my head abruptly from where I'd been leaning against the knees I have clutched to my chest. It is not very bright in the room. Clouds are still rolling in. The sunlight is spotty at best.

I asked her what I should call her, and she said *Mother*. It isn't a name, but it's what she told me to call her. Maybe, in doing so, it's *become* her name to me. I am me, and she is my mother. That is *who she is* to me. And maybe that's enough.

It's worth a try. I'm unusually good at naming; this is what I can do. "Mother," I whisper. Is it a trick of the scuttling clouds, or does the air shimmer around me?

I scramble to my feet, concentrating. "Mother," I say again, more loudly this time, making sure that I fill it with all my fury and frustration, with all my vengeance for Ben and for the seventeen years of my life I've spent without a mother, for the rest of my life that I have to spend without my mother, for my father who sacrificed his sanity, for all of *Boston*, huddled into defensive preservations of its history because of its terror of *my mother* and her people. Yes, that is definitely a shimmer, a contraction of the air, like it is struggling against something. I fling out my arm, the way my mother had when she had tried to name Ben, and I gather all of my angry intent. I make it the very opposite of the way I'd said Ben's name the night before. I shout firmly, "Mother!"

There is a sound like the splintering of glass, and then the air all around me seems to crash to the floor. I take one step, then two, and then I fling open my door. I have no real idea what I am going to do. I just know that I need, somehow, to get to Ben and get us out. Eventually, I hope, Will or my aunts will show up with a church bell, and when they do, Ben and I are going to be waiting right on the very edge of the cliff to hop onto Safford's hot air balloon. I don't know *how* I will accomplish this. I am just determined that I will.

I am Selkie Stewart of Boston.

CHAPTER 24

I keep shouting *Mother* as I march firmly down the hallway, keeping my anger wrapped tightly around me. The walls around me flicker, passages appearing and disappearing, and I realize that I am managing to break the enchantment that keeps the routes confused. Not entirely, but enough that I can mostly feel my way. I take only a few wrong turns before finding Ben.

I know that my mother must know by now that I've been able to break through some of her enchantments, and I know that I don't have much time, and I still don't have a plan. Maybe I can get Ben in good enough shape to put up an enchantment that will obscure us. It is the only idea I have. I wish I knew how to put up enchantments, rather than just dissolve them.

Ben's cell is *freezing*, and I am relieved. My little trick worked. The moat of water is frozen mid-tempest, the ice uneven, but I slip and slide my way across it, and it feels extremely solid. Ben is still curled in a tight ball, fixed into the film of ice that had once been the puddle he had been laying in. He is covered in a layer of snow that isn't melting, which is extremely alarming.

"Ben," I say, shaking him a bit. My teeth are already chattering in the frigid temperatures. "*Ben*." I try to infuse it with so much love that my voice actually trembles, but I wonder if the love is being drowned out by my terror. I force my hand into his. His hand is freezing, but mine may be even more freezing. Exactly how cold did she make it in there?

He opens his eyes blearily. They are a dull, mossy green. "Selkie," he says thickly. "You stopped the rain. I love you."

It is a testament to how panicked I feel that I don't even pause to register that. "You're just saying that," I tell him. "We have to go now."

"What? Go where?"

It's a good question, and I can't really answer it. "Anywhere that's not here."

"For an ogre, you're very bad at plans, you know that?"

"The moat is frozen. We can walk across it, and maybe you can come up with some way to hide us—"

Ben starts laughing, but it is horrible laughter, something closer to a coughing fit, really. "Oh, Selkie," he says around it. "I'm not sure I can even *walk* right now, never mind get an enchantment under way. If you think you've got an escape window, you should take it."

I stare at him. "Not without you."

"I'll be fine—"

"The entire *point* of coming here was to get you, Ben. I'm not leaving here without you."

"Selkie—" he begins.

"No, Ben. We *promised*. Say my name. Keep saying it. You'll get better."

"That is not going to work this time—"

"Shut up," I snap. I am so furious at him that I am crying, "I can't save you unless you *help* me. I am unusually powerful at naming, Will told me, so *say it*."

Ben is silent for a second. "Selkie Stewart," he says dully. "Selkie Stewart."

Even I can tell that it is having almost no effect. "*Benedict*," I say, wondering if the fullness of his name will help. "Benedict, Benedict, Benedict." I don't think, just lean forward to drop a desperate kiss in his hair to try to underline the love in my voice. "Benedict Le Fay."

"Stop it," he says thickly. "You're all over the place right now. It's hurting."

And now I've made things worse. "Sorry," I choke out, straightening. I seize in desperation upon the only idea I can come up with. "What if I give you my whole name?"

"Don't you dare," he says.

"Will it dissolve me?"

He hesitates. "No, but—"

"Then you're going to use it, do you understand me?" I command him fiercely.

"You shouldn't give your whole name, not to anyone, there's too much power—"

"I trust you," I tell him firmly.

He looks at me for a second. "You really shouldn't," he says finally. "You should never trust a faerie."

"I trust you," I insist. "Anyway, I know your name. You should know mine; then we'll be even."

"How many middle names do you have?"

"Two," I answer.

He nods briefly. "Fine. Give me one of them. You *don't* know my whole name," he cuts off my argument before I can begin. "And no offense, Selkie, but I'm not about to give it to you. So give me one of your middle names."

"Will it be enough?"

"Yes."

I pause. I *do* trust Ben, I do, but I have been infected by the thinking of faeries now. To give away my name seems like an unimaginably huge thing. I am literally handing him a large chunk of my life, trusting him to keep it safe. It is, somehow, more intimate and life changing and terrifying than anything I could possibly do with a normal human boy. I know it was my own suggestion, but I still take a moment before I lean over slowly, taking a deep breath, and press my lips to his ear and whisper it to him, and he whispers it back.

It is the first time that I have ever felt something when Ben's said my name. It feels a little like I just had a sneezing fit, emerging from it a tiny bit off-balance, in need of a good, deep breath. Ben sighs. And then, after a heartbeat, he sits up. He looks so alarmingly like his old self that I almost wonder if he'd been faking the whole thing.

"Excellent," he says, clearly delighted. "You *are* unusually good at naming. Now." He climbs to his feet and helps me up. "I'm assuming we have to get out of here before anyone discovers us, right?"

I blink at him in astonishment.

"Okay," he decides when I stay silent. "I'll figure it out. We can use that door over there." He skids his way across the moat, heading toward what looks like solid wall.

I collect myself, following him across the ice. "Ben, there's no door over there."

"Yes, there is. I noticed it when they first stuck me in here." He has his hands out, blindly feeling along the wall. "Can't keep a traveler away from a door. It was somewhere over here. They enchanted it away, it's—" He pitches suddenly through the wall, disappearing.

Wide-eyed, I run over to that spot, but I can't figure out how he got through. I try to do what he had been doing, feeling my way along the wall, shouting for him in the hope that he will hear me. There's a door there—there *has* to be—if I could just figure out the key to getting through it—

"What have you done with him?" my mother demands, skidding into the room with a small coterie of unidentifiable, copper-armored animals accompanying her.

I whirl to face her and back my way against the wall.

"Did he get through the door?" she continues, stalking slowly toward me, the animals behind her snuffling and growling, their armor clanging dully as they shift into what is undoubtedly attack position.

I force a smile, trying to look more confident than I feel. "Can't keep a traveler away from a door."

Maybe I shouldn't have said that. My mother seems to *expand* with rage, but at least she is focused on me and not finding Ben. I don't think Ben could handle another naming right now.

I brace myself for whatever is about to happen, but what happens is that from somewhere in the distance comes the gentle and unmistakable toll of a church bell. My mother's eyes widen in reaction, but I am unprepared for the fact that I feel it shudder through me too. I realize my mistake at that moment: part of me is Seelie. The church bells will affect me too. But I barely have time to digest this before the wall behind me disintegrates and I tumble through, falling in an inelegant heap onto a hard marble floor.

I make an involuntary *oof* noise, the wind knocked out of me. And I am still trying to recover from that when a voice gasps at me, "Selkie! I found you!"

I look up, wondering if I am ever going to reach the limits of my amazement, and ask curiously, as if it can't possibly be true, "Kelsey?"

CHAPTER 25

Will said the silver bough would lead me straight to you, but I didn't really believe him; he says a lot of stuff, and your aunts argue with basically everything he says, anyway."

I can't make this sentence make sense because there's too much else that needs to make sense first. "What are you doing here?"

"Saving you, of course," she says.

"We…What…" I feel like someone's hit me over the head and the world hasn't stopped vibrating yet. "But where are my aunts? Where's Will?"

"Will had to stay with the hot air balloon. And your aunts were busy arguing over which one of them would come save you, so I just took the silver bough and kind of…ran." She holds something up, and I notice it for the first time— what looks like a healthy branch of a beech tree, only forged entirely out of silver.

I blink at it. "*That's* the silver bough I sent you?"

"Yeah, it's amazing, isn't it? It was tiny when Fidelia brought us the package, but it's been growing ever since—"

"Who's Fidelia?"

"Oh, the bat."

"The bat has a name?"

"They *all* have names. Wait until I tell you everything that's happened since you left. It turns out the Boston Sewing Circle's not *entirely* evil; they're just mildly unpleasant— maybe slightly more than mildly. But it's mostly because Will broke the Threader's heart several centuries or minutes ago, depending on who's telling the story. And let me tell you, finding that out did *not* make your Aunt True happy. Apparently Will has quite the reputation. Anyway, once the Threader and your aunt bonded over hating Will, she *was* actually pretty helpful. The Threader was the only one who could figure out how to get through the Seelie enchantments to you. Apparently, the Threaders used to be in pretty constant contact with the Seelie Court, so the Threader managed to figure out how to slip through. But we don't have time for all this right now; we've got to go. Safford's waiting. And your aunts and Will are supposed to be holding the hot air balloon in place until we can get back. Once we're away from here, I'll fill you in on everything."

"You know Safford?"

"Just met him."

I have too many more questions that I want to ask, starting with how a sliver of glass had turned into a silver beech tree branch, but I guess escaping is the more important thing. I struggle to my feet. We are in an empty hallway.

The wall I'd tumbled through is solid once more, but I know it's only a matter of time until my mother and her army of animals—or one of the other Seelies—finds us. "Where's Ben?" I ask.

Kelsey looks confused. "I don't know."

"You didn't pass him, maybe, in the hall? Tall, dark hair, wearing several coats."

Kelsey looks at me like I'm crazy. I want to tell her that *she* doesn't seem all that sane to me right now, so she doesn't have to be judgmental about it. "I haven't seen anyone. Just you."

"This place is a maze. We'll never find Ben," I despair.

"Look what happens, though, when you ring the bell."

"Ring the bell?" I echo, because it occurs to me at that moment that I don't see a church bell anywhere in the hallway.

Kelsey pulls what looks like a walnut out of her pocket and tickles it. I decide maybe she really has lost her mind, but then the walnut abruptly becomes a huge church bell, suspended in space there in the corridor. Kelsey rings it enthusiastically.

The clang of it sends me careening against the wall, breathless. It feels a little like Kelsey rang my *brain*.

"Don't do that anymore," I manage to tell her. I vaguely register that she has stroked a finger down the side of it, that it's turned back into a walnut.

"We have to, Selkie. Didn't you see what happened when I hit it?"

I was too busy trying not to tumble to the floor in an

undignified heap to look around. "What happened when you hit it?"

"Almost everything disappears. All these doors, everything. You can see the way out clearly."

That makes sense, actually, I realize vaguely. The Seelies' enchantment is what makes this place a labyrinth; the bell is cutting through it. The problem is the bell is also cutting through *me*. I can barely think, and I have a new appreciation for how frustrated Ben must have been when he was trying to come up with a plan while wet.

"There you are! Come on!" Someone comes dashing into the corridor, grabbing my hand, and I realize it's Ben, although it could also be a hallucination, because it has that same quality. "Time to go," I hear him say to Kelsey, grabbing her hand as well. And then he looks at me more closely. I am stumbling in his wake, not quite able to catch my balance. "What's the matter with you?" he asks, sounding a little annoyed.

I shake my head because I don't have the words for what is wrong with me, not really. He slows, drawing to a halt and looking down at me. His eyes are bright and blue, no, green, no, gray, no—dizzy, I tip toward him.

"Selkie," he says sharply, catching my chin between his fingers so he can tip my face toward him. "Breathe. What happened to you? What did your mother do to you?"

My tongue feels thick. I realize that this whole thing is more like a severe allergic reaction than I had guessed when I had referred to it as such. And he's right: I am having trouble breathing. "Kelsey," I mumble at him, annoyed that I can't get my voice any louder, gesturing clumsily in her direction.

His eyes slide toward Kelsey, and I realize that Kelsey must have taken the opportunity of our pausing to ring her bell again. It sends a shudder through me, but I can see the moment when Ben connects the dots; it is there in his blue-gray-greenish eyes. "The bell," he realizes, and then urgently to her, "Don't ring that bell anymore."

It's too late though, because she's rung it that one more time, and I feel like I am falling. Maybe I *am* falling. I think that I hit the floor, and I can feel Ben over me, swimming in and out of focus, but I am so tired and I wish he would let me sleep.

"But why?" I hear Kelsey ask him.

"It's weakening her, can't you see?" Ben bites back impatiently. "Selkie," he says to me, but it sounds very, very far away, and I can't seem to answer him.

"The church bells never bothered her in Boston," says Kelsey.

"I was protecting her in Boston. And anyway, she's been here a long time; her Seelie blood is stronger now." Ben has stood up, is no longer in my vision, and I let myself close my eyes for a moment.

"Can't you protect her here?"

"No." Ben's voice is short.

"Can you carry her?" Kelsey's voice is so far away. I feel that I am drifting.

"I can't carry her and also outrun *Seelies*, and they're right on our heels now. You should go, get out. I'll take care of Selkie."

"I'm not leaving her. I didn't come all this way just to—"

"We do not have a choice," Ben snaps. "I cannot save both of you—"

"You don't have to save either of us, thank you very much," Kelsey retorts hotly.

I manage to get my eyes open—I have the vague idea that I am going to referee this fight that's going on, although I don't know what I'm going to say—and what I see is my mother suddenly swirl into the room with a jangle of chiming bells and snap, "Benedict Le Fay."

Ben doubles over with a gasp of reaction, reaching out a hand against the wall to keep from toppling over entirely. I try to tell Kelsey to ring the damn bell again, regardless of what it's going to do to me, and Kelsey seems to have the same idea, and she goes to lift up the walnut, but my mother descends upon her, moving with that fleet quickness of a Seelie, knocking the walnut out of her hand and beyond her reach. Kelsey gasps, struggling, but my mother grabs the silver bough and breaks it in half. Kelsey manages to get a solid kick in, and my mother lets her go, taking a step backward, and then she says silkily, "You don't belong here, do you? No. You don't. In fact, you should turn around and walk off the cliff of Mag Mell, fall into the embrace of the dark land below."

I stare in horror as Kelsey seems to go blank and limp.

She nods vacantly at my mother, turns, and seemingly walks straight through a wall.

"What did you do?" I cry, struggling to my feet. "Kelsey!" I shout. "Kelsey! Come back here! What did you do to her?" I whirl on my mother, desperate.

"I have done," says my mother, "what Seelies *do*. What *we* do. We get everyone else to do as we wish. Selkie Stewart."

I hear the small cry I make in reaction, but naming me is, oddly, the best thing she could have done, because the pain of it drives away the black sleepiness at the edges of my vision. I can see her clearly, her arms with her jingling bells folded, smiling her anti-smile. Behind her I can see the copper-armored animals and more Seelies, gathering now, their eyes all flashing pale fury at me. And I am not her. I am not them. I know that I am not. It crystallizes inside of me.

"Did you think it would be so easy? A Seelie escaping the Seelie Court? You *belong* here."

"No." I shake my head, trying to pull together my scattered thoughts. "I don't. I'm not like you."

"You *are* me."

"What have you done to my friend?"

"Nothing. I took away her church bell, of course, that was rude of her to bring here. And then I sent her home. Such a nuisance to have around, all these *vermin* underfoot. It's gotten awfully crowded here. We have *ogres* at our front door. And as for you. Did your precious Benedict abandon you?" she asks, smiling widely. "That is *so* like a faerie."

I look around, and she's right—Ben is nowhere to be seen.

"Oh, Selkie. This was foretold. This is part of your prophecy, my dear." She walks slowly forward. I stand my ground warily. She reaches her hand out, draws a finger along the curve of my cheek. I jerk my head away. "It was foretold, in this prophecy you want to come true so desperately, this prophecy where you silence the bells of the Seelie Court…" She leans even closer, her lips now directly at my ear, and she whispers, "Benedict Le Fay will betray you. And then he will die."

"No," I say, and then I shout it. "*No*."

Surprise widens my mother's translucent eyes, and then she is flung away from me, hitting the wall opposite us hard. The animals in their copper armor scatter in what I take to be fright, and the other Seelies behind her seem undecided what to do, unclear what has happened, the same way I am. My mother screams with rage, trying to collect herself from the tangle of her bell-chiming skirts. Thunder rumbles over our heads, and a white horse wheels around the corner, rears up. There is a brief pause, and I realize that Ben is riding it. Ben blinks at my shaken mother, still in a heap on the floor, and at the Seelies and their entourage, indecisive and clearly terrified. Then Ben spurs the horse onward, its hooves sending up copper-colored sparks along the marble floor as it gallops toward us. We all watch its breakneck approach, and I am as surprised as anyone when Ben, without breaking stride, leans down from his perch on the horse's back and swings me up in front of him, as if he has practiced this a million times before, this white-steed rescue of the damsel in distress.

"A horse," I say, clutching to his coats, because I am not steady to begin with and the headlong gait of the animal underneath us is not helping matters. "How'd you manage that?"

"I have my ways," he replies grimly. "Never mind that. How did you do that to your mother?"

"I did that?" I can't even process that.

Ben doesn't answer. "Hold tight," he says.

"Where are we going?"

"We're escaping."

"No. We can't. We have to find Kelsey."

"What?" He glances at me quickly then turns his attention back to the horse's headlong path. "Where did she go?"

"I don't know. My mother told her to jump off the cliff."

"Then she's going to jump off the cliff."

"What? Ben!"

He winces a bit. "Please watch my name. I'm a bit sensitive at the moment. And we'll intercept Kelsey at the cliff. It's the only thing we can do."

"Why would she jump off the cliff?"

"Because that's how Seelies *work*. They convince you that you want things you don't actually want. And it's easy to do when you've got no power of your own to contest it with. Now take a deep breath and keep doing it. *Breathe*."

Suddenly we are surrounded by *air*. It is fresh air, and I realize that I have not taken a breath of fresh air since stepping into the Seelie Court. Even the air coming in through the windows was too heavily enchanted to count as breathing. I take a deep, heady breath of it, and it seems to stop my head from swimming a bit. I twist and realize that Ben is heading for the hot air balloon suspended in thin air over Mag Mell. Will and my aunts are standing in it, and some of the copper-armored animals keep trying to launch themselves at it and are being repelled. Some kind of force field? Do my aunts have that capability?

But I don't see Kelsey. I twist around, looking to the other side, and there she is, moving relentlessly through the army of animals, unerringly toward the cliff. It's like she doesn't even notice they're around her.

"There she is," I tell Ben, gesturing.

Ben glances in her direction, changes the horse's path. He slows the horse as we reach Kelsey, but I don't wait for him to stop. I slide off as soon as I can, ignoring the grab Ben makes for me. I lunge for Kelsey, grab her, but it's like she's made of water; I can't get a grip. She keeps walking and walking and walking, and the cliff is ever closer. I scream her name, but she doesn't budge.

I turn to Ben, desperate. "Stop her! You have to stop her!"

"I can't," Ben says helplessly. "I can't break your mother's enchantment."

Kelsey is at the cliff's edge now. I reach for her, find my arms swiping through thin air. I scream her name again.

She takes a step off the cliff, but she doesn't tumble. It's as if she steps onto solid ground, even though she is standing in midair. I blink at her.

"I can't keep her afloat very long," Ben says behind me, and I look at him. His face is grim with concentration.

"You're doing that?"

"Yes," he affirms shortly. "But it's no good with your mother's enchantment on her. It's just buying us time. And I'm not a hundred percent yet; I can't do this for very long."

My mother's enchantment. I think of the last time I broke my mother's enchantment. It's the only thing I can do. The only chance we have. "*Mother!*" I shout at the top of my lungs, pouring all of my terror and hostility into it.

Kelsey shakes her head, looks down at the floor of the valley an impossible distance below her, then looks at me, her eyes wide with terror. She is herself; she is there; she is out of it.

"Oh, well done," I hear Ben breathe, and Kelsey is just starting to scramble her way back to the cliff's edge when my mother's voice snaps out, "*Benedict Le Fay.*"

Kelsey tumbles, and I react without thinking, throwing myself toward the edge of the cliff and catching her hand before she can fall entirely. I am sprawled out painfully on my stomach, rocks digging into me, and my arms are burning as I cling both my hands to Kelsey's. Kelsey looks up at me desperately, her legs scuffling uselessly against the edge of the cliff, trying to gain a toehold.

And then there is the hot air balloon underneath her, Safford piloting it, Will and my aunts in it. Will reaches up, grabs Kelsey around her waist, and I almost collapse with relief as Kelsey is pulled safely into the hot air balloon.

"Jump!" Aunt Virtue calls up to me, cupping her hands around her mouth.

"Jump!" Aunt True echoes her.

The hot air balloon's altitude increases, floating up toward me, and I know that it would mean safety, but I turn to look for Ben and find him several yards away from me, facing off with my mother warily.

I look back at my aunts, who read my thoughts.

"Leave him!" Aunt Virtue calls, but there's no way I can. There's simply no way.

I pull myself to my feet and walk over to where Ben is and stand next to him. His breaths are tearing and ragged, and I wonder how many times she's named him. He is, at least, keeping his feet, even though he seems to sway a bit as I approach.

My mother's eyes slide to me. She looks amused.

"What do you think you can do, either one of you, that will stop what has begun here? You will go into the human realm and try to hide from Seelie power, as so many have done, and how long has that lasted, for any of you? How well has that worked? No one can outrun a Seelie. Not forever."

Ben is stiff and unmoving. "Selkie Stewart," he says tightly, not looking at me, but I feel a small tingle and wonder if he's drawing energy from me, preparing for something. "You should have gotten on the hot air balloon."

"Not without you," I tell him stubbornly. "We promised, remember?"

"It's so touching, really," my mother says to Ben, "how loyal she is to you. How little she *knows* about you." Her eyes cut to me. "You should never believe a word he tells you, you know. He will betray you." She looks back at Ben. "And then he will die."

Ben's hand slides down, and his fingers curl through mine. "Do you know what you've done, ever since you *met* me? You've underestimated me. I am Benedict Le Fay." He smiles. "And I'm the best traveler in the Otherworld."

And then we are on the hot air balloon.

And I look back, worried that maybe we still aren't safe, and then I see something that surprises me. *Gussie.* I'd completely forgotten about her. Guilt twists into my abdomen. I should have gotten her out as well. But I'd been so busy—how was I supposed to save *everyone*? She is running toward the cliff, and I turn to everyone in the basket, almost hysterical.

"We have to go back."

Ben is panting for breath on the floor of the basket. "Go back?" he echoes. "I don't know if you noticed, but we barely got away. And we could get away a little faster."

"This hot air balloon is fighting me every inch, Benedict," Will replies tightly. "It would be nice if you could *help*."

"As if I have anything left," snaps Ben.

I interrupt their sniping, desperate. "But *Gussie*," I say and gesture.

They look where I am indicating.

Will draws his eyebrows together and says, "Is that Gussie Gregory?"

"Do you know her? She helped me. She—"

Gussie is exchanging words with my mother. I don't know what they are; we are no longer close enough to hear. Gussie is walking slowly backward, toward the edge of the cliff, and if she doesn't stop she's going to—

I go to shout to her, to tell her to watch out, and then she looks over her shoulder, and I could have sworn that I see her wink. And then she spreads out her arms and lets herself fall backward.

And then there is a furious, blinding flash of light, and the hot air balloon rocks almost sideways, blown clear across Mag Mell by the force of a gale.

CHAPTER 26

When we reach the slice of meadow on the other side, everyone staggers out. My aunts and Will collapse to the ground, and I rush over to them in concern.

"We're okay," Aunt True tells me, trying to sound comforting. "Just a lot of energy we used up there, and we're a bit out of practice with such active magic like that."

"But you're safe." Aunt Virtue reaches up and cups my cheek in her hand. "You escaped from Tir na nOg. You're safe."

I feel like I might cry. I am so happy to see them, I lean down and pull them into tight hugs.

Rain starts falling, sheets of it.

Ben groans audibly from where he too is collapsed in a heap. "Please stop the rain. Please."

It ends abruptly.

"Sorry," Aunt True says sheepishly. "It's just that we're so *happy*."

I blink in confusion.

"Ogre magic," Ben says sleepily. "Rain when you're happy. Rain when you're angry. Rain all the time with you guys. Bit inconvenient for me. I could sleep for a thousand years. Or a few seconds. Depending on which time you're keeping."

"Well, we haven't time for that sort of time," Will says impatiently, seeming to gather himself together.

"I don't understand," I say, straightening. "What happened to Gussie? Why did she do that?"

"Sacrificed herself," Will says brusquely. "Wizards can do that, send all the power left in them to the aid of those they wish to help."

"She was a wizard," I realized. "What was she doing in Tir na nOg?"

Will's eyes are sharp and glittery on me. "I was going to ask you that."

He is speaking very tersely, but there is something underneath it. He isn't angry; he's upset. "You really did know her," I recall. He knew her, and she fell to her death right in front of him, and he's upset.

"I—Yes. She was…" He clears his throat. "Doesn't matter. We have to get back to Boston before the Seelies regroup."

"It should take them a while." Safford sounds awed. He is staring at me. "You brought clouds to the Seelie Court. I've never seen clouds at the Seelie Court."

"Ogre magic," Ben says again. He is shaking his head briskly, as if to wake himself up, and drops of water are flying out of his thick, dark curls. "That's Selkie, getting angry and determined enough to bring clouds to block out the Seelie sunshine."

"And you," Safford says. "I've never seen anyone make a jump on Seelie land."

"Best traveler in the Otherworld, remember? And I had a little help." He winks at me then leaps lightly to his feet.

I am dazedly looking at the clouds. "But I didn't do that. How did I do that?"

"I already told you. You got angry and determined, and it spilled out of you. You just didn't *know*."

It doesn't make sense, that I could do that without knowing. Then again, I broke Ben's enchantment way back at the beginning of all this without having any idea that's what I was doing.

"How did all of you get here?" Ben is asking the rest of them.

"The long way," Will answers. "With a bit of help from the Threader. How do you feel? Well enough to jump us all to Boston?"

"Absolutely not. But I might be able to make Cottingley."

"We can't go to Cottingley," Aunt Virtue says stiffly. "We have to go back to Boston. We have to get Selkie safe. We have to bring Kelsey home."

"I'm fine," Kelsey says, but she says it shakily. She is sitting on the grass, looking as exhausted as the rest of us.

I sit beside her and give her hand a squeeze. "What are you even doing here?" I ask. "You didn't have to come."

"You were in trouble. Of course I had to come."

I experience an overwhelming surge of affection for her and lean over and hug her fiercely. I am surprised when it starts to drizzle. I hear Ben sigh good-naturedly. I draw back from Kelsey and say, "Sorry."

"I'm coping." He smiles at me.

"We can get to Cottingley because there's a strong faerie connection to Cottingley. Easier for Benedict. We can't get to Boston until Benedict's finished recovering a bit," Will explains to my aunts.

"We'd rather go straight to Boston," Aunt True says staunchly.

"We don't like being surrounded by so many *faeries*." Aunt Virtue looks at Ben and Safford suspiciously.

"We don't have a choice right now," Ben says, almost cheerfully. "Your only other option is the long way through the Otherworld, with faeries at every turn."

"And Seelies eventually on our heels," Safford adds darkly, looking over his shoulder at the Seelie Court with a shudder.

I look at it as well. It is storming over there, thunder and lightning surrounding the fortress, so that it is almost obscured entirely from view. I have seen storms like that move into Boston, rain in sheets so thick that the John Hancock Tower disappears into it, but very, very, very seldom. I stand, transfixed for a moment by the sight.

"I did that?" I say, because I have no recollection of doing anything like that.

"That's the thing about ogre magic coming up against Seelie magic," says Will. "It clashes, like a disturbance in the atmosphere."

"It literally makes it storm," realizes Kelsey.

"And Seelies are weakened by storms?" I say, confused, because my mother certainly hadn't seemed to share Ben's aversion to being wet.

"They don't mind a regular storm in the Thisworld. An Otherworld storm caused by foreign magic short-circuiting their power? That they definitely mind." Ben looks both amused and proud, looking across at the disturbance.

"Foreign magic in the Otherworld," breathes Safford. "I've never seen it like that before."

"Well," says Ben with a smile, "Selkie doesn't like to do anything the usual way."

"We should go," Will says. "I don't know how long it will take them to untangle the ogre magic from their own, and once they do that, they'll name us immediately."

"Let's get out of here," Aunt True says with a shudder.

"Fine." Aunt Virtue's voice is flat. "Cottingley. But after that we get to Boston."

Ben's hand slides into mine. "Hold hands, everyone."

And then we are standing on a cobblestoned street, outside a brightly lit convenience store. It is misty and damp. Ben sighs and says, "I hate England."

We sit at a table in a café, and although we are two faeries, two ogres, a wizard, a human, and a...whatever I am, to the outside eye, we probably just look like a normal group of people.

We are silent with a bone-deep weariness. Everything seems to be catching up with me. I can't figure out if I was at the Seelie Court seconds ago or centuries ago. Faerie time makes me feel perpetually jetlagged.

I think of Gussie, winking at me before falling backward to her death, or whatever they would call it. I feel like I will see her falling backward, tumbling through air, forever when I close my eyes. And if I'm not seeing her, then I'm seeing Kelsey, so close to plummeting the same way.

"She said someone else had hidden the other three fays," I say dully, eventually, into the heavy silence all around us.

"Who said?" asks Will.

"Gussie. That's what she told me. They're still hidden. I'm the only one who…asked questions. Or something."

"Who hid them?"

"I don't know."

"Well, didn't you ask?" snaps Will, sounding annoyed.

"Of course I asked. She said we needed some book. Some stupid book. I don't know. Something about a pickle or something."

"*A Pickle for the Knowing Ones*?" says Will.

I look at him in surprise. "That's it. Do you know it?"

"I knew the idiot who wrote it. Called himself Lord Dexter, because he was obnoxious."

"Well, can we get his book?"

"The Witch and Ward Society banned it, of course, so to get

the copy that would be any use to us at all, we'd have to get into the library. But I don't know how much good it would do us. It's a powerful book, but it tells the *past*, not the *future*."

"Whoever hid the fays hid them in the past," Ben points out.

"But we need to find them in the *future*."

"Maybe by finding whoever hid them in the past, where they put them," I say. "It's worth a try."

"Fine," Will agrees on a sigh.

"So we'll go back to Boston," Aunt Virtue says, satisfied.

"We were always going back to Boston. Boston was constructed for battle," Will says. "Boston was constructed for this."

My aunts shake their heads.

"It was never supposed to happen," Aunt True says, her voice trembling with something. Fear?

"It was *always* supposed to happen," Will corrects them.

"What is anyone talking about?" Kelsey asks, her voice full of exhausted exasperation. She is sitting with her head in her hands.

"Enchantment headache," Safford says, looking at her sympathetically. "That's a Seelie side effect. I've got one of my own going on. This helps." He holds up something that looks like a blob of phlegm.

Kelsey peers at it closely. "What is that?"

"Tangible moonlight," Safford answers.

"It looks gross."

Safford shrugs.

Kelsey hesitates, takes it, and then, screwing her eyes shut, tosses it in her mouth, swallowing it whole. Then she opens her eyes and says, surprised, "Tastes like chocolate."

All this faerie stuff is *so* weird.

"In the meantime, how long until you're well enough to jump us back to Boston?" asks Will.

Ben frowns, clearly thinking. "Depends on the time you're keeping. It's feeling very far away. Much farther than it should be."

Will and my aunts exchange abashed-looking glances.

"What?" I ask.

"We may have reinforced Boston's anti-faerie barriers," admits Will.

Ben makes an irritated sound. "Why would you do that?"

"Because you weren't the only faerie getting in, Benedict. And because you were in Tir na nOg."

"And you thought I was never getting out," concludes Ben.

"Well," says Will, "the odds weren't good." He pauses. "It's good to see you though."

Ben raises his eyebrows. "Really? Are you glad to see a faerie? They'll revoke your wizard classification."

"Why can't we go as soon as you dry off?" asks Aunt Virtue impatiently.

"Not that simple. I was also named."

"They only half-named you?" Will sounds surprised. "How did you pull that off? You must be better at enchantments than I thought."

"First of all, I am *definitely* better at enchantments than you think. Second of all..." Ben pauses and fidgets, then admits, "I have a hidden name."

Safford drops a fork with a clatter that is especially loud in the sudden absolute silence that has fallen over our party.

"Sorry," he whispers when everyone looks at him.

Will looks back at Ben and says, "Of course. Your mother. What a trick to be hiding up your sleeve. How did you keep secret the fact that it was hidden?"

Ben gives him a look, a look that makes me suppress a shudder. "I told you," he says. "I am much better at enchantments than even *you* think."

There is a moment of uncomfortable silence. Will looks as if he doesn't quite know what to make of what Ben has said. My aunts look almost fearful. Safford ducks below the table to retrieve the fork.

Kelsey says, "My head hurts."

Then she yawns, which makes me realize I am tired too. It's been a long...day? Week? Decade? Minute?

"If it's going to take you a while to recover, where are we going to stay in the meantime?" I ask. "We need to sleep."

Ben sighs and looks across at Will. "Will, be a wizard for a change and get us somewhere to stay."

Will convinces a family that they suddenly need to go to London to visit relatives. I suppose this is magic. The house he's procured for us is not enormous, but it is a decent size. Ben strips out of all of his layers except one, leaving a sodden trail of jackets behind him, and disappears into a bedroom, reappearing a short time later in a completely new outfit and clutching a hair dryer.

"Well done, Will," he says and sits on the floor and commences aiming the hair dryer at every spot on his body.

"Glad you approve," Will replies dryly and then sits next to Safford on the couch. Safford is curiously flipping through channels on the television, never pausing on any long enough to register what's playing.

"Thisworld magic," he says, sounding delighted. "This is *wonderful*."

I look at Kelsey.

"I have to go to bed," she says, looking white and drawn. "My head is killing me and I am exhausted. Can we catch up in the morning?"

"Yes," I say. "Sure thing." I give her a tight hug, and then she trails off into the nearest bedroom, collapsing onto the bed.

I look at Ben and Will. "We're safe from the Seelies here?"

"For now," Will answers. "The Seelies detest Cottingley; there's too much old magic here that interferes with them. We don't have long here, but it should be long enough for Benedict to get better."

"What if it's not?"

Will and Ben exchange a look that doesn't make me feel safe. But Will says, "It will be."

I look at Ben, still aiming the hair dryer at himself, and hear my mother's words. *Benedict Le Fay will betray you. And then he will die.* "My...mother said something," I begin, stumbling a bit over what to call her, because *mother* seems inappropriate.

I feel everyone look at me expectantly.

"She said it was prophesied for...for Ben to die." I leave out the first part. I can't deal with all of this at once; it just seems too much.

"She would have said anything, Selkie," says Ben. "Any powerful words she could find. Don't let the words have the power she intends."

I ignore him, looking at Will.

Will looks between the two of us. "Benedict's right. She could have just been saying it."

"You've never heard that part of the prophecy."

"No," Will says hedgingly.

I narrow my eyes, thinking. "But *would* you have?"

"Prophecies are incredibly tricky things. They're almost impossible to read. If they were easy, everyone would do it and no one would ever do anything that wasn't prophesied, and that's not how the world works. So...no, I've never heard that part of the prophecy. But that doesn't mean she was lying necessarily." Will says it reluctantly, awkwardly, looking at Ben.

Ben shakes his head and looks at me, pale eyes glittering. "She would have said *anything*, Selkie. Anything at that moment. If she knew so much about the prophecy, then how would we have been able to escape?"

It's a good point. But it doesn't quite ease the tight ball of nerves in my stomach.

In the morning, I wake without realizing I'd fallen asleep. My aunts are still snoring, but there is the sound downstairs of people moving about, so I get up and go down to investigate.

Will and Safford and Kelsey. Will is in the kitchen, and he is cooking something that smells heavenly. Safford and Kelsey each have an omelet in front of them.

"I don't understand," says Safford, frowning at it. "It tastes like strawberry jam."

Kelsey laughs, and Safford turns a pleased shade of pink in response. "It tastes like an *omelet*," insists Kelsey.

"This is what strawberry jam tastes like," says Safford. "The Thisworld is a strange place."

"Good morning," I say.

"Good morning," they all chorus. Kelsey blushes, which is interesting.

"Omelet, Selkie?" asks Will.

"You cook?" I've never really thought of Will cooking.

"I've lived several centuries. I spent a few of them perfecting my omelet," replies Will.

"Okay then," I agree.

"They taste like omelet." Kelsey grins at me.

"Strawberry jam," insists Safford good-naturedly, and Kelsey actually giggles.

I sit at the table with them, feeling like a third wheel. "Where's everyone else?" I ask awkwardly.

"As only Benedict is unaccounted for as far as you're concerned, you must be asking after him," remarks Will, whisking my omelet.

I might blush.

"Still sleeping," says Kelsey. "He slept with me last night."

I blink. "What?"

She grins. "Relax. There was an extra bed in my room. When I woke up this morning, he was in it."

"He needs his sleep," says Will, flipping my omelet, "so we'll let him sleep as long as he can."

I wish Ben had chosen *my* room to crash in, but I suppose it was already crowded with my aunts and we didn't have an extra bed.

Kelsey reads my thoughts. "Don't read anything into it. I don't even think he knows my name."

"I didn't sleep at all last night," says Safford. "I stayed up all night watching that magnificent thing." He gestures to the television.

"Safford thinks he's on holiday," says Will, sounding disapproving as he puts my omelet in front of me.

"I haven't left Mag Mell in years. Or minutes. I *am* on holiday. There is water in this house. On command. When you want it."

I pause. "Is he talking about sinks?"

Kelsey nods.

"Kelsey says it's very common in the Thisworld. Benedict must hate it."

"Safford's been telling me how Ben is allergic to water," says Kelsey. "How does he wash up? I'm so confused."

Now I am too. "You know, I've never asked him." I look at Safford. "So what did you think of the shower, then?"

Safford looks confused. "The what?"

"Oh, if you liked the bathroom sink, you're going to *love* the shower."

Safford brightens and leaps up and makes a beeline toward the bathroom.

"Now you've done it," sighs Will. "We'll have a flood, and I'll never hear the end of it from Benedict." Will goes after Safford.

I eat my omelet steadily. It's actually really fantastic.

"So," says Kelsey. She draws the word out playfully. "You and Ben, huh?"

"I don't know," I admit. "Maybe? It's confusing."

"You don't say," says Kelsey. "Odd, since everything else about your life makes total sense."

"Shut up," I say, knowing that I'm blushing.

"So I guess that's the end of you and Mike then, huh?"

"*Mike*," I exclaim, suddenly remembering him.

"Don't worry. He thinks we went to Europe. Which I guess we kind of did. But you'll have to break up with him when we get back."

I am perplexed. "Why does he think we went to Europe?"

"Everyone does. It's what Will made everyone believe, so it wouldn't look like we'd just disappeared. He said he's not as good at that sort of thing as Ben is but that it should hold. I asked him what his specialty is and he said remembering. What do you think that means?"

I look at Kelsey, so calmly talking about all these insane things. "I'm so sorry you're involved with this," I say honestly.

She looks back at me. "I'm not. You need help. At first I thought it was because you and everyone around you had gone insane, and now I know it's because *none* of you are insane. So I am with you here to the end of this little coup d'état everyone keeps talking about."

"This is above and beyond the call of friendship," I tell her.

"Well, that's me," she says. "Awesome. I expect really good birthday gifts from you for the rest of my life."

"Deal," I say and pause, then add nonchalantly, "Of course, it doesn't hurt that Safford's here."

Kelsey blushes crimson. "Stop it," she hisses and looks over her shoulder, where Safford is nowhere in sight. Then she turns back to me, eager. "He *is* cute though, don't you think? And funny."

I smile, and I'm about to reply when my aunts arrive,

and then there is bustling about as they make tea. Will and Safford come back, and Will makes more omelets, and Safford shows us the wonders of the television, and eventually Ben gets up. He sits at the table, looking adorably mussed with sleep, and eats his omelet mechanically, looking more awake when he's done.

"How are you feeling?" I ask him. I ask it just because I love him, of course, but I'm also anxious to get back home. I feel like it's been forever since I saw home.

"Better," he says and smiles. "Let's go for a walk."

My aunts both look alarmed.

"Is that safe?" Aunt Virtue demands.

"Just as safe as being in here," Ben points out. "It's not like this little cottage is going to hold back the Seelies."

Not the best way to reassure my aunts, who utter little cries of protest. "I'd love to get out of the house," I say, standing, and then glance at Kelsey questioningly, feeling bad about abandoning her.

Kelsey shakes her head, eyes on Safford. "I'm fine."

"I don't know—" Aunt True starts worryingly.

"I'll be fine," I promise her. "We won't go far."

I am delighted to be able to join Ben outside. The weather has cleared, and the day is bright and cheerful. It's been so many hours since the last time I was in immediate terror for my life, it seems to have faded a little bit for me.

"Do you want to see something lovely?" Ben asks me.

We are climbing up a gentle hill, wending into woods.

"Here we are," Ben says finally and sweeps his hand out in front of us. "St. David's Ruin."

It is still a little ways away from us, but it *is* lovely, a picturesque ruined tower, roofless, doorless, windowless, almost pointless, but lovely nonetheless, a circle of stone in the middle of the forest.

I am delighted by it, imagining it in medieval times, in times filled with faeries, when Cottingley was drenched with magic and faeries came here to convalesce, like a Caribbean resort. "How old is it?" I ask. We are nearly all the way to it now.

"Not as old as you'd think," answers Ben as we reach it. He watches as I duck into the tower itself. "It's a folly, built to be a ruin."

I look at the sky through its lack-of-roof. "Why would you build something to be a ruin?"

"Because you're impractical," suggests Ben. "The world used to be a much more impractical place."

I look at him. He is leaning against the stone of the open doorjamb, watching me. "Do you miss that? The world being a more impractical place?"

He shrugs.

Standing there, in a fake ruin, seems like the proper time to ask, "How old *are* you, anyway?"

"Is that important?"

"You sound like my aunts," I tell him.

He laughs like I have told the most hysterical joke ever, sagging against the doorjamb in his hilarity.

"What?" I ask, staring at him.

"Sorry," he gasps, trying to catch his breath. "It's just...if you'd been present for any of the numerous arguments I've had with your aunts over the years, you'd know how hilarious is the idea that I sound like them. Sorry." He clears his throat, attempting to become sober. "The thing is that time passes differently in each world. You can live a century in a minute and vice versa. Asking me how old I am is impossible. It isn't an age I could translate for you, not an age you could understand. We don't even keep track of things like that in the Otherworld."

Which explains my aunts. I lift myself up to perch on the open windowsill of the fake ruin's fakely ruined window. "So how old am I then?"

"You may be seventeen," he replies, "you may be four hundred and twenty-three, and neither one of those numbers is your age."

"Well, maybe that explains it then," I say.

"Maybe that explains what?"

"Why sometimes I feel so very young and sometimes I feel so very old."

"No," says Ben, his mouth tipping up in a smile. "I think that's just life, Selkie."

"Ah," I say. "How very philosophical of you."

"Why didn't you leave?" The question is abrupt, catching me off guard. The way he asks it is abrupt. His eyes are very serious, a storm-cloud gray in the fading light of the day.

"What?" I ask, confused. "When?"

"When we were trapped, outside Tir na nOg, and your mother was there, and I told you to go, you didn't go. I kept telling you to go, and you never went."

He is walking toward me very slowly, very deliberately, in that way he has, that way of making you realize that all of his attention has shifted toward this very moment, toward whatever he intends to do next. I curl my fingers into the stone of the windowsill underneath me, grabbing what little purchase I can, because tumbling out the window is the very last thing I would like to have happen at this moment.

"I wasn't leaving without you." My mouth is very dry. I have to make a huge effort to swallow to get the words out.

He has reached me now, stands in front of me and looks down at me, and he looks like I am a puzzle he is desperately trying to figure out. This confuses me, because usually I wonder if I can possibly be any more humiliatingly obvious in my interactions with Ben.

"I told you I was right behind you," he says.

I try to smile at him. "Never trust a faerie," I manage.

He chuckles and leans his head down, but he doesn't kiss me. "You should really, really remember that more often than you do," he murmurs at me.

"Should I?" My hands are fisted into his shirts. I wonder when that happened. But if I let go, I really am worried I'll just tumble bonelessly backward, so I keep them there.

"Yes. You're appallingly bad at it."

He leans his head closer, so close that I actually close my eyes, because he really is so close that he *should* be kissing me at this point, and I don't know why he's not. His hands are on either side of me, which makes me surrounded by Ben on three sides, which is kind of a lovely thing to be, much lovelier than this ruined tower.

"But you're the only faerie I trust," I am barely able to say, tipping my head a bit, so I can feel his breath across my cheek.

"I know." The words drift across my skin. "That's what makes you so appallingly bad at it."

And then he kisses me. It is so lovely to be kissed that I am light-headed with it. Kissing Ben is one of the world's best activities. I lean closer to him, and if time is confused, if you can live a century in a minute, then I want this to be the minute in which I live a century, I want this to be the only minute I have, if I can only choose one.

He draws back, and I think he is going to say something, which I desperately don't want him to, but all he does is shift slightly, lifting his hands up to cup the back of my head, and then he kisses me again, and I sigh with joy and wonder how it could ever possibly be wrong to trust him.

And just like that, I hear my mother's voice again, telling me that Ben will betray me. And then he will die.

I pull back, and he looks at me questioningly.

I take a deep breath, thinking about the prophecy, whatever it is, about the other three fays that are out there, hiding, waiting for us to find them. I think of all the faeries named for no reason, of all the terror in the Otherworld, of everything that I am supposed to do. I feel momentarily swamped by it. And I know that I have my aunts and I have Kelsey, but that is not as comforting as having *Ben*, who is always so coolly, calmly capable. Even when he's soaking wet in a prison cell, he has never been able to destroy my utter, complete, absolute, unwavering faith in him.

"We'll do this together, right?" And I mean all of it, everything. "You promised, right?"

He seems to know exactly what I mean. He smiles a little bit and says, "I promised." He leans forward, pressing his lips against my temple.

I lean forward as well, so that I'm settled heavily and comfortingly against him. It seems like the safest place in the world, and I never want to leave it. I squeeze my eyes shut and let Ben hold me, and I wonder if we'll ever reach the point again where our lives are normal and we're sitting on the Common and we're not in mortal peril.

To get there, I have to fulfill this prophecy and save the Otherworld. Which means I need to find this book. Which we can't do until Ben gets us back to Boston.

"When do you think you'll be ready to take us back to Boston?" I murmur against him.

"Wouldn't you know, I'm feeling much better?" remarks Ben.

I smile a little bit, not quite a chuckle, because I want to be able to just laugh with him, but there is still dread in my stomach over everything that has to happen first. And I could try to hide from it, I could, but I remember that poor little girl screaming as her brother disintegrated in her arms, and I squeeze my eyes shut and take a deep breath and then straighten away from Ben. "Good," I say firmly. "Let's go take down the Seelie Court."

CHAPTER 27

B oston looks exactly the way it has always looked, which is astonishing to me. With all that has *happened*, how can I just go back to the same townhouse with the lavender windowpanes and the non-working clock?

We sit in the conservatory that was filled with bats the last time I saw it, and we develop a plan of attack.

"They'll keep the book in the banned books room at the library," Will says.

"I'll be able to jump in easily," says Ben confidently.

"But you won't be able to jump *out*. They'll have taken that precaution."

"So I'll walk out."

"You don't think they'll have a goblin guard there?"

Ben frowns.

"What's the big deal about a goblin guard?" I ask.

"Goblins can stop a traveler from jumping away just by touching them," says Ben. "So needless to say, we are not usually friends, travelers and goblins."

"And that's why it's a good idea to protect a room with a goblin guard," I conclude.

"But I don't get it." I turn to Will. "Aren't the goblins on our side? You keep talking about them mounting armies. I assumed they were helping us. We need this book to win."

"Because a wizard who had no doubt gone mad from being in the Seelie Court told you we did," Will points out. "And it's a powerful book. One of the most powerful there is, after mine, of course." Will puffs up a bit with pride.

Ben rolls his eyes.

"The point is, they locked it up to make sure no one could get it, that no one would have the power contained in its pages. That was the point: we're all on an even playing field because none of us have the weapon. It maintains the alliance between all of us. It will look dubious to the goblins that we've suddenly decided to topple the balance of power our way."

"It sounds like you need diplomacy," remarks Kelsey.

"Kelsey's right. Why can't you *talk* to the goblins?"

"Yes, because Otherworld creatures are always so persuaded by logical arguments," drawls Will.

"Well, it's worth a try."

"It's not necessary," says Ben. "I'll go in, I'll get the book, and I'll get out before the goblins touch me. I'm the best traveler in the Otherworld. I can move a bit quicker than a couple of goblins can."

"I'm going with you," I say immediately.

Ben sighs.

My aunts immediately protest.

"No," I say staunchly. "We promised, and it's my prophecy, and this is what I'm doing: I'm going with Ben, I'm getting the book, and I'm saving the Otherworld."

I must be getting a lot better at standing up for myself, because no one really tries to stop me. They raise halfhearted protests, but I stare them down, and in the end, I take one of Ben's hands and Will takes the other and Ben jumps us to a large, high-ceilinged, marble room. The ceiling is so far over our heads you practically can't see it. Heavy, wrought-iron chandeliers filled with flickering, wax-laden candles seem to float in midair above us, the chains holding them up disappearing into the murk above our heads. One wall is lined with tall, narrow windows that stand open to sharp, cold air. Traffic sounds drift through them, and I walk over and peer out.

"It's Copley Square," I note.

"Well, yes," answers Ben. "We're in the library."

"I didn't think you meant the *real* library."

I turn away from the windows. Will has started moving farther into the room, and Ben has wandered over to the rows upon rows of books lining the wall opposite the windows as well.

"How are we ever going to find it?" he asks, frustrated. "It's *organized*."

"What?" I ask in surprise.

"It's like New York City, everything's so *sensical*; it's the only place in either world where I feel lost. It's so *devious*."

I peer at the books. Ben's right: they're alphabetized. Apparently, such a system stymies faeries. "Good thing you brought a wizard with you," says Will, coming up to us and holding up a book. "Here it is. *A Pickle for the Knowing Ones*."

Ben is looking at him with something close to awe. "How did you *do* that?"

"I could have done that too," I point out. "He just walked over to the Ds. It wasn't any sort of wizard *magic*." A bit disgruntled, I take the book out of Will's hand.

The first few lines read: *IME the first Lord in the younited States of A mericary Now of Newburyport it is the voise of the peopel and I cant Help it and so Let it goue.*

"It's…nonsensical," I say, flipping through the book. "I mean, the spelling is one thing, I know it's old, but there's no *punctuation*."

"The punctuation's all at the end," says Ben simply, as if that makes perfect sense.

There are indeed pages of periods and commas at the end of the book.

"What are you supposed to make of this?" I ask in exasperation.

"It's fluent Faerie," says Ben, and takes the book back from me.

I look down at the book, wishing that it made sense to me.

Shouldn't it? It's part of my prophecy. But it doesn't. "Can you read it?"

"Of course I can."

"Then let's get this over with," suggests Will. "Figure out who hid the other three fays."

"That way if I get detained by the goblins, you can still go on and fulfill the prophecy without me," notes Ben wryly.

"No," I say firmly and look at Will. "We are *not* leaving him behind. We do all of this *together*. Ben and I promised each other."

"Ah. I see. A promise from a *faerie*," says Will.

"Stop, she won't be dissuaded," says Ben distractedly, because now he is flipping through the book. His eyebrows are drawn together in dark consternation. "This...doesn't make any sense."

"In a faerie way or in a real-world way?" I ask, because I've noticed that the two are very different.

"It says it was my mother." Ben's voice sounds oddly detached for this pronouncement, like he can't wrap his mind around it.

"Your mother?" echoes Will, and then, "Well, that would make sense actually. A Le Fay enchantment has always been the best. That's why we went to you for Selkie here."

"No, you went to me because I was mentioned in your precious prophecy." Ben's voice is hard. He sounds furious all of a sudden. I look at him in surprise, but his gaze is still riveted to the book. "It says here that my mother hid all of the fays of the prophecy she could find, which might be all three or maybe not. But at any rate, for that she was imprisoned in Tir na nOg. From which she promptly escaped."

There is a moment of utter silence. The traffic sounds from Copley Square drift up through the windows.

Will looks evenly across at Ben. I swallow, uncertain.

"Did you ever hear," Ben asks, his voice silkily soft, "that my mother escaped Tir na nOg?"

"She didn't," Will answers after a moment.

"It is *here*!" Ben shouts. "In this *ridiculous* book of power that's been kept hidden from everyone! It is *right here*!"

"I know what you're thinking, that your mother is alive, and she *isn't*. If she's alive, where has she been all this time?"

"You want me to believe that my mother escaped Tir na nOg and *isn't* still alive? If she could escape Tir na nOg, what could possibly destroy her?"

"If she's still alive, why hasn't she ever contacted you?" Will asks gently.

Ben sucks in a breath and his eyes widen, twilight blue. "To keep me *safe*. To keep me…to keep me…to keep *herself* safe. If she escaped Tir na nOg, she couldn't exactly—I mean, look at us!"

"Benedict. It doesn't make any sense, and you know it."

"Sense? *Sense*? We are talking about the *Otherworld* here!"

I think of what Will told me, ages ago or just the other day, when I had first proposed rescuing Ben from Tir na nOg. "You told me she was rumored to survive, Will," I say, and my voice sounds small to me, but I know it must be said. I must be honest. I must give Ben all of the information.

Ben's head swivels toward me, and his eyes are gray and cloudy. "*What?*" he demands, his voice low and furious.

"She was rumored to survive Tir na nOg. She was rumored to be the only faerie to escape Tir na nOg," I manage. "Until us."

Ben looks back at Will. "Is this true?"

"It was a rumor, Benedict. It was never anything more than a rumor. Nobody was ever able to even find a *trace* of her, not a shred of evidence to—"

"*Evidence?*" echoes Ben. "William Blaxton, you have lived in the Thisworld too long. Do not speak to me of evidence, not in the Otherworld. If there was a rumor, I should have been told. If she is in the Unseelie Court, then there wouldn't have been *evidence*. There wouldn't have been a *trace* of her; there would have been only *rumors*. She is a *Le Fay*. She was the best enchantress ever. Do you think she couldn't have erased herself that way?" He turns his eyes to me, slicing like the dangerous silver glint of a well-polished sword. "I cannot believe you knew." His tone is accusatory and, underneath the thickness of that, hurt.

"Ben—" I try to defend myself.

"That you knew, and you knew what I thought, and you never once—That no one ever once—" He cuts himself off in sudden shock. "Lied to!" he realizes. "You were *lying* to me. I was...And I didn't...Never once..." He looks horrified. He turns back to Will. "You did this on purpose. You did this to protect your prophecy."

"Benedict," begins Will.

Ben sticks his hand out toward Will. "Take it."

Will blinks. "What?"

"Take it, damn you, before I change my mind and leave you here in this room," snaps Ben.

Will takes the proffered hand hastily.

I take the one Ben shoves at me.

We walk in silence. Well, it's more like marching. Eventually, we come to a surprisingly small door, all out of proportion to the height of the ceiling and the size of the windows. Ben hesitates with his hand on the doorknob then nudges it open a crack, and then he pulls all of us quickly through together.

I just have time to register that there is a single man there. He is an extremely attractive man in a black velvet suit and black riding boots, a cape jauntily flung back over his shoulder. He has one hand resting on the intricately jeweled hilt of a sword at his hip. On his head sits a large, bejeweled crown, flattening black hair into cowlicks that peek out from the back of his head. He focuses on us with eyes a brilliant shade of blue.

There is a moment when I feel sure that the man could have touched us, when I almost think that he is about to speak to us. But that couldn't have been possible; we were in front of him for the merest nanosecond before Ben whisked us away, and I find myself back in the middle of Beacon Street. A truck blares its horn as it screeches toward us, but Ben takes his hand out of mine and waves at it, and in front of my eyes, the truck lifts into the air like a feather and lands safely on the other side of Ben.

"Don't go, Benedict," Will says.

"I have to," Ben snaps, shaking Will's hand out of his.

"No. You do not."

"What is it?" I ask, staring at them. "What's going on? Where are you going?"

"He's going after his mother," Will tells me.

"I have to go," Ben insists. "All of my life, I have been trying to do *this*, and she has been out there, hiding, from *me*. And now that I've managed to track her down, you want me to stop because—"

"Because we have more important things to do," says Will.

"I have done the more important things for you, Will. Here is the fay I kept safe for you. Here is the book you needed me to retrieve. I've been playing at double agent for longer than a city has existed in your apple orchard. I almost got myself named several times in the process, and the whole time, you never once told me the most important fact about me."

"Because I knew you would do this," Will defends himself.

"Exactly. So you've manipulated me quite long enough, William Blaxton. I've done my part. When you liberate the Seelie Court, be sure to invite me for dinner at Tir na nOg, yes?"

"All right," says Will with the air of trying to interject

some reason into the conversation. "All right, I used you, you're right, and I'm sorry. But I'm not telling you not to do this because of the prophecy. I'm telling you not to do this because I don't know if you can trust her, Benedict."

"She's my mother, Will."

"She's a faerie, with a lot of very ancient faerie blood in her, Benedict. You know how these things work. Ask Selkie about her mother."

"I know about Selkie's mother," Ben snaps. "Selkie's mother is a *Seelie*. Selkie's mother is not *my* mother."

"If you wanted to trap Benedict Le Fay, can you think of any better way to do it than to dangle in front of you the promise of the mother you are so relentlessly compared to?" Will asks him pleadingly. "You have it in your head that she's better at this than you are, and she's really not. You're the most powerful Le Fay in existence."

Ben takes a deep breath and then exhales very slowly. Then he says, "I appreciate your concern. I'll be fine. You can wait for me if you like."

"Do it later," begs Will. "You can do it later, after we're done. You're not even thinking this through."

"Thinking this through," echoes Ben. "It's like you've never met a faerie before in your life."

I suddenly lunge forward, catching Ben's sleeve, terrified he's going to disappear and go somewhere.

He glares at me.

I have no idea what to say to him, but I want to talk to him.

I want to apologize. I want him to look at me without all that hurt accusation in his eyes.

"I didn't think it would help, to tell you. I was going to tell you, in Tir na nOg, and then I didn't think it would help, to get your hopes up like that, when I thought it was just…a faerie tale. I didn't think it was really true."

"It doesn't matter," he says.

"Of course it does." It's obvious that it does.

"It really doesn't," he denies again. "I am so very old, Selkie. It really doesn't."

"I know what it feels like, to want a mother so desperately and then to have her turn out to be…Even if your mother is alive, the fact that she never found you…I went looking for my missing mother, and look what happened. I didn't want the same thing to happen to you."

"It really doesn't matter," Ben snaps, finally looking at me. His eyes are dark and flat. "I made a mistake. It won't happen again."

"What mistake?" I ask blankly.

"Never trust a faerie," he says, and the words slice through me like he's cut me.

He shakes me off, but I grab for him again, refusing to be shaken, terrified that if I let him go, he will immediately jump somewhere else. Grappling, we move untidily across Beacon Street and onto the Common.

"Ben, listen to me. You *can* trust me. I would never hurt you. I was trying *not* to hurt you. I—" The words *I love you* get stuck in my throat. Can I say them now, like this, when he is angry and hurting and probably won't say them back? Can I bear that? I'm not sure I can.

He is not slowing down and he is still fighting me, and now I am no longer apologetic and desperate. I am *furious* that he's not listening and that he's doing this in the first place. So I gather myself and shout at him, with intent, "*Benedict Le Fay.*"

He stumbles, reaching out a hand to a tree to catch himself from falling completely to the ground.

He looks at me and narrows his eyes. "Not fair," he says.

"Shut up," I snap back. I am so angry with him I could shake him. "You're lucky I didn't use all four of them. What is *wrong* with you?"

"Wrong with me?" he repeats. "*Wrong* with me?" He sounds offended at the very idea.

"Yes! You're going to leave me, in the middle of all this, to go after your mother?"

"And now I know why you didn't tell me about her either!" he accuses.

"I didn't tell you about her because I was trying to keep you from getting hurt. Which is exactly why *you* lied to *me* about who I am for *my entire life.*"

He seems to acknowledge that point. "If I don't go after her now—"

"You're not the only one who never knew their mother, Ben," I remind him scathingly. "You're not the only one who was manipulated into staying away from her."

"That's different—" he begins.

"And when you asked me not to go to her, when you asked me to trust you and not her, I did."

"That was *different*," he insists.

"Excuse me," says someone to my right, and we both turn our heads. A smiling couple is standing there, looking cheerful and bundled up against the bright Boston cold. The male half is holding up a camera. "Would you take our picture?"

Ben and I both stare at them for a second.

Then Ben reaches out, snatches the camera, and flings it up over our heads, where it explodes into a million fluttering pieces of tinsel.

"Oooh!" exclaims the woman. "Was that a trick?"

"I will do that to *you*," says Ben, "if you don't walk away from us right now."

The couple's eyes widen, and they bustle away, and I would think it almost funny, except for the fact that I feel on the verge of tears, like their interruption has made all of my fury recede away from me, leaving nothing but a swamping sorrow.

"I knew what I was talking about with your mother," Ben tells me. "You've never met my mother. You want me to give up on finding her on the basis of some self-serving suspicion Will has that—"

"I want you to give up on finding her because of *me*, Ben," I interrupt him, and now I am worried that I *sound* like I am about to cry, and I don't want to sound that way, even if it is true, even if it is possible that I am crying already. "You're not supposed to leave me. You promised me that you wouldn't leave me. I know that you're upset, but I—but I—" All of the words refuse to come out. I gulp at them.

He is silent long enough for me to collect myself, for me to pull the tears back inside and grow furious at him again.

"I have to do this," he says. "The same way you had to find your mother. When everyone told you to stop asking questions, did you stop?"

"I should have," I say helplessly.

"And then you would never have known who you were," he points out. "And you wouldn't have been able to bear that."

I look at him, and he is looking at me so tenderly that I just say it. "Stay with me because you love me."

I decide, in that moment, that I will remember the look on his face for as long as I live, however long that is in the strange changeling life that I lead. And it's not that I'm going to remember it because it's plain on his face that he doesn't love me. That would almost be easier to take. Because I think that it is plain on his face that he does, and that it is never going to be enough for him—that he loves me, this little changeling girl, one of so very many that, for all I know, he has loved throughout centuries. *I* will simply never be enough. It could be that Benedict Le Fay loves me now, at this moment in space and time, in this human world, but his eyes dart, and he looks toward Park Street, and the clock ticks forward.

I let go of him and take a step away.

"Selkie," he says, his eyes returning to me. "I can't. Please. Can't you understand? I—" He reaches for me, and it's funny, because I was just clinging to him, but now I step backward, avoiding him as much as I can.

"Don't," I say, holding up my hands to keep him away.

"No, Selkie, listen to me. I don't *want* to—"

"Of course you want to. If you didn't want to, then you wouldn't." My voice sounds flat, and I *feel* flat, like everything inside me has retreated. "You promised me, Benedict Le Fay." I don't say it with much intent, but he flinches anyway. "Silly me. Never trust a faerie."

We stand on the Common, separated by a few feet, and stare at each other. Then he vanishes, and I realize at that moment exactly what that means: he is the best traveler in the Otherworld, and the best enchanter, and the strongest Le Fay. I may never find him ever again if he doesn't want to be found. And how did we get here?

I have never felt more lost in my entire life.

All of the emotion that had retreated inside of me barrels back, a tidal wave of it that had gathered force and momentum in the interim, but I don't let it. I tremble with the effort of refusing to let it, my hands deep in the pocket of my sweatshirt, standing alone on the Common.

"Selkie," Will says gently, and I feel his hand, tentative, on my shoulder. "Let's go. You'll freeze out here."

It seems like such a silly thing to say when I am already

frozen. I feel like everything stopped in the instant before Ben vanished, that I am just holding my breath now.

"Benedict Le Fay will betray you," I hear myself say, as if from a very great distance. "And then he will die."

ACKNOWLEDGMENTS

I admit that I kept putting off writing my acknowledgments because I wasn't sure what to say. At first I thought I would write this really witty acknowledgments section full of all of the little things that inspire a book—Andrew Belle's album *The Ladder* for being on constant repeat while writing; Tealuxe where so much of the book was written; the city of Boston and its inhabitants and all of its/their quirks for filling the book so entirely—but then I realized that, actually, while those things all deserve nods of acknowledgment for being true and real influences on the book, they were kind of taking the easy way out: they are easy for me to write about in the acknowledgments, because I know what to say about them.

All of the people who have been a part of this book are so much more difficult for me to write about, which is why it's taken me a full paragraph to get to them. Of all the words I've ever written, these are the ones that seem least capable of capturing the true depth of emotion I want to convey. I have decided that maybe all I can say is *Thank you* and hope that everyone listed here understands how wholly inadequate the words are. So:

Thank you, first, to my fantastic agent Andrea Somberg, whose enthusiasm for the book gave it life.

Thank you also to my delightful editor Aubrey Poole, whose particular brand of magic made the book better, and better again, and then impossibly still better!

Thank you to the entire team at Sourcebooks, especially Jillian Bergsma, Cat Clyne, Kay Mitchell, Katherine Prosswimmer, and Derry Wilkens.

Thank you to all of the friends who have read my writing over the years, listened understandingly to my venting, and cheered me on, including Hillard Bowe, Jean Bowe, Joanne Bush, Erin McCormick, Bill Mullally, Colleen Mullally, Chrystie Perry, Stephanie Pina, Laura Randall, and Kelley Walsh.

Thank you to everyone on the Internet—you know who you are—who has made me a better and much more thoughtful writer and has reminded me of the true rewards of writing at times when I needed it, including a special shout-out to Jennifer Roberson, who forced me to up my game.

Thank you to Claudia Gray, who has the distinction of having taken me for my first drink to celebrate my agent *and* my first drink to celebrate my book deal! It's a very good thing to have a guide in all this!

Thank you to David Hosp, who was another guide in all this, and whose tales of novel-writing during commutes were a source of inspiration for me to get this novel done. And who also, incidentally, still wins the award for Single Nicest E-mail I've Ever Received About My Writing (although I admit it's a close race and there are many, many runners-up).

Thank you to David Kowalczyk and his students, who provided invaluable feedback.

Thank you to Heather Wilson and everyone else who was an early reader of the book, whose words of encouragement, support, and advice were more important than can be said.

Thank you to Jennifer Mendola, whose Ben-for-Benedict-not-Benjamin inspired the idea of my Ben-for-Benedict-not-Benjamin.

Thank you to Kristin Gillespie, who was always excellent at asking just the right question to flush out the rest of the plot.

Thank you to Noel Wiedner, whose writing I genuinely admire and desire to emulate more than I think she realizes. Noel also deserves a special mention for being so incredibly selfless and giving whenever I have fretted over anything. She also drew several beautiful sketches for me. Yes, she draws too! Such is the extent of her talent!

Thank you to Larry Stritof, who puts up with an incredible amount of whining from me but nevertheless agreed to provide really excellent tech assistance, website building, and author photography. (Actually, maybe he agreed to do that *because* of the whining, not in spite of it.)

And while I'm on the topic of author photographs, thank you to George and Susan DoCanto for the gift of the pink coat, Helen Lantagne for doing hair, Caitlin Cabral for doing make-up and tagging along for the shoot even when she felt ill, Sonja L. Cohen for location suggestions, and Dunkin' Donuts for fueling the whole thing with its maple-frosted donuts. All of you made me feel like a celebrity! Okay, maybe Dunkin' Donuts didn't have much to do with that, but the rest of you did!

Speaking of Sonja: thank you to Sonja L. Cohen, who was this book's first editor and whose input at every step along the long and winding road here, whether it be swooning over Ben or reading fresh drafts while on vacation in Prague, has been vitally important. If you can, I highly recommend you find a friend who loves your book as much as you do. She has known, all along, just when and how to nudge me along and when to remind me to take a breath, usually with a glass of Prosecco and a hot British actor (on DVD, not in real life; her powers have *some* limits). Oddly, when thinking about the acknowledgments section of this book, the anecdote that I kept thinking of to explain Sonja's value has been this one: once I was eating dip at a party, and I said I was only going to have one more bite so as not to ruin my appetite for dinner, and she said, "You'll want to make sure it's a bite with a black olive in it." And she was right, of course, because black olives are the best.

Last but not least, thank you an incredible amount to my family. Selkie doesn't have the biggest family, or the sanest one, and in that respect she doesn't resemble me at all, because I have been blessed with the world's best family (and they are even mostly sane!). My family is large and extended and far-flung, and I love and thank all of them for everything, big and small, and they know who they are and how much they mean to me, especially Ma, and Jordan, my only nephew so far and therefore also, as of this writing, my favorite nephew. Some cherished family members have also been lost along the way, but I continue to feel their support and am so grateful to have had them in my life. I also offer a thank-you here to the rest of my Rhode Island "family," who may not be genetically related but are nonetheless family.

I must provide a special extended note of thanks to my parents and sisters. They have supported me in every crazy thing I've ever done, even the ideas I have that I know make them shake their heads and wonder where I came from. Perhaps more importantly though, they make me laugh, harder than anyone else in the universe, and in the end, that's what life should be about. This planet is a crazy place full of crazy people. Some of them I write about. The rest of them I talk to my family about, in giddy, hilarious, confusing conversations without equal, and I honestly have no idea what I would do without them. People ask me if I write about my family, and the truth is that I don't really, because I'm not sure anyone would believe me if I did; they are too amazing and fantastic. So Mom, Dad, Meg, Cait: Thank you for making me laugh, for loving me, for making sure I know I'm loved, for always being my home, through good times and bad. The world can be a big and lonely place. You may not be ogres or faeries, but you are magical in that you keep my world crowded with love and laughter and delight and happiness. You have made my life bright, exciting, unpredictable—as we would say, never a dull moment! And I genuinely would never want it to be any other way. You are the greatest gifts, and I am the luckiest person. We end every telephone conversation with "I love you," and I want, with these acknowledgments, to make sure you know how much I mean it every time I say it: I love you. And thank you.

ABOUT THE AUTHOR

Skylar Dorset grew up in Rhode Island, so she hates to drive more than twenty minutes to get anywhere. After receiving a law degree from Harvard, Skylar was an attorney in Boston for many years, where she wrote much of her first book during bouts of being stuck on the subway. Visit her at www.skylardorset.com.